P9-DEA-918

Adams Free Library

W. T. Adams Book Fund

Adams, Massachusetts

WITHDRAWN

PLEASE WASH
YOUR HANDS
BEFORE YOU READ ME
AND KEEP ME CLEAN

MAZATLÁN

E. HOWARD HUNT

DONALD I. FINE, INC.
NEW YORK

Copyright © 1993 by E. Howard Hunt

All rights reserved, including the right of reproduction in whole or in part in any form. Published in the United States of America by Donald I. Fine, Inc. and in Canada by General Publishing Company Limited.

Library of Congress Catalogue Card Number: 93-70905
ISBN: 1-55611-369-2

Manufactured in the United States of America

10 9 8 7 6 5 4 3 2 1

Designed by Irving Perkins Associates

This novel is a work of fiction. Names, characters, places and incidents are either the product of the author's imagination or are used fictitiously. Any resemblance to actual events, locales, organizations or persons, living or dead, is entirely coincidental and beyond the intent of either the author or publisher.

This book is for Morry Poummit,
teacher and friend.

He was a big man. So big that when he came through the doorway his frame blotted out the hallway light. His skull was shaved, and below the big, broken nose a handlebar mustache stretched across his ugly, damaged face.

In his ham-sized hand the double-barreled sawed-off looked as big and deadly as a bazooka. He waved it around like a feather, pointing it, finally, at the Preacher. "You," he boomed. "On your feet. We got travelin' to do. Miles to go before I sleep."

The Preacher got up slowly, face white and strained. Corpses have looked healthier.

The big man turned to me, smiling nastily, as Mean Muthas do. "You got objections, boy?"

I'd been considering counteraction, but even if I could hit him before he blew my head off, the effect would be like a fly landing on Mount Rushmore. So I shrugged. "Not me, friend. You got a beef with the Preacher, it's between the two of you."

He grunted like a bull moose, collared the Preacher, and dragged him away like a naughty child. When I closed the door I didn't feel heroic, just alive.

And grateful.

There was a bottle of José Cuervo on the basin, and as I swallowed a bracer, I reflected that the Preacher now faced a real challenge. Converting his captor to pacifism and brotherly love was going to require all the Preacher's extraordinary talents. And resourcefulness.

Swallowing more tequila, I shivered and wished him well.

That unsavory encounter came later, of course. After I'd met the Preacher's bodacious daughter.

ONE

I'd never heard of Tara Vaill or her father, Billy Joe, until the night Melody and I flew in to Miami from Cozumel. Over the two years since I'd rescued Melody and her mother from Luis Parra, Melody and I kept house between my place on Cozumel and her duplex in South Miami. The redecorating she'd ordered had fallen behind schedule, and she was determined to find out why. So, we were to spend a few days with her twice-widowed mother, Delores Diehl, a fine figure of a woman, and a free and calculating spirit if there ever was one.

Thomas, the houseman, let us into her big Bay Harbor house and said, "Welcome back, Mr. Novak. Nice to see you again, sir."

"Good to see you, Thomas. Keeping well?"

"Very. Mrs. Diehl is expecting you in the living room."

He took our bags and turned to Melody. "Will you be staying in your old room, Miss Melody?"

"Don't be ridiculous, Thomas. The guest room will be fine—for both of us."

"As you say, miss. There's mail for you on your vanity."

1

"First things first," I said as he started upstairs. "Let's dive into a cold drink."

"Let's." Melody bussed me briefly, then, hand in hand, we went into the sunken living room. It was as large as a doubles court, with thick beige carpeting and oversize leather furniture Delores had brought from Brazil. The death of her second husband had left her with a bundle, as they say, and far beyond the compromises of poverty. The Diehl home reflected this, as did Delores's designer cocktail pajamas and upscale coiffure. She was tanned from a recent Mediterranean cruise, and after greeting her daughter she kissed my cheek and pressed me to her shapely bosom. "Jack, it's so *good* to have you here, you've been quite a stranger."

"Unavoidably," I said. "Life on Cozumel isn't all mangoes and guacamole. Occasionally I have to work."

With an understanding nod she said, "Do build us some drinks, dear, I'm sure we're all in need. Tequila on the rocks will suit me splendidly. Melody, I suppose you're—"

"Yes, Mother. White wine. I'm still in training—no hard stuff for me."

I poured their drinks first, filled a short glass with crushed ice and added a satisfactory dollop of Añejo. Melody said, "Chin-chin," I said, "*Saludos*," and Delores said, "*L'haim*."

"*L'haim*?" I asked politely.

"Yes. At Haifa this attractive Israeli banker came aboard, and we did things together all the way back to New York."

"Whatever that means," Melody murmured, and met my gaze.

"*L'haim* means 'to life,' dear," her mother said unconcernedly. "The University of Miami isn't Vassar, but I *do* expect you to absorb a sense of the larger world." She sipped delicately. "Jack, you have an absolute *genius* for preparing drinks. This couldn't be more perfect."

"José Cuervo never fails," I told her, "and I brought a couple of bottles to tide you over until you visit us again."

"How very thoughtful." She glanced at her diamond-set wristwatch. "Fifteen minutes until dinner. I'm so glad your flight came in on time."

"Me, too," her daughter said, draining her small glass. "With AeroMexico one never knows." She stretched and arched her lovely body as though preparing for a competition dive. "I feel too grungy to enjoy anything until I've had a shower. Jack?"

"I'll postpone till bedtime," I responded, "and keep your mother company. Hurry back. *Rápido.*"

She blew me a kiss and walked sexily away, showing her petite, hourglass figure to advantage. When we were alone, I freshened our drinks and Delores said, "You both look exceedingly fit, Jack. Living in sin seems to become you both."

"Sin's in the mind of the practitioner," I remarked, "and mine's clear as London gin."

"Nevertheless," she said with a hint of reproval, "as Melody's mother I worry about her—now and in the future. Are you two *ever* going to get married?"

"I suppose. But Melody has another two years before graduation. Meanwhile, as a damsel, she can enjoy sorority life and girl-type friendships. Once we're married, I plan to lock her up and never let her see daylight again."

She nodded thoughtfully. "I know that's a put-on, but it's remarkably like what Melody's father, Olin West, tried to do to me. Brazil, after all, is both civilized and savage. Females are useful possessions and protectively cloistered, so I'm glad that my daughter is maturing in another environment entirely."

"We'll manage," I said, "and please give your daughter credit. She's got a B average, though she spends a week each month at diving meets."

Both of us glanced at the silver Olympic medal handsomely framed on the wall, and I remembered that my first glimpse of Melody was around back, in a spectacular dive

3

at the family pool. She'd come up looking like a diminutive, dark-haired Venus, all of sixteen years old. "Besides," I went on, "in Florida she can't drink legally for another two years. Should she be a housewife before she can sit at a bar?"

"Well—putting it that way . . . it's just that now and then I need to assure myself you're a serious person. Otherwise I'd be remiss in permitting Melody to fritter away her life, miss opportunities she'd later regret."

"I can't speak for my roomie," I said, "but I try to see that she lacks for nothing. We get along extremely well, you know, and either of us is free to alter the equation at any time."

She sighed. "Sometimes I feel your attraction to violence will end in tragedy for you both. What Melody's told me about your activities in Guadalajara and Puerto Vallarta are enough to make a person faint. And I'm sure I don't know the half of it. Still, I can't deny that you've had a steadying effect on my rebellious child—but why not? After all, you're almost twice her age."

"Ah, but she's wise beyond her years, and I'm not yet infirm."

She looked at me admiringly, then her expression became prim as Melody entered the room. She was wearing an *après-swim* playsuit and still toweling her hair. The other hand held a letter and what seemed to be a tape cassette. "Did I interrupt conversation I should know about?"

"Just a family exchange," I said and drained my glass. "Your mother was reminiscing about how she first thought me a pedophile."

Melody looked sharply at her mother. "I thought Jack was pretty terrific—that's why I offered him my baby bod. Now, let's be serious. Mother, you remember Tara Vaill?"

Delores looked perplexed. "The name's vaguely familiar, but—no, offhand I can't place it."

"Well, she came here occasionally when I was at Ransom—helped me with swimming strokes. Slender blonde, snub nose, broad pelvis . . ."

"Dear, I can do without gynecological descriptions. Yes, I do recall her now. Dressed rather shabbily."

"Well, Army and Navy surplus was the in-thing. She'd had to leave community college for financial reasons, supported herself waiting tables and giving swimming lessons. I liked her, and we got on really well."

"So," her mother said, "I gather you've heard from Tara. Is she married? In trouble?"

Melody glanced at the letter. "Her father's boat was seized by pirates, and she's afraid he's dead."

"Good Lord!"

"Mother, does that huge electronic setup have a tape player?"

"I suppose it does. Somewhere. Jack?"

I opened the big wall cabinet, exposing an array of expensive electronic gear. Yes, it included a cassette player.

Just then Thomas came in to announce dinner. Delores rose and said, "We'll listen later."

I snapped the cassette into position while Melody shook her tresses like a spaniel. A natural air-dry.

We went in to dinner.

Over black, Brazilian *cafezinhos*, Melody summarized the letter from her friend. After years of wandering, Tara's father, Billy Joe Vaill, had struck it rich in Southern California. As a radio evangelist.

I saw Delores's nose wrinkle in disdain. "Don't knock it," I said. "Those electronic preachers make nothing but money. I'd like a piece of his action."

"But it's so—seamy," Delores objected. "Luring lonely souls to contribute for God knows what reason."

"It's a cockamamie world. At least the contributors get a

5

little spiritual satisfaction—or a lot. Which is better than the return from mail-order breast creams." I stirred my syrupy coffee and sipped. Melody said, "May I go on? Tara's father decided to branch into TV and bought air time, but contributions fell off and he couldn't afford to continue. With what money he had left Billy Joe bought a sailing ketch and named it *Paz Paloma*—that means Peace Dove, Mother."

"What on earth for?"

"To take food and medicine to Central America, hoping to start a movement toward peace and reconciliation in those troubled countries."

My eyes rolled heavenward. Sharply, Melody said, "Jack, you're always discounting people's good motives, and that's very mean-spirited of you."

"One question," I said, "does the Preacher speak Spanish?"

She shrugged. "I don't know—the letter doesn't say. But he took along his assistant, Sister Grace, who does. She's a South American."

"Guns might have served him better," I remarked gratuitously. "Let's get to the hijacking."

She nodded, and we went into the living room. Melody said, "The Coast Guard recorded this distress signal from the *Paz Paloma*," as I turned it on.

Through static and electronic shrieks I heard a man's strained voice: "They've got a machine gun trained on us—fired a few bursts to show they mean business. Their boat has no flag . . . don't know who they are, just pirates. Sister Grace is lowering sail, and in a minute we'll be stopped in the water. This is Preacher Billy Joe asking for help—anyone, *please help us*. My boat is the *Paz Paloma* on a peace mission to Central America, but when they find out I have no money, just medicine and food for the starving . . . I'm afraid. *Please help us*. SOS *Paz Paloma*, SOS *Paz Paloma* . . ."

Then, nothing.

Delores uncrossed her legs. "So dramatic," she observed. "Those poor people—I suppose they're long since dead."

"Probably," I agreed. "The Caribbean's a battlefield these days. Every marina has its own hijacking story. People put out to sea—whole families—and simply vanish. And it's not because of the Bermuda Triangle. The hijackers are smugglers who pick up boats that way—cheap."

Delores said, "You mean, for running drugs to the States?"

I nodded. Melody said, "Well, what are we going to do?"

"Send postcards to the Coast Guard, Navy and the President. Where was the ketch when it was hijacked?"

Melody shook her head. "That's the awful part—nobody knows. It stopped at Mazatlán for water and supplies—after that . . ." She shrugged expressively.

"Wonder why he didn't give his position? Any skipper with half a brain knows how to make a distress call."

"That man was frightened to death," she said defensively. "He didn't have your U.S. Navy training, Jack. Try to be more understanding."

"Another simpleton at the helm of an oceangoing boat," I muttered. "Probably doesn't even know the Rules of the Road."

"Probably not—but Tara's father was well-motivated. A humanitarian—"

"—in an ugly world," I finished. "Sounds like an authentic California looney."

"Perhaps—but what are we going to do?"

"What do you want to do?"

She stared at the letter in her hand. "Help her, of course. She's broke and distraught, and wouldn't have turned to me except as a last resort. The least I can do is bring her here so she can sort things out. By then, there may be some word on her father."

"Where is she now?"

"San Diego."

Her mother said, "You mean, bring Tara here, in *my* house, dear?"

"Exactly. She won't eat much, and for once I think you could do something in a spirit of charity. I'll pay for her plane ticket." Melody eyed her mother unblinkingly.

Delores sighed. "Very well, if you insist—but I do hope she'll keep a low profile, not be underfoot all the while. And as soon as possible, please move her into your duplex."

"Agreed." She looked at me. "Jack?"

"Space allocation is up to you and your mother."

"I don't mean that. The point is whether you have any ideas how to help my friend."

"Not a one," I confessed. "But if I were going to get in-volved—government agencies having failed to locate the peace boat—I'd head for Mazatlán, pick up what I could on the spot."

Her expression brightened. "Terrific. We'll take Tara with us."

"We? Us?" I shook my head. "No job for a woman."

"Oh, c'mon, Jack, don't be an old chauvinist ogre. I can take care of myself, and there was a time when I saved your bones . . . Or is that an inconvenient memory?"

I thought it over while Delores radiated disapproval of the whole idea. Hell, if Melody was that determined to help her friend I had an undeniable obligation to join in. Besides, nothing was going to come of any search for Tara's dad. How could I succeed where everyone else had failed? "Okay," I said finally, "I'll check out Mazatlán on condition I go alone. No Jesuitical arguments, that's it."

Delores breathed a sigh of relief. Frowning, Melody said, "Somehow, you always seem to get your way. Very well, *mi amor*, do what you think best. Now, how can Tara help?"

"Have her bring photos of the yacht and her dad, anything else she thinks could be useful."

Delores shook her head resignedly. Melody gave me a hug

and kiss. "You won't regret it, dear," she promised, and I felt her body flow against mine. "Even if you didn't volunteer."

Door chimes sounded, and presently Thomas came in and said, "A Mr. Forrester, madam. Shall I show him in?"

Slightly flustered, Delores rose. "Say I'll join him in a moment." Turning to us, she said, "You wouldn't approve of Lance, and I don't want an uncongenial start for the evening."

"Why wouldn't we approve, Mother?"

"Lance dresses in current fashion and wears gold chains. We met at the Racquet Club where he lives. Tonight we're going to a party at the Grove Isle. In case you need me." She kissed Melody lightly and glided away.

When she was out of the room, Melody said, "Another gigolo, I suppose. Jack, you'd never be a gigolo, would you?"

"Not unless it pays better than I think." I pinched her rump. "Room and board ain't enough."

"That hurt!" She rubbed her behind. "How do I get Tara a ticket fast?"

"By phone, credit card and Telex. And while you're on that I'll have my shower. I need it."

"I noticed." She picked up the phone. "Join you, if you'd like company."

"Always," I said, and a few minutes later, she did.

We hadn't made love since morning, so we were hungry as honey-bears. Concentrating on Melody, I forgot the problems of Tara Vaill.

Until next afternoon, when she arrived.

TWO

I spent the morning on Miami's Calle Ocho, negotiating with a Cuban-American food exporter who had tight connections in Central America. The problem at my Cozumel ship chandlering business was that I had to buy imported supplies with dollars, although not all the cruise ships I serviced were willing to pay me in hard currencies. Several pursers tried paying with pesos at the official dollar rate, which was less than the street rate. So I had a surplus of pesos, which were as unwelcome to me as Polish zlotys.

This Cubano—Mariscal—turned out to have property in Zihuatanejo where his brother-in-law was building two resort hotels. Because of certain complexities in cross-border currency transactions, Mariscal was willing to credit my pesos at a fair exchange rate. I'd transfer them to his *cuñado*, and Mariscal would ship me canned goods, delicacies and liquor in return. We shook hands on the bargain, and he said his lawyer would draw up the papers within two days.

We lunched at La Tasca on chunks of pork bedded in Moros y Cristianos—rice and black beans—washed down with icy *sangría*, ending with savory *flan* and a chota peg of

Añejo. Then I drove back to the Bay Harbor manse in an excellent frame of mind.

Melody wasn't around, and Thomas told me she'd gone to the airport to meet Miss Vaill. I got into swim trunks and did a few underwater lengths in the pool. When I surfaced, Delores was just coming out of the poolside exercise room where a Haitian masseuse had been pounding her zaftig frame.

Delores had on a silk happi coat and a minimal bikini. The scanty halter did heavy duty restraining the maternal bosom as she bent forward to splash water on my face. I noticed a couple of hickies on her neck and inquired if she'd had an enjoyable evening with Lance. With a shrug, she said, "The Grove Isle was a big blah, so we went on to the Racquet Club. Jack, you can't imagine the overdressed old yentas who put the eye on Lance while we were chatting on the terrace. Both of us were uncomfortable so we repaired to the Jockey for late supper and privacy."

That explained the hickies. I said, "Lance must be a very attractive chap."

"Oh, he is—indeed. Led such a fascinating life—Hollywood extra, Hawaiian surfer—all-around sportsman."

"I'll bet," I said, and did four more laps. By that time Delores was ordering drinks on the poolside phone, called, "Anejo okay?" to me, and I nodded.

We drank at a poolside table, and I became aware that Delores was giving me the covert eye. Very casually she said, "I've always gotten on so much better with younger men, Jack. Do you find that odd of me?"

"Not at all. You're what—three years my elder?"

"If that," she nodded, and sipped. "As I've said before, I can hardly blame Melody for latching on to such an attractive man. I remember thinking, the first time I saw you, how compatible the two of us could be."

"Ah, but Paul Diehl was warm in his grave, and your comforter was Larry Parmenter."

"Ugh—how could I have been so stupid? That criminal. But whatever your faults, Jack, Melody and I, Thomas—the household—all of us owe our very lives to you. So I just want you to understand that you can always count on me."

"Well, I have," I said, and buried my face in my glass.

"For anything," she added, as a car came up the drive.

It was Melody's Mercedes coupe. Melody got out on one side, and from the other a blonde girl seemed to unreel. She was taller than my diminutive darling, and her freckled face wore a questioning expression that I attributed to myopia. From the neck down she was garbed in a San Diego State sweatshirt, flannel warm-up trousers, and running shoes. Thomas carried her bag into the house as Melody and Tara approached.

After preliminary introductions, Tara gave me a firm, warm hand and told me how surpassingly grateful she was. I mumbled something equally gracious as she turned to Melody. "Mmmmm, the pool looks wonderful. Shall we?"

"Absolutely." They disappeared into the bathhouse and emerged in tight-fitting tank suits. Melody hit the high board for a three-and-a-half gainer in pike position. As effortlessly as going down a water slide. Tara took the water in a shallow racing dive, butterflied to the far end and backstroked back. Spinning water from her hair, she cried, "That was *great*! Let's race."

So they did, freestyle, two water babies. Tara was larger and slightly more muscular, but Melody was in magnificent condition and cleaved the water as smoothly as an otter. Panting, they pulled up at pool edge. "Who won?" Tara gasped.

"Dead heat."

"No visitor's preference?"

"Only for drinks."

"Rye and water for me, thanks."

I made drinks all around and carried them to the table. Tara was sprawled back in her chair, legs parted enough to display shapely loins. Flat stomach and nicely curved breasts for a female in her early twenties. Large, white front teeth kept her lips parted most of the time, giving her mouth an innocent sensuality. Her blonde hair sported a gamin cut, and I noticed that she had asymmetrical dimples—right cheek and chin.

Melody saw me looking at her and frowned slightly. Delores said, "Tara, you'll stay in Melody's room. I hope you'll find it comfortable."

"Oh, I'm sure I will, Mrs. Diehl. Some of the flops I've lived in you wouldn't believe."

Delores's lips quivered, and Melody said, "Tara's been waiting table and attending night classes."

"Sounds an exhausting schedule," Delores remarked archly.

"Oh, not really. When you're young, you can do anything."

Delores's eyes smoldered, and I suppressed a smile. Preliminary sparring was underway, and I anticipated a great main bout. With a frosty smile, Delores got up, drew the happi coat around her torso. "Well, I'll leave you young people to talk. I'm sure there's much to go over, and I know I couldn't add a thing." When she passed the pool's far end Melody said, "Tara, don't mind her, she's just that way. You're *my* guest—and Jack's."

"Hmmm. Always bear in mind that Delores has a matchless ability to rise above the sufferings of others. Where were you working in Dago?"

"At the Westgate—and it's *San* Diego."

"I know, I've flown out of North Island."

Her face relaxed. "Melody said you were Navy, so of course you'd use the Navy word."

"Affectionately. Just how long has your Dad been missing?"

Her face sobered. "Thirty-two days ago he sailed out of San Diego harbor—no, thirty-three."

"With Sister Grace."

Her mouth twisted. "Unfortunately."

"Why so?"

"Since she began working with Dad he hasn't been the same. Her real name is Graciela—Graciela Rodriguez. They're secretly married, so she's really Mrs. Vaill."

"Secretly?"

"Dad thought publicity might reduce donations—from some of the ladies who've been regular contributors. The ministry was already losing money."

"How did Sister Grace meet your Dad? When did they marry?"

"Oh, it was about a year ago. He was at Tehachapi for a few days' ministry and met Graciela—she'd been writing him and sending small amounts of money. She asked Dad for a job and a parole recommendation, and he agreed." She sighed. "She was paroled to Dad, and three months later he married her." Turning to Melody, she said, "Tehachapi's a California prison."

As Melody frowned, Tara said, "I haven't anything against reformed criminals, if they're truly reformed, but why he had to marry her I couldn't begin to guess."

"You and your father were close?" I asked.

"Always. Mother died when I was ten, and Dad took me wherever he went. So we were really close—until Graciela."

"Is the feeling mutual?"

"We can't stand each other."

"Understandable. So she came to work for the radio ministry, then the TV program. Was she on camera?"

"Yes—she's fairly young and attractive, and of course she speaks Spanish. So she'd interpret Dad's preaching for the Mexican audience."

"Sounds perfect for the locale. How come the ministry went bust?"

"Dad blamed it on contributions falling off—lot of competition in the field, you know. I figured Graciela was siphoning money—a lot of it came in cash—but I couldn't prove it. When I mentioned it to Dad he got furious, said I was jealous of Sister Grace."

"Were you?"

"I suppose—but mainly suspicious of her, and resentful. I didn't want him to buy that damn boat, but they went ahead, and got enough donations to stock it with food and medicine for the trip." She looked away, eyes moist. "Melody said you'd know how to find him."

I looked at Melody.

Tara said, "I brought along literature and photos to help." She rubbed her eyes slowly. "I'm so grateful to you both. Melody, if you hadn't come through, I don't know what I'd have done."

"How old is your father now?" I asked.

"Forty-three, and I want him to live a lot more years."

"Without Sister Grace—Graciela."

Her face tightened. "I'd be a liar if I pretended I care what happens to her."

"Though the same is likely to happen to your father."

She looked away. "Then I hope they're both alive and well."

A thought occurred to me, but I suppressed it. Telling her that the crews of hijacked boats are usually deep-sixed wouldn't improve her spirits. I made fresh drinks, and when I went back to the table Melody asked, "When can you leave for Mazatlán, dear?"

"After I take care of Mariscal's contracts. But I thought Tara was going to rest up here, get things together."

"She wants to go right away."

I sat down with them. "Let's be realistic. If they survived the hijacking, they're probably still alive. If they didn't, charging off half-cocked won't help them now." I sipped my iced Añejo. "Conceivably the pirates have them on an island somewhere, holding them for ransom. Kidnapping Americans abroad is widespread and profitable."

"But Dad hasn't any money and the ministry doesn't exist any longer, so there's not even anyone to contact with a demand." She shook her head sorrowfully.

"The kidnappers don't know that," I told her. "And if your Dad is hip, he won't tell them. After all, he's lived by the spoken word—knows its value."

"That's true," Melody said, "and I'm not sure just when I'll be able to leave. I have papers for two courses that are almost overdue. On Cozumel I can never bring myself to deal with what I have to do in Miami."

Tara said, "I'd hoped you'd come with us."

"What I can do is join you there if you stay more than a few days," Melody suggested.

I put down my glass. "Everything considered, it's better I go alone. Shouldn't take me more than two days to check the waterfront." I turned to Tara. "You didn't say where *Paz Paloma* was headed."

"Puerto Padrón—that's on the Guatemalan coast by the Salvador frontier. Dad's supplies were to be taken inland to refugee camps inside the Guatemalan border. Conditions there are horrible, so he decided to do something to help."

"Graciela's idea?"

She shrugged. "You read about it in the papers all the time."

"And while there your father was going to do some close-in evangelizing?"

"Of course—it's his calling."

Melody said, "Honey, I don't like you going alone to Mazatlán. I wasn't with you in Guadalajara and you got beaten up and almost killed."

"That was a job for Manny," I reminded her, "for which I was paid. Taking it, I assumed those risks."

Tara's expression was perplexed. "What kind of job?"

Melody said, "Jack used to be with DEA. Now and then they get him to help out—unofficially."

"DEA—that's . . . ?"

"Narcotics," I said. "I'll tell you about it sometime. Do you have the photos and such?"

"I'll get them now." She bounded out of her chair and ran lithely across the lawn. As she climbed the outside staircase Melody said, "What a terrific figure. I'm just as glad the two of you won't be together in an exotic Mexican resort."

"Never crossed my mind," I said "Besides, looking out for Tara would only slow me down." I eyed her. "But for you I wouldn't be doing this, you know. I don't need it, and neither do you."

She sighed. "Actually, I'm having second thoughts, but it's too late now. She's here, and we agreed to help her."

I grunted. "She doesn't seem to have anyone but dear old Dad in her life. She's so attractive I have to wonder where her boyfriends are. Did she ask around for help before appealing to you?"

"I don't know—she didn't say. And now that you mention it, it's strange she's never said anything about a boyfriend. Perhaps she asked and was refused. A girl like Tara wouldn't want to admit something like that, you know. Or perhaps men walk all over her. Right now she seems pretty defeated by everything."

"Keep her here then. Help heal her psyche."

Melody nodded thoughtfully. "Good idea, hon. Do you think you'll be able to learn anything in Mazatlán?"

"A couple of religious flakes put into port, buy stores, and shove off for a place I never heard of. What's to learn?" I drank lengthily from my glass. "My guess is that about five minutes after Pop made that SOS call he was dead in the water with Graciela, and the pirates sailed on. I can show around a picture of the ketch, but in the two weeks since it was captured, it probably picked up a few tons of Mexican pot and ran them into Southern Cal. After that, if the pirates liked the boat, they'd keep it; if not, sink it offshore. No evidence, no prosecution."

17

"*Please* don't be that frank with Tara. All she has is hope."

I saw her coming down the staircase as Melody continued. "She's had a transient, rootless sort of life, so I feel sorry for her."

Tara handed me a rumpled envelope. Glancing inside, I saw brochures and newspaper clippings. I didn't take them out. Melody said, "Tara, I'm starved—aren't you hungry?"

"Uh-huh. I'd love a salad or a sandwich."

"We'll have both. C'mon." She led her guest toward the manse.

Alone, I finished my drink and emptied the envelope on the table. The brochures were what I expected. Cut-rate printing job in black and white, advertising the True Word Gospel Church, with testimonial letters from several who had received spiritual help from Preacher Billy Joe. Photographs showed him at a studio microphone, arms outstretched. His angular, masculine face looked as though it had absorbed more than its share of wear and tear, but it was topped with curly locks that added a youthful touch. The back of the folder was a cut-out coupon for sending contributions to a San Diego P.O. box. In return, the donor was promised on-air blessings. Broadcast times were listed on station KXSD's AM band.

I picked up the next brochure.

This was the TV promo. Same testimonials and box address, but the photo was more interesting.

Seated beside white-robed Billy Joe was white-gowned Sister Grace. Her soulful face was framed by a white band that merged into what seemed to be a nursing sister's coif. With its high cheekbones and full lips the face was provocative. Graciela Rodriguez, late of Tehachapi, transformed by the True Word Gospel Church into Sister Grace, the Preacher's bilingual assistant.

Or accomplice?

For a while I gazed at their photograph. I could understand

how the elderly and infirm, the abandoned and the hopeless would be moved to respond to their appeals. Billy Joe will say a prayer for you (in English), and Sister Grace will do likewise in her native tongue.

Native of where? I wondered. Meskin wetback, or Dago-born chicano? Tara should know, but why inquire? After hearing the Preacher's SOS, I figured they were both dead meat. Shark food. Making my trip to their last-known port of call confirmatory at best.

Glancing at the house, I wished Melody hadn't included me in her uplift program for Tara. Still, it was her money and her mother's house; I was the live-in fixer.

One short article from the Religion Section of the San Diego *Express* announced the advent of Billy Joe's radio ministry. Another, his and Sister Grace's TV debut. A third and larger piece in Local News was a more recent write-up of Billy Joe's humanitarian crusade to Central America. The illustration was a starboard photo of the *Paz Paloma*. Ketch-rigged, it looked about fifty-five feet from stern to bowsprit. The mainsail was decorated with a large version of Picasso's peace dove, which should make the boat easy to spot in any harbor. As I looked at brochures and articles I realized that I'd learned nothing of the man or his background. Divinity school credentials could have been mentioned, perhaps something concerning the Preacher's education and spiritual qualifications. Still, lack of formal training never prevented store-front shepherds from gathering a humble flock. So long as they helped the less fortunate, I had no quarrel with them. It was those who exploited religion against the vulnerable that I detested.

All the material revealed of Sister Grace was that she was willing to pray for contributors, in Spanish—a service that might interest some. That the brochure told readers nothing of her origin or qualifications didn't bother me particularly, for she hadn't founded Billy Joe's electronic ministry. But an organization dealing in sin and redemption shouldn't have overlooked her prison background. After all, one repentant sinner—as presentable as Graciela Rodriguez—was a clear gain for righteousness, and should have been claimed.

Strange.

I used the cabaña phone to call the San Diego *Express*, but the Religion Editor only worked part-time and the Managing Editor wouldn't give me the number of his home phone. I said I'd call another time, and placed a call to station KXSD. When the operations manager asked who I was, I said, "Jack Diehl, Miami *News*. I've got the Coast Guard beat, and I got curious about a preacher your station used to carry—Billy Joe Vaill, presumed lost at sea."

"Yeah, I heard that tape, too. I hope the hump is alive, because he owes us close to eighteen thousand dollars' air time." He paused. "You pick up anything on him? Any hope he's alive?"

"Not according to my sources. Still, it's an intresting story—if I can get a little background on his ministry. Got a few moments?"

"I'm a little rushed right now, mister, so why don't you phone the DA's office for an earful?"

"Gimme a break," I pleaded. "Calls cost money. What would the DA tell me?"

"That Preacher Billy Joe jumped bail and skipped town ahead of a couple of warrants."

"Yeah? What crime?"

"Mail fraud's one. Lifting a check from a thousand to ten's another—little old lady, too, the hump. I'm damned sorry I ever let him use the station, you can bet."

"Well, yeah. So, Billy Joe's a fugitive, you say?"

"Every way, mister. What does that do to your story?"

"It's certainly a new angle," I said reflectively, "and mucho thanks for your help."

"Okay, so do me a favor. Anything you publish on the Preacher, send me a clip, okay?"

"That's a promise," I told him, and hung up.

At the nearby bar I poured myself a shot of Añejo and drank. A new angle, I'd told him, and it was all of that.

Tara couldn't be unaware of her father's difficulties with the law, not while living in the same town. She hadn't come clean with Melody, or me. I didn't like the way she'd entered our lives under false pretenses, and I wasn't sure whether I should tell Melody what I'd just learned. But I could understand Tara's withholding derogatory info, for whatever else Billy Joe was, in her eyes he was, above all, her father. And it wasn't as though she'd lied to us. She just hadn't told the full story.

As I drank, I reflected that the equation was different now. Instead of searching for a starry-eyed do-gooder, I would be looking for the trail of a hardened thief.

Better all around if he were dead, I mused. The little I knew of Tara suggested she deserved better than a fugitive father. And if Billy Joe was still alive, the odds were high he didn't want to be found. Not by me, not by anyone.

His daughter had been with us barely an hour, but that was long enough to make me wish she'd never come. And whatever else I did, I wasn't going to go poking around Mazatlán unarmed.

THREE

On the way to the airport I stopped off at Mariscal's office to pick up the signed agreements. He'd had them notarized at the Mexican Consulate, a thoughtful touch that could spare me aggravation later on, and I felt that for once I'd concluded an agreement that wasn't going to fall apart.

Once aboard the flight, I reflected that even though I'd been away from Cozumel only three days, I'd lived there so long that returning gave me the excitement of going home. For I had formed ties of affection and blood with the Migueleños, and except for Melody there was no one in the States I cared for.

In addition to my ship chandlering business I owned the *Corsair*, a charter boat that catered to sport fishermen. Ramón was its second skipper, the first having been killed with Melody's stepfather, Paul Diehl. I still helped out Manuel's family, for in Mexico a widow with children to house and feed doesn't have an easy time.

I'd gone to Cozumel originally as a DEA agent tracking narcotics smuggling through the Caribbean. After resigning I'd managed to sink Luis Parra's cocaine-processing yacht,

killing him after he'd taken Melody hostage. As a peace
offering, DEA had let me keep the safehouse that was now
my home and refuge. I'd had to defend it, and the blood that
had been shed there made it all the more symbolic to me.
DEA had also conceded me the old four-place amphibian
that was tethered at my pier. The Seabee hadn't been manufactured in more than forty years, and without replacement
parts, DEA hadn't known what to do with it. But at the
Mérida airport a resourceful mechanic with a machine shop
kept my plane airworthy.

Through the late Paul Diehl, Melody had come into my
life and we'd gone through a lot together. She was intelligent
and fearless, and one of the nation's top competition div-
ers—her Olympic Silver proved that. And she was a sorcer-
ess in bed. So, my life seemed complete and serene.

Until Tara Vaill's project intruded.

Unlike her teflon mother, Melody couldn't turn away
a friend, and so I was commencing a sleeveless errand to
Mazatlán. I hoped to wrap it up quickly and negatively; no
news of the Preacher and his consort would be excellent
news for me.

We came down to the San Miguel airport at midday, and
I was cleared quickly through Customs and Immigration.
The deference shown me resulted from an unsubstantiated
rumor that I'd done away with a former airport chief. I
had—after Captain Jaramillo had twice tried to kill me,
slaughtering Chela, my housekeeper and lover, instead. So,
even the island cops left me alone. I had earned respect,
which is often more useful than friendship.

A taxi took me to my warehouse near the cruise ship pier,
where I explained the currency transaction to my manager
and filed the papers in my office. As I rode the rest of the
way to my place, sights and sounds churned memories in
my mind.

Only last month I'd visited a grave in Sonora—Sarita Rojas, the film star I'd known and loved in Guadalajara when

Melody was off in Europe. But I expected that Melody and I would be married for a long, long time.

I paid the taxi driver and whistled up my Dobermans, César and Sheba. Guard dogs, for a time they were my only companions, and I'd felt badly over selling their first litter—but I'd inspected the homes beforehand to make sure the pups would be appreciated and well-cared-for. Besides, Ramón's wife, María, who took care of my place when I was away, complained that seven *perros* were just too much for twice-a-day feedings.

The dogs jumped and bounded against the chain-link fence until I unlocked the gate. Then they licked my hands and face and tugged at my trousers until I fed them in the house.

That done, I poured a double shot of Añejo and thought about my mission to Mazatlán. I had a supply of weapons cached around the house, and I considered what I might need over the next few days. I had an Uzi 9-mm semiautomatic issued by DEA for assault boardings, but the Model 11 Ingram I'd acquired from a dead cocaine cowboy had double its rate of fire. Both, however, were too bulky to wear under my guayabera, so I decided to settle for my Browning 9-mm pistol. It was enough gun to intimidate any *cabrón* who thought me easy pickings. I extracted it from its niche behind the baseboard and packed it in my suitcase. Then I took a shower and a long siesta, and drove my jeep into town for an aperitif at Pepe's Bar on the waterfront, then a candlelit dinner at Morgan's.

In the morning Ramón drove me to the airport, where I took a feeder flight across the Sierra Madre range to Mazatlán on the Pacific coast.

Rather than a four-star tourist hotel, I selected an inconspicuous waterfront *posada* that catered to Mexicans. From my room I could see the shrimp fleet at anchor. Landward rose the gray-brown Sierra Madre *cordillera*. The once simple fishing village was nicely situated between sea and mountains. After unpacking I got out the Browning and shoved it between my belt and spine. The starched guayabera concealed it nicely.

At an open-air waterfront restaurant I ordered beer-steamed shrimp and quenched the flaming Tabasco with two bottles of chilled Tecate, my favorite Mexican beer. Seined overnight, the shrimp had that sea-fresh taste of iodine, and I happily shelled two dozen until my mind returned to my mission.

The waiter was a polite young man with a wispy mustache, and when he dropped off my third Tecate I showed him the photo of Billy Joe's ketch and asked if he remembered it.

"*Sí, señor.* A big boat. I remember the *paloma* on the sail." He stared at it intently. "The captain and his woman ate here. He didn't speak Spanish, but she did."

I palmed him a ten-thousand-peso note. "Mexican accent?"

"*No, señor.* Venezuelan, I think . . . or Colombian. It was—well, I had no reason to pay attention. But she was good-looking, and young for the captain. *Muy guapa.*"

I showed him the studio photograph. "This couple?"

"*Sí, sí.*" He nodded excitedly. "Even in religious garb I would know them."

I laid another bill on the table, where the breeze stirred it slightly. "How long were they in port?"

"Not long—maybe only overnight. Two nights, perhaps."

"And then they went where?"

He shrugged. "I don't know. You could ask down there." He pointed at the rows of charter boats along the docks. I said, "I'm staying at the *posada*, so if you think of anything else, look me up."

"*Sí, señor.* Gladly." With an almost unseen movement he made the banknote disappear. "Your name?"

"Just ask for the *gringo*, okay?"

"*Estámos*. Another plate of shrimp?"

"Later, maybe." He moved away and I sat back and tilted my Tecate bottle. Beyond the overhead canopy the sun scorched the harbor, but in the shade where I sat breeze kept the air tolerable.

Where Cozumel had one pier scaffold for hoisting a prize catch, I could count a score out by the boats. One held a sun-shrunk octopus that, alive, must have topped two hundred pounds. Its desiccated arms showed rows of knobby suckers that could grip and hold a swimmer until he drowned. Fishermen feared *El Pulpo*, but they ate him, too, and I enjoyed the tasty flesh that was tough only when badly cooked.

The abundance of trophy scaffolds reflected the abundance of Pacific sailfish—*pez vela*—off Mazatlán. They bred north in the Sea of Cortez, waters that teemed with plankton, shrimp and fry that fed on them. In the Caribbean, where I fished, the sail were smaller and hard to find. So I encouraged my charter sportsmen to tag and free their catch, though they seldom did. For the sake of a photo posed beside their prize.

I paid my bill, bought a reed hat from a sidewalk vendor and strolled down to the boats. For the next hour or so I showed captains and crew my photos of Billy Joe and Graciela, and the *Paz Paloma*. Most recognized the boat, but none knew where it had gone. I let them know there was a reward for information, and said I could be found at the *posada*.

Next, I showed the photos around nearby stores that sold bottled water and provisions, and checked a nautical supply store as well. There, Billy Joe had bought three solar water purifiers, an assortment of batteries, two boxes of shotgun shells and one of .30-caliber rifle ammunition. The shopkeeper remembered the purchases, having thought it odd that a peace boat would carry weapons.

"Did he say where he was going?" I asked. "Next port of call?"

"*No, señor.*"

"Did he buy handgun cartridges?"

"I don't sell them. Ah—one thing else. A machete. With *vaina.*"

Perhaps the scabbard was to protect the blade at sea. Aboard, a machete was useful for killing and cutting up fish. On land, for hacking through brush. I thanked him and went to the store next door.

Behind the scarred counter sat a very large woman with pillow-size breasts and thick, muscular arms. In a shadowed corner I could see a man of normal size. Except for occupying a chair and smoking a corncob pipe, he was doing nothing at all. I judged he was her husband, and it was easy to see who was in charge.

So I showed her my photographs.

She recognized the couple and acknowledged that they had bought a few things. Lip balm, suntan oil, jugs of water, a case of canned soups and four cartons of filter Marlboros. "It was all the lady selected."

"When she came in was she smoking?"

"Yes. And kept lighting cigarettes. No wonder she needed four cartons."

"Did you happen to hear where they were headed from Mazatlán?"

"South. The lady said the sun would be stronger there, so they needed protective oil."

"*Agradecido, señora.*" I laid two fifty-thousand-peso notes on the counter. Quick as a piston stroke, her arm shot out and the *billetes* disappeared. "I'm staying at the *posada,*" I told her, "in case anything else comes to mind."

"*Sí, señor.*" Her smile stretched from ear to ear. I paid for an iced Tecate and swigged it as I left the shop.

The missing couple's purchases were routine enough, I thought as I walked back to the *posada.* At four packs a day,

Sister Grace had stocked a ten-day supply—enough to get her to Puerto Padrón. Otherwise, no clues at all.

The air's dry heat was enervating; besides, it was siesta time, working people relaxing in the shade. In my room I turned on the ceiling fan and stretched out on the bed until sleep came.

When I woke it was evening, and someone was knocking on the door.

Quietly, I left the bed and picked up my pistol.

FOUR

Straw hat in hand, there stood the little man with the corn-cob pipe, the stout *señora*'s lesser half. Through the crack in the doorway he saw the Browning and started back. "Don't go," I said, and opened the door.

Still staring at my pistol, he came in and I locked the door, then tucked the pistol in my belt. "*Qué pasa?*" I asked.

"*Señor*, I have information for you, information my *señora* doesn't know about."

So he'd been eavesdropping on us, the old rascal. "Have a chair," I invited. "Why wouldn't she know?"

Uncomfortably, he sat down, looked up at me, eyes wide. "She told you only what the couple bought in her—our—store. Not what they bought in another place."

"Ah," I said, "that could be interesting." I got out some banknotes. "Tell me all."

"*Gracias, señor*, I will do so." He smiled tensely.

"What's your name?"

"They call me Pablo, '*El Chico*.' "

"I'm Juan, '*El Gringo*.' What is it you want to tell me?"

He fanned his face with the shabby hat. "The couple asked

29

where they could buy snorkeling equipment. We have no call for such things, but I was able to name a diving shop along the waterfront." He paused. "I took them there."

"And saw what they bought?"

Nodding, he glanced at the money in my hand. I peeled off a ten-thousand-peso note and gave it to him. Four bucks were finally going to buy me something.

"Two face masks," he told me, "two pairs of fins, and two snorkel tubes."

"Air tanks?"

"No."

"Did they bring any to fill?"

"Not then—I don't know about later."

"Think about this," I said. "Were they interested in snorkeling, or deep-diving with air tanks?"

He shrugged. "Shallow swimming, I think, though the woman spoke to her husband about a keel."

To make sure I understood, I said, *"Quilla?"*

"Sí. Exacto. La quilla." His hand made a descriptive gesture.

Maybe they were planning to scrape off sea growth. "Did they buy metal brushes, scrapers?"

"Not to my knowledge, *señor.*"

They could have had those things on board. The snorkeling gear could be for recreational use after they reached Puerto Padrón. *"Gracias,"* I said. "I appreciate the information."

He didn't get up, and I wasn't going to pay for more marginal information, so we stared at each other until El Chico said, "There is more to know, *señor.*"

"Oh?"

His eyes glittered at the money in my hand. "I'm listening," I said.

"The woman," he said, "the man's young, dark-haired wife—"

"Go on."

"I saw her again."

I stood up. "That's possible. They were here for a couple of days."

"I mean recently."

I stopped moving. "How recently?"

He was still staring at the money, so I gave him five thousand pesos. With a smile, he said, "Four days—nights—ago."

"How could that be? She and her husband were lost at sea, presumed dead."

"This *mujer* is alive," he said, folding the banknotes into his shabby shirt. "I saw her with my own eyes."

That was my cue to get out Sister Grace's photo and have him examine it under a light. Finally he said, "*Cierto, señor.* Even in this nun's habit I recognize her. I swear it on the life of my wife."

"Where did you see her?"

"At the big hotel—Camino Real."

The story he told was that he had an *amiga*—a serious, congenial person like himself—who worked in the hotel's kitchen. Nights when he could slip away from his wife, he would go to the hotel and they would enjoy a late supper together, food courtesy of the Camino Real. Then they would wander off in the darkness, and . . . He left that much to my imagination. Resuming, Pablo said they liked to watch the rich patrons on the terrace, and at a table near the shrubbery the woman had been sitting. Her hair was combed, her nails colored and lacquered; she wore an expensive-looking gown, and jewelry. The man with her at the table was a tall, strong *morocho* with a triangular scar on one cheek. He wore a lot of jewelry.

"Her husband?"

"Who can say? The brown-complexioned man is not the man she was with in our store, the one in this picture."

"Two different men."

He nodded.

31

"That was four days ago—nights—and you haven't seen the woman since?"

"No, *señor*—I first recognized her four nights ago. Last night I saw her again, and with the same man. In different clothing, but the same couple."

"All right," I said, "you did well to remember. Have you seen the husband recently?"

"No, *señor*. Not since I left him at the diving shop. Two weeks ago—a little more."

"What time is the woman and her companion on the terrace?"

"Both nights, around ten. *Más o menos*."

"I'll check it out. There could be a bonus for you."

"Ah, *señor*, I pray she has not departed the hotel. The money would be very welcome. My wife . . ." A sad expression took over his face.

"Say no more, Pablo." I pumped his hand vigorously and pressed an extra ten thousand against his palm. That made him a lot happier, and we parted on excellent terms.

Showering, I thought things over. Work the street, ask questions was the investigator's golden rule. I'd done so, and for the moment felt rewarded.

But what did I actually have?

The *Paz Paloma* had been in Mazatlán for a couple of days, and its owners had made some purchases around town, generally routine. What seemed a little offbeat was the rifle and shotgun ammunition, the machete and the snorkeling gear. Or maybe I was oversensitive, grasping at little, having nothing solid to go on.

Until Pablo "El Chico" identified Graciela Rodriguez. If she was the piracy's sole survivor, why keep it secret? Shouldn't she be running up and down the streets screaming for justice and reprisal? Where was the boat? Her husband, Billy Joe?

But was I letting imagination overwhelm logic? I had

nothing but the word of a little man who smoked a corncob pipe in the corner of his wife's store—a man with an *amiga* and no money to buy her presents. Why not pry a few pesos from the *gringo*?

Having come this far, I wasn't going to stay in my room and indulge in philosophical riddles.

Maybe Graciela was alive and at the Camino Real, maybe not. I'd find out for myself.

It was a large deluxe resort hotel of the kind that had sprung up all over coastal Mexico. Polished tile floors, glitzy decor, and too much lighting. It reminded me of Puerto Vallarta, whose memories were both sweet and bitter.

Mazatlán wasn't yet a prime tourist destination, so the hotel was far from crowded. Thus, the bartender was polite to me and generous with the Añejo he poured over my cracked ice.

As I sipped, I looked around and saw that the bar lounge extended onto an outside terrace that had candlelit tables, caged macaws and a mariachi band. Foliage bordered the terrace, separating it from the hotel grounds. Somewhere just beyond the ixora and flame trees, Pablo and his *amiga* had watched the jet-setters at play. The corner table had a Reserved sign on it, and I wondered if it was where Sister Grace and her dusky escort customarily repaired.

Nine o'clock.

I left my drink and went to the main switchboard, where I had the operator place a call to Miami. I said I'd pay in cash and demonstrated that I could. She said she'd call me at the bar.

I was enjoying a second drink when the call came through. Thomas, in his wisdom, divined the call was from me, and had summoned Melody. When I heard her voice I said, "Anyone listening, hon?"

"Just me, precious."

"Keep it that way. And by no means tell Tara any of what you're about to hear."

"Bad news?"

"Don't know yet. At the moment I'm in the Camino Real following a lead."

"Ahhh. So like you. Go on."

"Don't interrupt, the connection could vanish forever. Now, a source of unknown reliability claims he's seen Sister Grace in recent days. On the premises. If she hasn't checked out, I'll have more to tell later. Meanwhile, I'm lodged at a roach-bin called El Gran Camarón. Got it?"

"Marvelous name—unforgettable."

"A humble *posada* befitting my station in life. No room phones, natch, so I'm calling from here. Working on your papers? Tara okay? Everything tight?"

"She's—ah, apprehensive, Jack, very nervous."

"Has reason to be. Her tragic tale left out a lot—but that's for another time. Love you."

"*Te adoro.*"

I waited for the toll calculation, paid the cashier and returned to the bar. After finishing my drink I laid pesos on the *maître* and got a table close to the suspect one. Then I ordered dinner.

The cold, veined jumbo shrimp were almost as fresh as the steamers I'd enjoyed earlier. The Tabasco-laden sauce was less incandescent, but it cleared my sinuses and sharpened my vision without inducing headache. So far, so good.

A cold glass of crisp Etiqueta Blanca freshened my taste buds before the *huachinango* filet arrived. Salad greens were advertised as chemically washed, but I wasn't going to gamble my GI tract, so I passed.

The corner table was still unoccupied, *Reservado* sign in place. Time: nine forty-eight.

Before leaving Miami I'd managed to reach the San Diego DA's office, where an assistant DA told me more about Billy Joe Vaill than I was prepared to hear.

Born William Joseph Vaillant in Tesla, Oklahoma, he had a long rap sheet as petty thief, gambler and con man, stretching across five states. Deserted by his common-law wife, Madge Brinker, Vaillant had brought up their daughter, Tara, in an itinerant, picaresque life. During periods when he was jailed the daughter was cared for by county, city or state in a dozen different localities. Vaillant's longest jail time was a trey for car theft. Throughout, he had always been a model prisoner, attending high school and college-level classes. While in the Pico Correctional Institute he had developed interest in religious matters and worked as chaplain's assistant.

Two months ago, Preacher Billy Joe had been arrested for mail fraud and check-kiting, as I already knew. Bond for eighty thousand dollars, plus a lien on the Preacher's yacht, on which he'd paid only a thousand down. So, after sailing surreptitiously from San Diego, Billy Joe was charged with grand theft, and the bonding company's money forfeited. Outstanding fugitive warrants converted his relief mission to Central America into a headlong flight.

Although the assistant DA said that her office viewed Sister Grace as a full accomplice, there was insufficient evidence to bring charges against her beyond parole violation. So it was the Preacher they wanted—alive, unlikely as that now seemed.

I pondered these findings as I ate broiled red snapper and sipped white wine. It would be heartless to reveal all that I knew to Melody, and pointless to challenge Tara for what she'd concealed. So the optimum outcome would be the verification that her father was dead.

And Graciela would know.

The mariachi musicians filed out, and more congenial music flowed from the bandstand. Bass and rhythm guitars,

35

keyboard, conga drums and flute. The tempo was Afro-Cuban and the flute soared like a jungle bird. Couples took to the floor, and I reflected that the setting and rhythm would appeal to Melody, given her Brazilian upbringing.

Dancers obstructed my view of the corner table, and when the number ended I saw the *maître* removing the Reservado sign and seating a couple at the table. The man was tall, brown-skinned, and sturdily built. When he turned to reward the *maître* I made out a small, light-colored scar on his right cheek. Reaching across the table, he took his companion's hand.

Her complexion was lighter than his—*café au lait*—and I judged her height to be between Melody's and Tara's. Her arms were well formed, as was her half-revealed bosom; straight, charcoal hair, full lips and a slightly curving Indian nose. As she spoke, I glimpsed white teeth.

So far I'd seen only her profile, and it wasn't until she rose and glanced at the band that I saw her almond-shaped face. I compared it to the photo in my hand and decided Pablo had earned his bonus. The woman *was* Billy Joe's wife.

The intense, sensuous way she danced with her escort suggested that any mourning for her husband had been brief. Or, if the Preacher were still alive, fidelity was history.

I wanted to question Graciela about her husband and the boat, but she was enjoying herself, and I doubted that her escort would tolerate a prying *gringo*. Direct approach was out.

Don't push, I thought, something may drop into place. She didn't know I was watching her, or even that I existed, and that gave me an advantage.

All I had to do was use it.

They were ordering dinner when I paid my check and strolled into the lobby. Bell captains have a deserved reputation for comprehensive knowledge of their premises, and this one was no exception. Rafael "Call me Rafe" Peregil accepted twenty thousand pesos. In border English he said, "If you're a divorce dick, keep me out of it, okay?"

"No problem. The girl's family hired me to check whether the boyfriend is a suitable lifemate."

He covered his mouth to suppress laughter. When he could talk without snickering, he said, "That big *morocho* has heavy connections in Colombia." He simulated a snort. "But if it's rich they want, he's it. Name's Federico Gomez—goes by Freddy."

"So would I. Are they rooming together?"

"Does a snake suck eggs? He was there two days before she arrived. Ordered up girls like they was beer bottles—by the case. After she came, no more of that."

I tugged my earlobe. "Doesn't sound too steady a marital prospect, Rafe."

"Like I say, you get what you see, and rich it is."

"What about the *señorita*?"

"Like what?"

"Like a quick look at her passport?"

His eyes narrowed. "You know her name, what do you need the passport for?"

"To check her travels," I said with a pained expression. "Can do?"

"For another ten thousand."

I patted his shoulder. "I'm contemplating early retirement myself. Okay, ten."

"But you don't keep it—I stay right with you."

"Absolutely. While I make a few notes."

"Wait in my office—that door beyond the registration desk."

I nodded. "One other thing—they spend all their time around the hotel?"

"They do the pool, lounges, bars—eat here, like now. But afterward they usually get into his Maserati and take a drive. A long one."

"How long?"

"I'm off at four. I've only seen them not come back once."

"Probably sifting the moonlit sands for trinkets."

"Yeah, to pay expenses."

"Maserati, you say. The roads around here look pretty rough for a low-slung formula car."

"Maybe they don't go far."

"That's the answer," I said admiringly. "You've done it again, Rafe. Freddy wouldn't want to risk such expensive wheels, would he?"

He grunted. "The kind of dough he's got, he can buy Maseratis the way I buy tortillas, okay?"

"Gotcha." I headed for his command post while Rafe sauntered over to the registration desk.

His office, slightly larger than a closet, also served for lost-and-found. Sawed-off desk and phone. In a corner a stack of hand luggage, airline bags, mostly, forgotten by— or lifted from—guests. I wondered how many Rafe had "forgotten" to return.

Two minutes and he was with me, a shiny Colombian passport in hand. The photo showed Graciela Rodriguez— the woman on the terrace wth Freddy Gomez—but the name on it was Marta del Campo. The passport date of issue was just ten days ago, and it bore no entry/exit stamps— not even for Mexico. That meant it had been brought to her from Bogotá.

Rafe and I were thinking the same thoughts, but I said nothing about the blank pages. If the birthdate was correct, Graciela/Marta was thirty-one years old, and from what I'd seen of her face and figure, in the splendor of her prime.

Rafe said, "It might be worth a lot to Freddy—quite a lot—to know a *gringo*'s been asking about his woman."

"Might at that," I agreed, and handed him the passport. "But if he were to find out, I'd make your face impossible to repair."

Eyeing me, he muttered, "Forget it, bad idea." He licked his lips. "Anything else, *caballero*?"

"I have a craving to know where they drive after supper."

"Yeah. Got wheels?"

"No."

"Get back by four and you can rent mine."

"How much?"

"Fifty *mil*."

"Be reasonable."

"Forty."

"Thirty's the magic figure."

"Cool. You buy the gas."

FIVE

Something was better than nothing, but the best feature of Rafe's old Fiat was its shabby inconspicuousness. The seat springs were sprung, the tires knobby, and the engine wheezed in terminal emphysema. The windows hadn't been cleaned since the day the car came off the assembly line. But for 20/20 vision, I could never have spotted the orange Maserati after it flared out of the hotel drive.

I counted on Freddy's having to slow to avoid busting his tires on potholes, and presently I was able to glimpse him proceeding south at more reasonable speed. Between palm trees, moonlight revealed occasional orange streaks, verifying that we were on the same road even though I was far behind.

Freddy Gomez had arrived in Mazatlán for the purpose of meeting Graciela/Marta, and had probably brought her new passport. He'd expected her to leave the *Paz Paloma* and join him, so at least two people had known that Billy Joe's boat was not going to reach its advertised destination, Puerto Padrón. How many others knew? The high-seas pirates—if they existed.

I'd sniffed bad joss when Billy Joe's SOS hadn't included his location to aid possible rescuers. Assuming the omission was intentional led to the possibility that the hijacking had been simulated. Why? Because a "dead" Preacher had no further worries about California warrants for his arrrest. His stateside existence had ended, and a new, less complicated one could begin.

If he was still alive.

He might well be, because the scam was consistent with everything I'd learned about the Preacher's life and times. Still, how explain his wife and Federico Gomez? They shared a suite, they were bunkies. How did that sit with Billy Joe?

If he knew.

And why was it permissible for Sister Grace to surface back in Mazatlán without her husband? Wouldn't that raise the kind of questions I was pondering? Did she feel that make-up, new hairdo and passport would shield her identity? Couldn't the Preacher also wear disguise? What was the point of it all?

As I asked myself these questions, I realized I should have asked more about Sister Grace. According to Rafe, Freddy was a *narcotraficante*, and Graciela/Marta had done a stretch at Tehachapi. But I'd neglected to ask why. Perhaps her photo in religious garb had made me slide over the possibility that she had been involved with drugs. If that was why she'd gone to prison, her pairing off with Freddy made more sense.

Then I reminded myself that I wasn't on narcotics detail. I'd come to learn the truth about Tara's missing father. My interest in Sister Grace should be limited to what she knew about him—dead or alive—and she was my only lead.

A cloud covered the moon, and I lost all sight of the Maserati. The farther from Mazatlán, the worse the road. I'd kept the headlights low, and missed seeing a trench-like pothole that jammed my jaws and almost snapped what was left of the Fiat's axle springs. The Maserati, I mused enviously, must have flown over the ditch.

Slowing to a stop, I turned off the engine and listened. Off in the distance came a powerful burbling roar. Freddy hurtling through the night.

At twenty-five mph I resumed the chase.

Clouds cleared the moon, but by now the Maserati was too far ahead for visual contact. My only hope of spotting it again would be after it came to a stop. That had to be fairly soon, because the thin threading of roads around Mazatlán ended either at the sierra foothills, the rocky coast, or petered out like tendrils in the jungle.

Besides, Rafe said the couple usually returned by four, so there had to be a destination where they stopped and passed some time.

Where? And why?

The road rose gently, hugging the coastline, and through scrub and foliage I could see the Pacific's phosphorescent rollers. I didn't have to worry about cattle and burros along the roadside, because the Maserati would have frightened them away. For another ten minutes I concentrated on the narrow, rocky road, then at a high point I stopped, turned off the engine, and listened.

As my ears adjusted, I could hear geckos chirping in the jungle, the soft whoosh of breaking waves below, sea wind rustling ceiba branches, but no Maserati engine. Only the sounds of nature drifted through the night.

Wherever it was, the Maserati had stopped running.

Far off at sea, lights of the shrimp fleet twinkled like distant windblown candles. A peaceful, moonlit night.

Where was Sister Grace?

My spine was numb where the hard seatback pressed against the Browning. I got out of the car long enough to readjust the pistol's position, then I started the engine and drove slowly on, scanning both sides of the road.

If the Maserati was stashed in thick foliage I'd never see

it, but why would Freddy want to conceal his car? For that matter, why did they leave the comforts of the hotel for the hazards of an unimproved road, and do so every night?

As I inched along, I thought of Manny Montijo, my old DEA pal. Last seen, he'd headed the Guadalajara operation and hired me to look into the narcotics traffic and the corruption of high state officials. I reflected that I'd fulfilled my contract, and more. The more had put me in a basement dungeon where I'd been brutally beaten until Manny managed to extricate me by freeing Colombian drug kingpin Omar Parra from US jail. The three-nation deal never made the press, and though I was glad to be free, it grated me that Parra had been released to continue his lethal trade.

I wondered what coverage, if any, Manny had been able to develop in Mazatlán. Probably very little, because he'd had to rebuild the informant network that was severely damaged when his consulate predecessor was murdered by narcotics dealers.

So, I concluded that if I picked up anything of value I'd pass it along to Manny. Like finding Freddy Gomez in Mazatlán, far from Colombian haunts. Manny might know, and he might not care—unless Freddy associated with Omar Parra. That would be worthwhile news.

There had to be a motive behind Sister Grace's moves since leaving Tehachapi. Chance meeting with Preacher Billy Joe Vaill had converted him into a parole guarantor who provided her a visible job as his assistant. Marriage, then, while collections diminished. The *Paz Paloma*'s humanitarian mission, aborted by apparent disaster, the Preacher and his wife presumed murdered or lost at sea. Finally, her reappearance in Mazatlán, looking neither distressed nor devout, and no sign of husband or boat.

Now, like the boat, the Maserati had disappeared.

Slowly, I guided the old Fiat as far as the road seemed passable, and then I turned around.

Through the dirty windshield I glimpsed something I

hadn't seen before: a light in the jungle. To make sure it wasn't dash reflection I stopped the car and got out.

Moonlight flooded a jungle hillside, showing the almost invisible roof of a distant house. Light filtered from a top-floor window but I couldn't see the rest of the building through the heavy foliage. I got up on the car's hood and managed to scan more of the house. It was old Colonial style with whitewash patches clinging to gray stone walls. Barrel-tile roofing and barred windows. The place was so isolated that I wondered how it had electricity.

There had to be an access road or path, and the Maserati might have taken it, but I wasn't going to stumble through the dark and disturb some poisonous *vibora* slinking up on an unsuspecting frog. My natural aversion to snakes had escalated ever since Sarita Rojas died from a coral snake's bite, and now I feared snakes with near phobia.

So, having decided against nocturnal exploration, I turned and started to get down from the hood, then stopped.

At road level I hadn't been able to see the cove below. Protected by fallen boulders, it was formed like a shallow V, and toward the ocean opening a fair-sized yacht was anchored. The sails were furled, but the masts showed it was ketch-rigged, and about the length of *Paz Paloma*.

To make sure, I would have to see the boat broadside, check the name on the stern. No lights showed **through** cabin portholes, so I decided to go down the long, steep bank and check it out.

But for the moonlight I couldn't have kept footing on the rocky side, and had I fallen the full fifty feet to the boulder-edged beach, there would have been no rescuers available. Rocks tumbled beneath my weight, a clinging shrub gave way, but by working slowly and carefully down, I made it to the sand.

With the bow pointing seaward, the boat's stern faced me, but it was darkly shadowed, any lettering invisible.

In shadows I stripped to my shorts and left my Browning in the bundle of clothing. Then I crossed the beach and waded into water as warm as the night air. Quietly, I began breaststroking toward the stern of the boat, but I couldn't make out the lettering until I was almost close enough to touch.

The entire transom had been recently painted with white enamel. Across it, in large black script, *Delfin*, and below the name, the home port: *Guaymas*.

With light I could have discerned the outline of whatever lettering the fresh enamel now obscured. It wasn't unusual for boats to bear new names chosen by buyers, but registry papers and entries had to be made out accordingly. And displayed aboard.

As I stroked around the waterline I saw a small skiff tethered amidships by a small ladder. I went up the ladder and stepped onto the quarterdeck, moved into shadows and listened. All I could hear was the creaking of the hull, strained by the rising tide.

Moving aft, I stepped into the cockpit and looked around. The big mahogany helm turned listlessly as I went around it to peer at the panel's framed certificates. Cowling shadowed them from moonlight, so I turned on a panel lamp, knelt and looked closely at the registry certificate.

Crimmins-designed, the boat had been built in a Maine shipyard twenty years ago—and badly tended since. Nearly thirty tons displacement, fourteen-foot beam. I focused on the name.

Sure enough, still *Paz Paloma* out of San Diego.

I was reaching to turn off the light when a voice barked, *"Manos arriba. Qué hace?"*

My arms shot upward. Turning slowly, I saw a man on deck. Pointing a shotgun at me.

It would not, I thought, serve my interests to pretend I didn't speak Spanish. So I shrugged, tried to look shamefaced and said, "Sorry—I didn't see anyone aboard, so I swam out." I glanced around. "I didn't take anything, I'm not a thief."

"Maybe I stopped you."

"No," I said calmly, "the boat looked like one belonging to a friend, so I decided to check it out."

"Eh? What friend?"

"Licenciado Moisés Guzmán of Guadalajara. He keeps a boat down here. Mazatlán, I thought, but maybe he keeps it at Manzanillo. If his boat was here I was going to look for him in town." Attorney Guzmán had helped me get out of jail, and his name had come quickly to mind. Besides, Moisés was a renowned criminal defense lawyer, and mentioning him couldn't hurt.

The gunman was undecided what to do. Maybe I was okay, maybe not. Even in Mexico, where murder was a casual matter, I didn't think he wanted to kill me. So, I dropped my arms and climbed out of the cockpit, putting us about five feet apart. He didn't like that, and his hands tightened on the shotgun. I raised my arms again and tried to look helpless and concerned.

He said, "The Licenciado don't own this boat."

"So I found out. Sorry I woke you. I'll be on my way."

"*No!* You stay here until morning."

I put on my perplexed expression. "Why?"

"Maybe the owner knows you."

"I doubt that," I said, "but to save time for all of us, let's call the police."

He didn't like that either. My right leg snapped up and I grabbed the foot. "Cramp!" I howled and hopped around on the other, gradually nearing him as he watched my antics. When I judged I was close enough, I spun and kicked the shotgun barrel upward. The gun went off as it left his hands, spraying pellets over my head. Off balance, he moved backward, and I jumped forward, hitting his chest with both feet.

He slid down the deck, grunting. I picked up the shotgun's hot barrel and slammed the stock against his head. His body convulsed, lay still.

I swallowed and leaned against the rail. The guard, or crewman, whatever he was, would be out of play for a while, so there was time to search the boat.

I jacked a shell into the shotgun's firing chamber and set the safety. Then I began looking around.

The first thing I noticed was a set of tank racks along the portside gunwale. In them stood four yellow scuba tanks, snubbed by elastic cord. I went forward and saw nothing out of the ordinary, except that lines lay loose, the deck was dirty, and the impression was of slovenly shipkeeping. Unsurprising considering the couple's un-nautical background. Next, I went down the companionway and found things equally untidy in the saloon. Clothing and bedlinen were scattered across pull-out bunks; the table held an unwashed plate, a metal knife and fork and a dirty glass. Near it, a bottle of Bacardi rum. I wiped the lip and drank deeply. Then I searched both cabins.

Both had unmade beds, and the second held a scattering of brochures advertising the True Word Gospel Church, material I'd seen before. No question that I'd found the right boat.

An ash tray held the short butts of crudely made cigarettes. I pinched one apart and sniffed the shreds. High-grade pot. I visualized Billy Joe and Sister Grace toking their way south, wheel lashed, stars and moon above. An idyllic tropic voyage.

Above the bunk, an old Marlin .30-caliber lever-action rifle was set into spring clips. Its ammunition had come from Pablo's store.

I wasn't looking for anything in particular, except possible signs of violent struggle, and I'd seen none.

As I returned through the saloon I took another pull from

the rum bottle and capped it. The crewman would need the rest for a very sore head.

I ejected the shotgun's shells and shoved them under the bunk mattress before taking the weapon on deck. He'd have to explain a missing shotgun, but if it was there he might forego mentioning me and our altercation. I didn't really care.

But to make life a little more difficult for him I decided to row the skiff ashore. Kneeling, I listened to his shallow breathing and felt for his carotid pulse. Around his neck was a thin circlet of white and red beads, probably strung on animal hair. A *santería* amulet against misfortune. His pulse was strong, so maybe the amulet had helped him stay alive.

With that thought I left him sprawled in the moonlight. Then I stepped from the ladder into the little skiff, untied it, and unshipped the oars. Light rowing and the thrust of the tide soon ground the skiff against sand. I shoved the bow further onto the beach, squeezed out my wet shorts, and got dressed.

I was just starting to climb back up the face of the cliff when I heard the Maserati zoom by with the sound of a low-flying jet. Holding onto outcrops, I swore. Wherever Freddy had gone, I'd missed him, and now he was heading back. Still, it was worth something to know the *Paz Paloma* was safe in the cove below. Its still-unpaid owners in San Diego might be the most eager to know its location, and I might earn myself a few bucks by helping them out.

Still, I thought, as I gained level land, I hadn't learned where Billy Joe was, or whether he was alive or dead. And that was why I'd come to Mazatlán for Melody and Tara.

Under strong moonlight I drove back to town and returned Rafe's Fiat a little before three. He was glad to see his heap intact, and gladder for the thirty thousand pesos I laid in his hand.

It had been a long, active night. I took a taxi to El Gran Camarón and flopped onto my bed.

Around midday, repeated knocking at my door wakened me, and when I opened it, there stood Miss Tara Vaill.

SIX

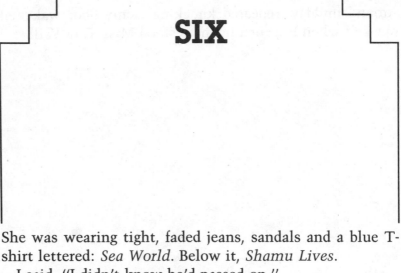

She was wearing tight, faded jeans, sandals and a blue T-shirt lettered: *Sea World*. Below it, *Shamu Lives*.

I said, "I didn't know he'd passed on."

"Who?" Her freckled face tightened. "My father?"

"Shamu, the killer whale."

"Oh." She picked up a tattered rucksack. "Aren't you going to ask me in?"

"I haven't decided. I don't think I should encourage you. Anyway, why are you here?"

"Melody bought me a ticket."

"That's not why, that's how. So you flew in. Why?"

She shrugged. "Because I wanted to be close by—in case you get any information. And maybe I can help."

"Think I'm not competent at skip-tracing?"

Her eyelids lowered. "It's not that, Jack, it's—well, I need to feel I'm *doing* something."

Resignedly I shoved the door so she could enter. Once inside, she closed it and stared at the room's one bed. "What did you expect?" I asked. "The executive suite? Waterbeds and blue movies?"

She swallowed. "I—I don't know what I expected. But I'm willing to share, to save money—if you won't try any funny business."

"Sex is funny?" I said wearily, and began rinsing my face at the washbasin.

"Well, it's not funny ha-ha, but you know what I mean. And even if I wanted to get it on with you, I owe Melody a lot—too much to come between you. So—"

"Don't get complicated, get another room. If you don't have traveling money, I'll pay."

I thought that might send her on her way, but I was too optimistic. Through a corner of my eye I could see her kick off her sandals. She sat on the edge of the bed and began to massage her feet. I lathered my face and began to shave.

She said, "What can I do?"

"Run down to the corner store and bring up a couple of iced Tecates. Make it three."

"What's Tecates?"

"Beer."

She didn't move. I said, "You asked what you could do, I told you. What's the delay?"

"I don't speak Spanish. Besides, that's not—"

"When you get there, hold up three fingers and say 'tay-cah-tay.' Got it?"

"If that's what you want."

She got off the bed and stepped into her sandals. "I bet you're not so curt with Melody."

"When necessary," I told her. "And that relationship is totally unlike yours and mine. Money in my trouser pocket," I added. "Remember: three fingers, tay-cah-tay."

She shook her head. "How much should I take?"

"Five thousand will cover. Buy yourself a taco with the change."

Without further instruction she left the room, closing the door unnecessarily hard. I finished shaving, took a tepid shower, and got into clean clothes. Last night's clothing showed cliffside stains and dirt.

Returning to the room, Tara placed three brown bottles in the basin. "Shall I open one?"

"Two, if you're thirsty. Cap puller's on the wall." That kind of place.

She handed me an open bottle and sucked at hers while regarding me thoughtfully. "Save your feet," I suggested. "Use the chair."

She did, and I sat on the bed exercising my toes. A couple of them ached from kicking the shotgun. The beer went down smoothly as cream sherry, and I opened the second bottle. As I was tilting it, she said, "How much have you found out?"

"About what?"

"About where my father is."

"Nothing," I said. "*Nada.*"

"What did you think I meant?"

"Well, hon, I wasn't sure. I thought you might be wondering how much I've found out *about* your father. After all, you gave me a minimal scan, and revealed nothing of importance. Is that any way to brief an unpaid investigator for his mission?"

I swallowed more beer and gazed at her, but she wasn't meeting my eyes. I kept on sipping beer while Tara stared at the floor. When my bottle was empty I tossed it at the trash basket, missed, and said, "Well?"

"Well, what?"

"Well, are you going to come clean?"

"About what?" she asked, and her voice was surly, all little-girl pleading gone.

I sighed. "We keep asking each other questions. I'll ask another. Are you going to come clean about your father's background? If not, I'm flying back to Miami and you can have the room."

She swallowed and finally looked at me. "You're very difficult, aren't you?"

"About average," I said. "And I don't like lies or the aggravation they produce."

Her lips formed an unattractive smile. "Knowing Melody, I thought you'd be a gentleman."

That made me grin. "Haven't had to be since I left the Navy. What do you think of that?"

"I think it's too bad—and not very nice."

"Nice, I'm not, and never pretended to be. Okay." I got off the bed and began shoving dirty clothing into my suitcase. "Tell the maid to change the sheets." I snapped the bag shut.

Her body stiffened in the chair. "You're—really going?"

"Why not? My coming here was your idea and I didn't ask you along. Since I've been here I've had to do things the hard way. Why? Because you failed to tell me the full story. Knowing it, you shouldn't have much trouble back-tracing Dad. You've conned Melody, but you're conning me no more. *Adiós.*"

She shot across the floor and caught my arm. "Please—I was wrong—I admit it. But I couldn't tell Melody everything, could I?"

"You think she'd have turned you away? I know her a lot better than you, and I doubt it. I don't think she'd have dumped you because the Preacher is a crook, a con man, a forger and a thief. She knows the kind of life he gave you, and it engaged her sympathy. All Melody cares about is that the father you love is missing. I found out about Dad before I left Miami, but I came here anyway. I don't hold his crime career against you, but I'm not going to deal with you so long as you cover up and pretend. But I'll tell you this— on my own I've found out a few things, and you're not entitled to share them. I won't tell Melody, either, and that will spare you embarrassment, and prevent her from turning away the next desperate friend." I looked around the shabby room. "You're on your own, kid. Do your thing."

Lugging my bag, I left the room.

She caught up with me in the lobby as I was getting ready to pay my bill. Her cheeks were tear-streaked, eyes reddened. "Don't go," she said huskily. "Please, Jack, I'll tell you everything."

"Everything?"

She nodded, and I gave her a handkerchief. While she was drying face and eyes I noticed that the desk clerk was staring at us with fascination. I snapped my fingers and he segued into reality. "A room for the *señorita*," I told him, "who happens to be my cousin."

His smile was sly. "Cousin?"

"Cousin."

"Of course, *señor*." He shoved over the register and asked for her tourist card. He looked at it, then at the key boxes behind. "A room near yours, *señor*?"

"Inconsequential," I said. "House draw. So long as it's clean and has a bath."

"Certainly, *señor*. *Para servirles*." He glanced admiringly at Tara, who was trying to look less like an urchin, more like a cousin. Family pride.

She took her room key and we went back to my room. There I sat her down and said, "Let's have it."

For the next quarter-hour she told me what I already knew, adding detail here and there, filling gaps in her father's travels not provided by his rap sheet. It was painful for her, I could see, like pulling a hook out of a fish's gullet, but all she did was sniffle a few times, then apologize again for her deception. She didn't ask if I believed her—the sure sign of a liar—so I made no comment. When she finished she said, "Now, will you tell me what you've found out?"

"No—for reasons given."

She swallowed. "Is my father—dead?"

"I don't know. But the fact that I'm still here means I haven't found him."

She nodded slowly. "At least there's hope."

"There's always hope," I said and changed the subject to lunch.

She hadn't eaten either, and on the way to the waterfront café I bought her a reed sun hat like mine. I didn't want stepmother Graciela spotting her, and with shades and wide-brimmed hat Tara was just another touristy *gringa*.

I noticed the way she shelled steamed shrimp, using her long thumbnails, and she told me she'd learned the technique working kitchen at the Del Coronado.

"While Dad was raking in big bucks?" I asked.

"I never asked him for anything," she said. "Dolls or toys, maybe, when I was a kid, but while my father was in jail he didn't have any money, and when he was out he had less." Deftly she veined a shrimp and dipped it in Tabasco. "Besides, he taught me to be self-sufficient—expected me to be. That was his way."

"Still, it wouldn't have hurt him to kick in now and then, pay night school tuition, for example."

"I guess Sister Grace got the money."

"Were you at the wedding?"

"*No!*" Her cheeks reddened. "I didn't know about it, wasn't invited."

"So you can't say they're actually married."

"No—but what makes you ask?"

"Just wondering. Why was your stepmother doing time?"

"You mean, at Tehachapi?"

"You know what I mean. Stop stalling."

She licked sauce from her lips. "It had—I think—something to do with marijuana."

"You think—or you know?"

"I—I overheard them talking about how hard it was getting to bring in large quantities of pot."

55

I shelled a shrimp and began gnawing the large end. "Ever see Sister Grace toke up?"

"I've smelled it in their apartment. That's not a crime," she said defensively.

"Maybe, maybe not. But it's not a practice your father's flock would approve of."

She shrugged.

I said, "And as for the True Word Gospel Church—any comment?"

"What can I say? My father created it—for a while it was a good thing."

"Meaning a profitable enterprise." I selected another shrimp. "So it wasn't as though a blinding light filled his cell, and a resonant baritone instructed him to go out among the world and evangelize the heathen."

"You're cruel," she said breathily. "You didn't need to say that."

"Sorry. I talk too much."

After a while the waiter came over and asked if we required more shrimp and beer. "Not for the moment," I said, and gave him six thousand pesos. "One's for you," I told him, "if you'll deliver five to Pablo 'El Chico' over there at the store. Know him?"

"Of course, señor." He smiled. "But one seldom sees him."

"For which reason, give him the money out of sight of his wife. Or we'll be seeing him even less frequently."

The waiter said he understood and set off at a trot down the waterfront. Tara said, "What was that all about?"

"Paying a bet."

"Lottery?"

"Sort of. I got lucky."

Her nose wrinkled. "It's lucky to lose a bet?"

"Sometimes. What's your boyfriend's name?"

"Boy—? I don't have one."

"Hard to believe. Good-looking chick like you . . ."

"I'm *not* a chick. I'm a woman and a human being. Like you," she said angrily.

"Apologies."

"Anyway, what business is it of yours?"

"Only that I've been wondering why you didn't enlist your boyfriend in the search for your father. It didn't seem reasonable that you'd be fighting the world all alone."

She thought it over. "I can see why you wondered. But until he married, my father and I were very close."

"That's not quite the same."

Her head tossed. "After Mother died, he took care of me— as best he could. I wanted to do the same for him—but then he got married."

"First marriage," I said.

"What do you mean? He and my mother were married."

"Uh-uh. Madge Brinker left him—and they weren't married. So don't bullshit me."

Her shadowed face looked frozen. "You take pleasure from that, don't you? Why not come straight out and call me a bastard?"

"Why bother?" I said. "I was just testing your veracity. I don't care if you were born out of wedlock, and few people would. Except yourself, of course. It's no big thing, Tara, so unburden yourself. You're not responsible for what your parents did or didn't do, and names don't mean anything." I tilted my Tecate and drained it. When the waiter came back with Pablo's thanks, I ordered two more beers.

She rose from her chair. "Drink them yourself. I'm going to my room."

"Fine—siesta time."

She paused. "What are we going to do tonight?"

"You're going to stay in your room, out of sight. What I do doesn't concern you. Got it?"

"I'm part of this—he *is* my father."

"Or was," I said casually, "as the case may be."

"Then just tell me why I should hide," she demanded.

57

"Because people responsible for his disappearance may be hanging around Mazatlán. If so, you could be the next target."

She strode away until her sandal caught on a cobblestone and came off. She freed it, jammed her foot into the sandal and marched off toward El Gran Camarón. Peeling another shrimp, I wished her a good snooze.

In the tropics, a person hadn't ought to get so worked up. Bad for blood pressure and liver, Mexicans said. Especially on a load of shrimp, Tabasco and beer.

Behind me a car stopped, and presently I saw a man walk past the café. I tilted my hatbrim forward and drank more Tecate. There was a thick bandage across the left side of the man's head and he wore dark shades. He walked slowly and delicately, as though every step was painful. I imagined it was, being no stranger to concussion, and wondered how long he'd lain on the deck after I'd cooled him. He made his way down the pier and stepped carefully into the cockpit of a big sport-fishing boat. Another man greeted him, and they disappeared into the companionway.

Now was my chance to inspect the *Paz Paloma* by daylight—if I wanted to. But I had other things in mind. I paid for lunch, gave the waiter a memorable tip and pointed out the boat the bandaged man had boarded. "Ask around about the boat and its captain," I said, "and—"

"*Sí, sí, señor.* Right away."

"No, no," I said. "With calm and tranquility. I'll stop by this evening."

He bowed, and I walked over to where an old taxi sizzled in the sun.

I left it at the Camino Real and went to the telephones. The call came through while I was sipping iced Añejo at the bar, but it was Thomas who answered. Miss Melody was at the university library and not expected home until the evening meal. Was there a message for her?

"Let her know I'm not particularly pleased that Miss Vaill is here. Otherwise, things are moving along."

"Yes, Mr. Novak. As soon as she arrives."

I finished my drink and strolled out to the hotel pool. From a shaded table I scanned bathers and sun worshipers until I saw, lying on twin pads, hands clasped, the Colombian couple I'd failed to find last night.

Sister Grace—Marta—had a spectacular body, perfectly curved to Latin taste. Freddy Gomez was stroking it with sun oil, reaching intimate places a little too frequently for happenstance.

I wanted to meet and converse with the former Sister Grace, but for that I had to finesse Freddy from the play. That would take a little doing, but I thought I had a way.

I'd used it at Cancún one evening, and it involved a cooperative bartender and doctored drinks.

But all that went out of my mind when I saw a nattily dressed Latino come out on the terrace and look around. He was wearing an ice-cream suit, white Panama hat and gleaming white shoes. And in that lush, tropical setting he looked as cool as a frozen daiquiri. His gaze settled on Freddy Gomez, and for a while he stared at him. Then he stepped back into shadows and beckoned over a waiter. Pointing at Freddy, he spoke briefly and disappeared into the hotel.

The waiter went over to Freddy and gestured at the doorway. Freddy nodded, spoke to Marta and got up. Towel around his waist, he padded off toward the doorway, and I felt suddenly chill.

For the well-dressed newcomer was my old pal, the chief DEA agent in Guadalajara, Manuel Montijo.

In contact with a bigtime drug dealer, Federico Gomez.

So they'd corrupted Manny, too.

It made me want to throw up.

Instead, I began walking toward Sister Grace.

SEVEN

Whatever his reasons for showing up just then, Manny had detoured Gomez from my scope and taken the play away from me. Still, I'd been given an unexpected opportunity to move on Marta del Campo, alias Sister Grace, a/k/a Graciela Rodriguez. The variety of her names didn't bother me as she lay there in the sun; it was the voluptuous curvings of her body that commanded my attention.

Unlike Manhattan fashion models, Marta had more to offer than a lean and hungry look. There was flesh on her bones, and it was smoothly sculptured without being plump. Her bikini bottom and top would have fitted into a light airmail envelope, and I got the impression of a female who was proud of her body and enjoyed showing it off. I liked that outlook because it implied related possibilities.

I chose a table a few yards away, so she would have to notice me when, eventually, she sat up and looked around. I ordered a Coco Loco from a waiter, laid my hat on the table and leaned back as though to soak up rays. Marta rolled down her string bikini a fraction of an inch for better tanning, and I reflected that if she dropped the hint, I'd gladly join her nudist camp. Motionless, she lay there, arms outstretched, thighs apart. Without lifting a finger, she was transmitting. I was receiving her subliminal signals, and if surrounding males were even partially alert, they were getting the covert message too.

The Latin female mystique was involved in all this, and it was perfectly consonant with tropic heat and the ageless rhythm of the sea.

But my musings weren't getting me any closer to their subject, and Freddy could return at any time. So when the waiter delivered the topped coconut, I took it awkwardly from his tray. Liquid slopped over the coconut, and I let it slip from my hand so that it rolled toward Marta, coming to rest against her shoulder. I hurried over as she half-rose and glanced, startled, at the emptying coconut. Mumbling Spanish apologies, I picked it up and tried dabbing the spilled drink with her towel until my waiter intervened. Before leaving, I made further apologies, which she accepted with a casual smile, murmuring, "No es nada, señor. No se preocupe."

I bowed and saw the waiter hurrying off for a replacement. That gave me reason to leave, and when I caught up with him I paid for the spilled drink and told him not to bother with another.

The timing was good, because while I was smoothing things with the waiter, Freddy Gomez came past us, face set in thought. Ignoring him, I strolled through the lobby and looked around for Manny. I didn't want him to see me just then, and I didn't want to encounter my onetime buddy. His being with Freddy told me much more than I wanted to know, and disillusion was a bitter, nauseating pill. But if the right moment ever arrived, I'd call him for complicity with the very narcotraficantes our government was trying to nail. And, if it came to that, shoot it out.

In my book, a corrupt DEA agent was far lower than a

dealer who sold nose candy to kids. Ironically, there was a time when Manny Montijo felt the same way.

Still, bitter thoughts about Manny weren't getting me closer to Billy Joe, so I erased him from my mind. The day had begun badly with Tara's arrival and deteriorated on seeing Manny. On the plus side, I'd managed to give Marta a close look at me, ostensibly by accident.

Before leaving the Camino Real I looked around for Rafe, the bell captain, then realized he didn't come on until later. My business with him would have to wait.

I was standing near the front steps, adjusting priorities, when I noticed Marta walk by, wearing a tropic-print sarong. She went down the steps and paused at the curb, surveying the far side of the street. The big, flashy-looking disco wasn't open, so I decided she was considering an expensive-appearing resort-wear boutique beside it. Before Marta could step from the curb she was approached by a short Indian woman whose brown face resembled a walnut shell. A worn gray shawl covered her hair, draped down over a faded red-brown dress. A second shawl held a black-haired baby close to her breast, and a small, nearly naked child clutched the woman's skirt while sucking a thumb. The woman held out a clawlike hand to Marta and her lips moved. One of Mexico's countless indigenes uprooted from unproductive cornfields, come to the city for charity.

I wondered what Marta would do.

To my surprise, Marta opened her clutch purse and got out a roll of paper money. Without a word she gave the old woman four fifty-thousand-peso notes—a month's salary for a teacher—and smiled. As the woman thanked her, Marta knelt and gave the child a handful of coins. The child accepted them gravely and tucked them in the woman's skirt. Then Marta crossed the street and disappeared inside the boutique.

The act of generosity by so unlikely a donor stunned me. Not that Marta would miss the money, but to react so sympathetically to the old woman's plea added a facet to Marta's character that I wouldn't have believed if I hadn't seen it take place. I was going to have to revise initial impressions of Sister Grace because she wasn't, as I'd thought, all bad.

Meanwhile, I was late for siesta, so I returned to my room and surrendered to national and local custom.

At dusk, Tara's knocking on my door brought me off the bed. She had the quaint idea that dinner began at nightfall, so I enlightened her irritably, yawned and rinsed my face and hands.

She sat in the chair watching me. Same sandals and jeans, but a new T-shirt: black, with *Awesome* across the front in light-catching spangles. Her idea of evening wear in a resort town.

She said, "Have you talked with Melody?"

"Not since yesterday." I stared at my face in the cloudy mirror and rubbed bristles. They'd pass for the night.

"Melody said you were a very reliable man."

"That's only partly true. I'm reliable when I want to be. Otherwise I don't care if school keeps or not."

In the mirror I could see her chewing her lower lip. Finally she said, "Where are we going for dinner?"

"We're dining together? In that case, some waterfront joint that's passably clean."

"Can I get a hamburger?"

"Don't even try. America is the only country on the globe where hamburgers and hot dogs are what they should be. Enjoy a taco instead. You don't seem to realize that this isn't San Diego. You're in a foreign land with its own customs, cuisine and language. If you can't accommodate, bug out."

"This isn't my first time in Mexico. I've been in Tijuana, too."

I turned. "The Tijuana Trolley makes you a world traveler? I'll feed you tonight, and in the morning I'll put you on the plane."

"I'm not going back yet, Jack. If you'd let me leave that room I could mingle with people, find out things."

"Speaking what language?"

She colored. "Someone has to speak English here."

"Sure. Hotel workers, bartenders, charter boat captains, people in the tourist trades." The subject bored me so I dropped it. "Anyway, until more is known about your dad I don't think it's safe for you to be on the streets. Your clothing makes you as noticeable as a nude in a nunnery."

She flushed. "So, I might as well sleep around the clock, while you do all the work."

"That's one solution. The alternative is flying home."

"What home?"

"Melody's. She's sort of adopted you."

"I can't sponge off her forever."

"Get a job." I was looking at Tara's figure but thinking of Marta's more ample charms. Trash like Freddy didn't deserve them. I smoothed my guayabera. "Got a flashlight?" I asked.

"A small one. What do you want it for?"

"To hunt armadillos under the bed. May I have it? Now?"

Sulkily she left the room, giving me an opportunity to answer nature's call and fit the Browning against my spine. When she returned I took the light and shoved it in my rear pocket. "Ready? Let's go."

The restaurant was a block from the *posada*. The tables had gingham tops, fake flowers and uneven legs. The open window framed a postcard view of the fishing fleet, reminding me of the sorehead and the boat he'd visited at lunchtime.

It was early for dinner in the tropics, and there were only two other couples at tables. As we sat down a man came in and took a corner table. I noticed him because he wore a brown suit, brown tie and brown straw hat—overdressed for the climate. He had a mustache and a pale complexion, and his hands looked as though they might be able to perform delicate knife work in the dark. After glancing at us, he looked away and fidgeted with the sugar bowl.

In a low voice I said, "Tara, ever see him before?"

"The man in brown? Uh-uh. Never."

So, he was only giving Tara routine *macho* scrutiny. I ordered for both of us while the waiter wiped a Corona beer tray in a circular motion that distracted me. Finally I gripped his wrist gently and asked him to desist.

He said he could remember the order without writing it down, and when our plates arrived, I agreed. Grilled swordfish steak, soggy french fries (that I shoved aside), white asparagus and a bottle of overly sweet Oaxaca wine. Aside from that, and the fries, the meal was a success. For dessert Tara had pineapple sherbet but I passed in favor of a chocolate-dark Vera Cruz cigar that looked better than it tasted.

As I smoked, I realized that Tara reminded me of Inge, the road urchin I'd once befriended on the road to Guadalajara. Both girls were blonde and equally rootless, but Tara had a more discernible background. I'd used Inge as unwitting camouflage for my work in Puerto Vallarta. As a result, she'd suffered dangerous and hair-raising episodes that cooled her enthusiasm for me. Understandably.

Well, comparisons were odious. Tara was excess baggage, and I wanted her out of town. If she and Marta were to recognize each other, my problems would explode.

So I walked Tara back to the *posada* and told her to lock her door and retire early. That was not at all what she had in mind as she frowned and said, "I'm going with you. I can take care of myself."

"Either way, I don't want to find out. Go to bed, we'll talk tomorrow." I left her and walked back to the waterfront.

At the seafood café the waiter saw me coming and gave

me a sly smile. I took a table and asked for Añejo. When he set down the iced glass, he said, "The boat you asked about is *El Chango*. Captain Miguel Ramirez."

I sampled the chill rum. "What about him?"

"They say he makes—special trips."

"How special?"

His nostrils made a soft snorting sound.

"Ahhhhh, so." I nodded. "*Polvo blanco*." White powder.

"*Cierto, señor*."

"And delivers it where?"

He shrugged. "Somewhere up the Baja peninsula—near the *yanqui* frontier."

"Or across it," I mused. "Well, he's not the only one. What about the fellow with the head bandage who went aboard?"

"That one is Pedro Ramirez, his brother."

"Same line of work?"

"*Sí, señor*. After all, they are *Colombianos*."

The linkage was primitive, but apt. Like assuming all chefs are French. "What else?"

"Concerning the Ramirez brothers, that is all I know."

I was reluctant to let him go. For a few moments I thought back, then asked, "When the man and woman of the *Paz Paloma* were in port, did you see them with either Ramirez brother?"

He nodded. "They all ate shrimp together at that table." He gestured with his napkin.

"Did they go out fishing on *El Chango*?"

"No, *señor*. But the woman seemed to know the brothers. All four were comfortable together, laughing and making jokes. Later they went out to where the *Paz Paloma* was anchored."

"Excellent." I handed him sixty thousand pesos. "Let me know if *El Chango* leaves port."

"With pleasure." He bowed his thanks.

Chango was the *santería* cult's god of thunder and tur-moil, and Pedro Ramirez had been wearing a *santería* amu-let. In primitive contrast to Billy Joe's clerical collar.

The waiter hadn't moved on, and I wondered if he was expecting further payment. I glanced up at him and he grinned uncomfortably. "*Señor*," he blurted, "there is some-thing further you might want to know."

"Like what?"

"This afternoon a man came here and showed me the same photograph that you showed me. He asked if I had seen the captain of the *Paz Paloma*."

There was no breeze at all, but my face was suddenly chill. "What did you tell him?"

"Nothing."

"Why not?"

"I thought he might be a dangerous man. And he offered no money."

"Where did he go?"

He gestured at the piers. "Down there."

"You'd never seen him before?"

"No, *señor*."

"What did he look like?"

The waiter shrugged. "About my size. Everything he wore was brown, even his hat."

Turning, I gazed back at the restaurant. The table where the man had been was empty. "Perhaps he's an old friend of the captain's. If so, maybe we could look together. *Gracias*."

"*De nada*," the waiter said and moved off.

I didn't like two of us working the same slim Mazatlán lead, and I didn't really think the brown man was an old pal of Billy Joe's—unless they'd done time together. So far, all he'd done was stare at me, and I couldn't shoot him for that.

So I finished my after-dinner drink, emptied the sugar bowl into my handkerchief and stowed it in a pocket for later use. As I walked away I pondered the fact that Billy Joe, Sister Grace and the Ramirez brothers had been together in Mazatlán and appeared to be on cordial terms. Last night I'd encountered Pedro Ramirez aboard the old *Paz Paloma*, so it seemed reasonable that if, indeed, the boat had been hijacked, the brothers Ramirez were involved.

All of which suggested strongly that Preacher Billy Joe was no longer among the living.

Even though his wife or widow was.

I took a taxi to the Camino Real to look up Rafe.

At the hotel I tried to call Melody, but Thomas said she'd phoned to say she was going to work through dinner with her diving coach, then stay late at the university library. "I did give her your message, sir."

"Here's another. Tell her not to be surprised if Tara returns abruptly. She's not needed here."

"Certainly, sir."

"Also that Tara's stepmother is enjoying life in Mazatlán."

"That *is* surprising. And the father?"

"Still missing," I said, and paid for the call.

I was getting low on pesos, so I cashed several traveler's checks at the cashier window and tucked the money away, grumbling at the poor exchange rate. Rafe was in his closet office and seemed pleased to see me. After closing the door I said, "Spot me the Gomez Maserati."

"Sure—around back, this side of the beach *cabañas*."

"Next question, I need a small car for the night—two-seater roadster, like an MG or Alfa. Can do?"

He thought it over. "Suppose I could 'borrow' one?"

"Ownership doesn't concern me."

"Can you hot-wire?"

"Like shaving."

"Good. There's a little Triumph stored in the garage—

owner stays here when he's not on his boat. Right now he's away on his boat with a couple of broads."

"We should be so lucky."

"Yeah. When do you need it?"

"After Freddy splits."

His eyelids narrowed. "You're not gonna—?"

"I got a long look at his woman today, poolside. She's too much for him."

"And just about right for you." He grinned lecherously. "I can almost admire *gringos*."

"That's an improvement, *chamaco*." I peeled forty thousand pesos from my roll. "I continue to appreciate your cooperation. Check with you after dinner."

He took the money without changing expression, and I opened his door, then froze. Beckoning to Rafe, I said, "That fellow crossing the lobby—any line on him?"

Beside me, Rafe peered toward where I was pointing. "Latino in the white suit? Haven't seen him before, but I'll ask around."

"He may be an old friend of mine—then, again, he may not."

"I'll get on it." Rafe headed for Registration, and I started walking toward the bar without looking again at Montijo.

I took a bar seat away from two young couples who were downing frozen daiquiris and celebrating something or other. Possibly a honeymoon—or a prospective orgy. The bartender brought me a generous shot of Añejo, and I sipped it feeling resentful over the way Melody had saddled me with Tara's problems, then isolated herself to concentrate on her own. It didn't seem fair, and I began to appreciate her mother's inhospitable attitude. She'd had her fill of freeloaders over the years.

Tilting a glass, I sensed someone sliding onto the stool beside me, and when I glanced sideways I saw Manny carefully removing his Panama hat. "*Hola, amigo*," he said. "*Qué pasa?*"

"Minding my business," I said curtly, "which is more than I can say for you."

He gazed at me with dark Andalusian eyes. "Meaning what?"

"I'm surprised to see you without your banker." I finished my drink and gestured for another.

"What the hell's with you, pal? I thought we were friends."

"We were," I said harshly, "until I realized you'd sold out. Be more choosy where you meet Freddy, away from hostile eyes." I stared at him. "Like mine."

There were white spots on his cheeks. He swallowed and said hoarsely, "Keep your damned voice down, Jack. Appearances are one thing, reality another."

I grunted. "Don't feed me clichés, Manny. This isn't even your territory, *pal*. You're on the take from Gomez."

"Oh, shit." He turned away, shaking his head. "Whatever happened to benefit of the doubt?"

"In our business it has to come down on the side of the good guys." I pointed at his Panama. "Just wearing a white hat doesn't make you one."

"Ever hear of operational disguise—fitting in with the *ambiente*? And what do you know about Freddy, anyway?"

"Colombian trafficker."

"Right. And who would he likely work for?"

"The Parra family."

"Right again. If you saw him, you probably noticed his lady friend. Know who she is?"

"Sure. As Graciela Rodriguez she did time at Tehachapi. As Sister Grace, she worked an evangelism scam in San Diego. Down here she's Marta del Campo, with a shiny new Colombian passport."

His eyes widened. "All true—but what's your interest in her?"

"What's your interest in Freddy?"

He edged closer. "Informant."

70

I smiled tolerantly. "What would convince a wise guy like him, living the abundant life, to turn informant?"

"Easy. We've got a hook in his kid brother, Hector."

"How?"

"He's doing two dimes at Leavenworth. Hard time, unless I say the word."

Slowly I said, "I'd like to believe you—but I'm not convinced."

"Anyone but you, Jack, I'd tell him to screw off. So, hear this—you omitted one little detail from Marta's bio."

"Such as?"

"She's a Parra. Omar's first cousin."

I stared at him. He said, "DEA pushed her parole to get her out and back with old contacts. We ran Gomez against her to learn her plans. Organizationally, she's Omar's executive officer. We lost track of Marta until she phoned Gomez in Medellín and issued instructions. Gomez notified me, and that's why I'm here. What's your interest in her?"

As I told him, he listened without changing expression. Then he said, "As simple as that. Tara Vaill to Melody to you." He shook his head wonderingly.

I said, "You'd better order a drink, maintain cover as a free-spending pachuco."

He asked the bartender for a tequila highball and turned to me. "I didn't expect to find you in Mazatlán, much less mixed up in this."

"All I want is Billy Joe's whereabouts."

"Which Marta undoubtedly knows." He touched the side of his nose. "Naturally, you want to question her."

"That's why I came. How long are you staying?"

"Wish I knew. Yolanda—that's her true name—has been closemouthed with Freddy. He gets the feeling she just wants to unwind after prison, and all that time with Billy Joe. He has a further feeling she's waiting around for something."

"Something to happen, or something to arrive?"

71

"Not clear. And I can't stay away from the Consulate much longer—too much to do in Guadalajara." He gave me a slanting glance. "So, I don't want you gaffing the setup."

"You mean Freddy and Yolanda?"

He nodded.

I said, "Every night around eleven they whip out in Freddy's Maserati and tool down the coast road. Where do they go?"

"I don't know."

"Then you ought to find out. Following them, I chanced on the *Paz Paloma* with the name painted out. It's the *Delfín*, now, out of Guaymas."

"They went on board?"

"No. I did. Found souvenirs of the electronic ministry. And a guard named Pedro Ramirez."

Manny's drink arrived, and he waited until the bartender moved off before saying, "The Ramirez brothers are well and unfavorably known to us. Baja runners."

"I thought they might be. In addition to the *Paz Paloma*, I spotted an old house to hell and gone in the countryside. It's big and fitted out like a fortress. Maybe that's where the pair's been going."

"I'll ask Freddy."

"Without letting him know he's been tailed."

He sipped moodily. "Despite the chair job, I can still handle an informant—occasionally."

"Then you can save me some trouble. Ask Freddy what he knows about Yolanda's erstwhile spouse, Billy Joe Vaill."

"That's all?"

"It's all I contracted to learn."

He smiled. "Melody's okay?"

"A joy to behold. So I'm anxious to get back. When's next meet with Freddy?"

"Tomorrow PM. Until then he's occupied with Yolanda."

"Understandably. Well, that may be too late for my needs." I looked along the bar at the foursome grown suddenly quiet. It seemed to me that, as the men paid their tab, they had also switched partners. Magical Mazatlán.

After they traipsed past us Manny said, "To repeat, Jack, I'm handling a very delicate situation here, and for the sake of a twenty-hour wait I don't want you butting in."

"If the couple was, ah, disengaged, I'd ask you to introduce me as an out-of-town buyer—it's worked before."

"Yolanda's never seen me."

"She'd accept Freddy's word."

He shook his head wearily. "Jack, this operation is far more important than your problem with Daddy Vaill. We know the Parra layout—the marijuana acres, the curing sheds, the poppy hills, how coca base gets there from Bolivia and Peru. What we don't know is where the processing labs are located. Every man we've sent in has failed to make contact. We've tried aerial photography, satellite thermo-scans, everything. Until we can find the labs we can't dent the operation. Making Freddy the key."

"And, once having found the labs, what will our government do?"

"Well, we tell the Colombian government, and offer help with agents and choppers and jeeps."

"And if certain Colombian officials are less than anxious to take action . . . ? That's a road we've followed before."

"I don't want to hear that nightmare."

"Well, it's not a new one. I can't accept sending man after man into a meatgrinder when their deaths are meaningless. You know how hard it is to find a man willing to go into the Guajira *llanos*, brief and launch him—then have nothing to put after his name but a gold star."

"I know," he said quietly. "Which is why it's so crucial to have Freddy romancing Yolanda. If he produces what we want, it could be a whole new deal. The final solution to the Parra enterprise."

"I've heard that before, too," I reminded him, "after I sank Luis Parra's floating lab. And that turned out no more than

73

a temporary inconvenience." I grunted. "I wasn't even supposed to be around."

"I know—but that was Phil Corliss."

"Prompt to take credit for my accomplishing what he'd
refused to authorize."

"What can I say? We know he's a scumbag."

I grinned. "If Phil gets in my way one more time, I'm
going to lay a contract on him."

Manny chuckled. "And do the job yourself."

"Cheaper."

We laughed conspiratorially, and Manny glanced at his
wristwatch. "I'd like to spend a lot more time with you,
Jack, but I'm expected elsewhere." He eased off the stool.
"Boat still running? Plane okay?"

I nodded. "What's your alias?"

"Fernando Camacho. Room five forty-five. Next to
Freddy's."

"Which you've bugged."

"To keep him honest."

"Maybe that's why they take long drives."

He didn't like that, opened his mouth to say something,
and moved behind me. "*Hasta*. Keep well."

"Likewise. Oh—one thing. New man in town—all brown
but for a black mustache and sallow face. Would he be
working for you?"

His lips pursed. "Not by that description. What's he look
like?"

"Tijuana pimp or guinea hustler."

He smiled tolerantly. "Not mine, Jack. You keep him."

"He's looking for Billy Joe."

"Which makes two of you. Lotsa luck."

I didn't watch him leave, and I was glad my thoughts
about his taking juice from Gomez were wrong. Still, I'd
found too many fellow agents on the take to be anything
but suspicious of a covert meet.

Manny hadn't specifically told me not to follow Freddy

and Yolanda or stay away from the jungle house. And I didn't think that what I had in mind would prejudice his plans.

But I wasn't sure.

Rafe came up to me and said, "I see Camacho found you."

"We had a drink together."

"I've got a few minutes. Let's find the Triumph."

We did, and with his penknife I cut through the ignition wiring, pared the ends and joined them. The engine started like a dream, and Rafe looked at me admiringly.

I had wheels for the night. Now to take care of fast Freddy's.

EIGHT

The orange Maserati's gas tank cover had a flush lock that Freddy neglected to use. Mexican gas was cheap, so he wasn't concerned about theft by siphoning. While Rafe stood guard I unscrewed the top and let sugar from my handkerchief slide down the filling pipe. After wiping off stray granules I replaced top and cover and shook out my handkerchief. As we walked back to the hotel, Rafe said, "What's that for, *jefe*?"

"A surprise for Freddy."

"Where'd you learn it?"

"I had a duty tour with the SEALs. Learned all kinds of useful things."

"For a *gringo* you're something. Anything else, *jefe*?"

"A spare key to Freddy's suite."

"It'll cost you."

I gave him an additional twenty thousand pesos and recommended he spend it wisely. We entered the hotel separately, and while I was cooling off at the bar he palmed me the extra key.

I had some hours to kill before Freddy and Yolanda were likely to begin their nocturnal drive, so I decided to rack down in my room. I shorted the Triumph's ignition and drove the little car back to my *posada*, parking half a block away.

As I walked up to the second floor I was wondering how the evening was going to work out. For one thing, I'd gotten the impression that Freddy wasn't coming totally clean with Manny Montijo. Gomez wasn't required to turn in clinical descriptions of his hours with Yolanda, but where they drove to every night, and why, was information he should be sharing with his boss.

I was unlocking my door when I decided to look in on Tara, make sure she was in her room and not roaming the streets. So I walked two doors further and was about to knock when I heard, inside, heels drumming on the floor. Flamenco practice sans guitar seemed unreasonable, and when I heard a muffled cry I turned the doorknob and pushed in.

Tara was lying on the floor, bound and gagged. Kneeling beside her was the brown-suited man. There was a long knife in his hand, and the point was pricking the side of her throat.

His head snapped toward me. Under the brown hat brim his eyes flashed. Rising, he pointed the knife at me, then slashed out, fast as a striking cobra. "*Fuera!*" he snarled.

Blinking, I grunted "Huh?" and took a sideways step toward the bed.

"Get out," he grated and came toward me, pigsticker carving empty air. That was supposed to terrify me. So, before he was close enough to cut me, I grabbed a pillow from the bed and shielded my left arm, while my right dug the Browning from the back of my belt. I didn't want to shoot him, but when he saw the pistol his eyes went crazy and he began lunging and stabbing until the blade hilt caught in the pillow. While he was trying to jerk it free, I was levering it away, and when his concentration was absolute I kicked him in the crotch.

Staggering backward, he tripped over Tara's legs, and lay gasping on the floor, face contorted with pain, hands clawing his groin.

I picked up the knife and tossed it on the bed. Then I went to him, kicked the small of his back, and with a howl he rolled face down. I slammed the pistol barrel against the bulge of his head, and he lay still. The next sound was the low whistling of air in his nostrils.

With the knife I cut Tara's bonds and helped her sit up, shaking and sobbing. The side of her neck showed a few drops of blood, then as she pointed I saw blood coming from a slash in my guayabera sleeve. He'd managed to nick me while we struggled.

The cut was about two inches long, but shallow, and partway between my left wrist and elbow. I dabbed blood away and saw a slow red ooze return. Huskily, Tara said, "You're hurt."

"You could have been hurt worse." I lifted her to her feet and guided her to the bed. "Lie down," I told her. "Take it easy."

I yanked out the brown man's shirttail and cut off a long piece. Tara wound it tightly around my forearm and tied it in place. "You need a doctor," she said worriedly.

"Fast clotter," I said. "No problem." I sat on the bed edge beside her. "Who's our friend? What did he want from you?"

She stared at me, starry-eyed. "God, you were good. The way you used that pillow—"

"Gaucho trick. When they're out spearing jaguars they wrap one arm with a *serape*. What about him? What did *he* want?" I repeated.

"My father—Billy Joe."

"Does he know something we don't?" I went over to him and rolled him on his back. Then I pulled out his wallet and emptied his pockets, inside, outside and trouser. Patting him down, I discovered a .25-caliber derringer holstered around his right ankle and concealed by calf-high buckaroo boots. His left leg sported a sheath for the bowie knife he'd used on us, and among his pocket litter was a switchblade stiletto from Palermo. This fellow seldom worried about muggers.

His wallet held a little less than a thousand dollars in crisp green bills, and half that in peso notes. I divided the money and gave Tara half.

"What's that for?" she asked.

"Pain and suffering. Buy yourself a bracer on tomorrow's flight."

"You mean, you're sending me away?"

"After *this*?" I gestured at the unconscious man. "You think I want problems every night? Face it—you're a magnet for trouble."

She sniffled a little, but I ignored it while I examined his documentation. Nevada driving license in the name of Domingo Ferré Sanchez with a Carson City address. Across it was stamped the reminder: *Paroled Felon Must Report to Local Authorities.*

I liked that.

Business cards from half-a-dozen casinos in Vegas and Reno. A plastic card identifying Sanchez as an employee of the Casa de Oro casino in Tahoe. Both photos fit the man on the floor.

There was a grimy brochure that showed Billy Joe and Sister Grace in better days, and last of all a grainy photo taken from above. It showed a roulette table crowded with players, two faces circled. One was Billy Joe, the other— Tara Vaill.

I tossed it at her. "How about this? I didn't know you were a gamester."

She stared at it, lips trembling. Finally she murmured, "I'm not—my father is. He's a compulsive gambler."

"Every casino photographs heavy bettors," I said. "Especially those who sign checks or markers. That your Daddy's practice?"

She swallowed. "When he lost."

"And he lost more than he won—right?"

"I—I'm afraid that's so."

"So, Dom Sanchez, here, would be the casino's collection agent. The enforcer. How much did Dad drop at the Casa de Oro?"

"I—I don't know."

"Think hard."

"Twenty—more than twenty thousand," she blurted.

"Well, hoist me for a swordfish—and him a practicing Reverend." I shook my head. "No wonder the ministry went bust—and you blaming poor Sister Grace."

"She took a lot—I know she did."

I shrugged, and opened the folded airline ticket. It held a return flight to San Francisco and Carson City. I decided to let him use it—when he felt able. By torturing a defenseless female he'd removed himself from humane treatment, so I considered how best to get rid of him. The bowie knife was half as large as a machete; I had no use for it, but the switchblade might come in handy. I was fond of unconventional firearms, so I decided to keep his derringer too. Maybe Melody could be persuaded to carry it in her purse those nights when she had to cross the dark U-M campus alone.

The closet shelf produced a dusty paper laundry bag in which I stowed Sanchez's ID and bowie knife, then rolled it in a bundle. The airline ticket I returned to his pocket.

"If he moves, yell," I said, and went to my room. From my bag I extracted my first-aid pint of Añejo and dribbled some into his mouth and over his shirtfront, then drank a slug myself. "You could use a shot," I said, and handed Tara the pint. She drank reluctantly, coughed, and gave me back the bottle. "On your feet," I told her. "We're going to give this galoot Finnegan's salute."

"What's that?"

"The bum's rush. Out the corridor—down the stairs."

She got the idea, and as she leaned over to grasp his arm we both noticed what I'd missed before. Sanchez's knife had opened her T-shirt to the waist and her breasts swung charmingly free. She gasped, and tried to cover herself, but I said, "No time for false modesty—I've seen breasts before. Now, lift."

Together we brought his slack body upright and dragged him down the hallway to the head of the stairs. There was a jog at the landing, so I aimed his body for it, pushed, and returned with Tara to her room. His hat was still on the floor. I tossed it from the open window and picked up my rolled bundle. "I'm going now," I told her, "and you keep the damned door locked. Shove a chair under the knob and get a good night's rest. You've got money for your room and a taxi to the airport. There's breakfast on the morning flight."

"What about—Sanchez?"

"They'll jail him for drunk and disorderly. Wipe the blood from your neck and go to bed."

Her voice and features softened. "Jack—I don't know how to thank you."

"Easy. Take the morning plane."

She took a half-step toward me, and for a moment I thought she was going to offer me her bod. Instead, she said, "You will—keep in touch?"

"Until I find out about Dad—one way or another."

That brought fresh sniffles, so I said, "I want to wind this up in the next twenty-four hours, so—"

Her eyes brightened. "You have a lead?"

"I do."

She swallowed. "You've been keeping things from me."

"Of course. What would life be without its little secrets?" I walked to the door, opened and closed it, and waited until I heard her key turn in the lock.

Then I went back to my room.

As I fitted key into lock I heard coarse voices on the landing. From what drifted down the hall I gathered that a couple of cops were collecting Domingo Sanchez and not liking it. Dom should have expected trouble when he violated parole and left the USA for foreign shores. Let it be a lesson, I thought, as I opened the door and went in.

Before hitting the sack, I dabbed drying blood from my forearm and applied a pair of Band-Aids. Then I downed a swallow of Añejo, turned out the light and sprawled under the ceiling fan. After a while I fell asleep, and when my wrist alarm woke me it was ten-thirty and time to move along.

By now Big Freddy and the fair Yolanda should be finishing their after-dinner brandies and getting ready for the moonlight drive. Somewhere along that wretched road I intended to play Good Samaritan. Yolanda should recognize the role, I reflected as I walked down the stairway. As Sister Grace she must have lent many a helping hand.

No sign of Domingo Sanchez. The lobby was quiet. I strolled along the street, dumped my bundle in a trash can and got into the Triumph. The engine started with a low, satisfying burble, and I drove away.

Heading for the big hotel.

NINE

I parked in the shadows of the cabañas, well away from the lighted area, but not so far that I couldn't watch the Maserati.

Couples strolled the outside walks, music drifted from the dance terrace. "A Letter from My Brother in Brazil" was the melody I recognized. Dick Hayman style, with subtle Afro beat and the harsh grating of a *reco-reco* to keep dancers awake. Man, *my* kind of music.

Yolanda's, too, because she was still swaying and snapping her fingers as she moved rhythmically toward the Maserati a few steps ahead of Freddy. They got into the orange projectile and I listened carefully, praying the turbocharged engine would start and speed them on their way. My gamble was that the sugar hadn't yet gone into solution with the gasoline, that it wouldn't until road bumps stirred up the granules and mixed them with the fuel sucking through the feed line. Gradually the carb would clog, the turbos overheat and combustion fail.

With the roar of a concussion grenade the engine caught and Freddy raced it, building volume until even the dancers must have been deafened. He backed around, skidded, double-clutched and laid a month's rubber as the car spun down the drive.

I listened to its sound grow fainter, listened until it was lost in the distance, and then I left the TR and went into the hotel. The elevator let me off at the sixth floor, and I walked casually down the corridor to six forty-six.

My borrowed key opened the double-width doors, and after a glance around, I stepped quickly in. Moving to the center of the sitting room, I looked around for possible mike sites and said, "Don't get upset, Manny, I'm just having a look around while the place is unoccupied." And having made my good faith statement, I went into the bedroom.

The enormous bed could have accommodated three couples and a mama-san. There were ceiling mirrors, and pier glass sections around the walls, a Servi-Bar and simulated lionskin carpeting. The place was adequate for a honeymoon bower or an orgy.

Open luggage in the walk-in closets. I didn't bother with Freddy's, it was Yolanda's that interested me. Her new clothing, some still price-tagged, swung on hangers. Her suitcase held an assortment of nylon trifles, and as I groped through them I felt something hard, unwrapped it and found myself holding a small Beretta pistol. I sniffed the barrel and decided it hadn't recently been fired. The magazine was full, no cartridge in the chamber. I snicked the magazine back into the grip, wiped off my prints and re-rolled it in her panties.

The zippered bag divider contained a large estate checkbook, checks imprinted with the name and P.O. box of the True Word Gospel Church. There was no current balance on the tally side, but from the amounts on some of the check stubs, withdrawals had been substantial, most of them made out to Cash. Well, it wasn't their financial affairs that interested me, just the whereabouts of the man who had conceived and run the airwave ministry. And, of course, what lay behind the radioed distress call that brought Tara to Miami. And Domingo Ferré Sanchez to Mazatlán.

I explored further, finding a California Parole Board document that paroled Graciela Rodriguez to the custody of Rev. Billy Joe Vaill, and a court-endorsed pre-trial agreement releasing Billy Joe against $80,000 bond provided by the Acme Bailbond Co., for which an attached receipt showed that Billy Joe had paid Acme 10%, or $8,000, to secure his freedom.

Lastly, temporary sale papers for the ketch *Wanderlust*, indicating a deposit by Billy Joe of a thousand dollars against an agreed price of $97,500. So, he'd slipped out of San Diego owing at least $168,500, a tidy sum by anyone's reckoning. To which add his gambling debt, and Billy Joe was on the minus side of two hundred thousand dollars.

Ample motive to head for Mexico.

As I replaced the papers, a tissue-thin half sheet slipped out. It was a penciled list of P.O. boxes in Baranquilla, Cartagena, Santa Marta and Uribia, the latter the town nearest to Parra's holdings in the Guajira peninsula. The list would be of interest to Manny Montijo, but not to me.

So far I'd come up with nothing that might lead me to Tara's father. I hadn't expected the search to produce much, so I wasn't overly disappointed. But it was a routine that had to be done.

Now to locate the target for tonight.

Driving the TR, I spotted the Maserati's motionless lights when I was still half a mile away. As I neared it I began to slow, and came up carefully alongside so both Yolanda and Freddy could see me. He had a gun in his hand. I braked and looked over. Vapor rose from the Maserati's hood. I said, "What's wrong?"

Freddy pointed the gun at me. "Who are you?"

"Just a fellow taking a drive."

Yolanda said, "Freddy, he's from the hotel. He—sir, didn't you spill a drink on me today?"

"Coco loco? Matter of fact, I did. I'm sorry about that, but maybe I can make it up to you now, ma'am."

Freddy put away his gun. "How?"

"Out of gas? Need a mechanic? I can take one of you back."

They exchanged glances. I said, "Even if I had a cable, your car is too heavy to tow."

"Yeah." Freddy turned to Yolanda. "Honey, you better go with him."

She said, "Are you sure you don't want me to stay?"

"I'd feel better if you were at the hotel. I've got the gun—I'll be okay until help comes."

I said, "Know of a garage that might be open?"

"There's a *gasolinera* you could try. She'll show you."

Yolanda got out of the Maserati and opened my passenger-side door. Freddy said, "What's your name, *amigo?*"

"Jack Reynolds."

"Staying at the hotel?"

"Drinking there." I gazed the length of his gleaming Maserati. "Didn't get your name."

"Gomez. Federico Gomez." He didn't offer to shake hands, so I looked at Yolanda, who smiled. "I'm Marta del Campo. I appreciate your help."

"Pleasure," I said, and to Freddy, "I'll send someone as soon as possible."

"Do that. I'll make it worth his while."

I backed around, gunned the little car and drove back toward Mazatlán. Yolanda said nothing, so after a few minutes I said, "I thought Gomez was your husband."

"Oh, no. He's a—very good friend."

"Great—I wouldn't want to think you were driving around with an enemy." Her divided skirt showed a becoming length of tanned thigh. She saw me admiring it and did nothing to alter the view. "How long will Federico be around?" I asked.

"What's it to you?"

"I'd hate to have you spending long afternoons at the pool—alone."

"Does that concern you?"

"If Freddy leaves, I'd be glad to take his place."

She thought it over, frowning slightly. "You move fast, don't you, Mr. Reynolds? Don't waste any time."

"Time's to be used, not wasted, don't you agree? And my guess is that you enjoy life too much to miss many opportunities."

"I suppose that's true." Wind rippled her long hair. Hard to believe this was Sister Grace beside me, for Yolanda was carnality personified.

Turning to me, she said, "You're an adventurer, aren't you?"

"I guess."

"So you—recognized it in me."

"Kindred spirits." I raised her hand to my lips. "How urgent is it to rescue Freddy?"

She smiled casually. "We should do something about it, shouldn't we—eventually?"

"I'll bet there isn't a service station open this time of night."

"You're probably right. But Freddy should take better care of his machine. If it hadn't been for you, I'd still be sitting there, waiting to be attacked by *bandidos*."

"Dreadful thought," I remarked. "Instead, you're safe with me."

"How safe is that?"

"How safe do you want to be?"

She drew my hand to her lips, nibbled the thumb and licked it. After a while she said, "You like that?"

"I like anything you do. Shall we have a drink at the bar? Get acquainted?"

"There's a bar in my room."

"How convenient," I said. "Let's take advantage of it."

When we reached the hotel I parked in shadows down the drive and untwisted the ignition wires. The engine died and Yolanda eyed me. "Lose your key?"

"Car didn't come with a key, it's borrowed. Why drive my car all the way from Houston when so many cars are already here?"

"And available."

I leaned across her to open her door. My chest brushed her breasts, and as I leaned back I paused to kiss her full lips.

She responded calmly and said, "Shouldn't we go in?"

I kissed her again, and her response was several degrees warmer. Then she slid over and got out. As she closed the door she said, "Are you a car thief?"

"Would you care?"

She shrugged.

I said, "I'm not, but I have a compulsion to take what I want."

"Even if it doesn't belong to you?"

"Particularly if it doesn't belong to me." The Spanish equivalent was translatable as: I like to lend things to myself. Street argot.

I took her arm and walked her through the lobby to the elevator. On the ride up she got out her room key and handed it to me. "What do you do for a living?" she asked.

"Buy and sell."

"What?"

"Commodities in demand—where the price is high and profits worth the risk."

"You do all this in Houston?"

"Now and then I take a trip to scout up supplies."

"And that's why you're in Mazatlán?"

I nodded, the door opened, and I looked around as though unfamiliar with room numbering. "This way," she said, and I followed her to the double-width doors I'd closed less than an hour ago.

I opened them and when we were inside I closed and locked them. She stretched and pointed to the Servi-Bar. "Over there. Scotch for me. A little ice."

I poured Añejo for myself, Black Label for my hostess. Carrying our drinks to the sofa, I said, "You work for Freddy?"

"No—he works for me." Our glasses touched and we drank. I said, "Sounds interesting. Maybe you'd like to hire me."

"To do what?"

"To take Freddy's place."

"Ummm. You mentioned that before." She sipped lengthily.

"In a different context. Anything he can do, I can do better."

She laughed. "You sure of that?"

"Well, look at the evidence. Freddy screwed up and stranded you. I drove you back. When I go out, I usually get where I'm going. Freddy's too casual"—I nuzzled the side of her neck—"with a precious cargo like you."

She smiled. "God, you're super-confident. I'm not sure I like that. In my country I get more *machismo* than I can take."

"Those *macho* studs—they get off in girls' underwear."

She laughed encouragingly. "But not you, Jack."

"Maybe when I'm over the hill. By the way, what's your country—you're not Mexican?"

"Please—I'm Colombian."

"Ahhh," I said, "that sort of explains things."

"Meaning what?" Her fingers began unbuttoning my guayabera.

"Oh, I'm thinking of Colombia's most famous products."

"Beef cattle?"

"Sure. Maybe we could do business."

"I doubt it—but we're not here for business, are we?"

"Not that kind." I began undoing the top of her blouse. She knocked back more of her drink and said, "You didn't ask permission, Jack."

"Seldom do."

"Afraid of refusal?"

"Do I look timid? Dialogue wastes time." I reached around and unhooked her bra. She traced a finger idly around my forehead and over my cheek. "You'd rape me, wouldn't you?"

"With pleasure." She was naked to the waist. I lifted her breasts and kissed them. She shivered. "Then I'd better give in, hadn't I?"

"Preferably."

She gave me a long, hard kiss, rose and began walking away. "I'm hot from the road," she murmured. "All sweaty. Let's have a shower together."

"*Momento.*" I waited until she disappeared and I heard the shower running. Then I took the Browning from my belt and slid it under the nearest bed pillow. I undressed and joined her in the shower stall. Her arms went around me as we kissed, and her fingers were like small, hungry animals. The water was pleasantly warm, and before things were too far advanced I reached for a soap bar and used it on both of us. After a while she shivered and backed away. "I'm ticklish—I'll do the rest."

After a good soaping she gave me the bar, rinsing herself while I finished up. She was using a perfume stick on her body when I stepped out and reached for a big fluffy towel.

There was a single small light in the bedroom, but I could easily make out the fan of dark hair across her pillow.

I pulled down the sheet and said, "You shouldn't hide such a fantastic body."

"Is that why you're here?"

"Of course. I gaffed your car and stopped by to rescue you."

Abruptly she sat up. "You know, I wouldn't put it past you."

I got in bed beside her. "But the whole idea's bizarre, isn't it?"

"If Freddy ever got the idea you did something to his car he'll kill you."

"Well, then," I said, taking her into my arms, "we must keep him from finding out."

For a while, no more talk of Freddy or anyone except ourselves. Sister Grace was no bedroom amateur, and her body gave no promise it couldn't fulfill. For a while I thought I might be in an expensive Cartagena cathouse, and the strategically placed mirrors enhanced the impression. But Yolanda was no jaded pro, just a normal, healthy female who exulted in the pleasure her body could take and give.

Finally, she separated from me, kissed my lips and padded off to the shower. I dozed off for a few minutes, and when I woke she was standing at the foot of the bed pointing her Beretta at me. "Now, you sonofabitch," she grated through bared teeth. "Who the hell are you, and what do you want from me?"

TEN

My right hand slid under the pillow, gripped the Browning. "Hey," I said, "you don't actually think I sabotaged the car, set things up? I was only kidding."

"Oh? I got to thinking about that Coco Loco spill, then the way you drove up out of the dark road. Very convenient."

"Well, sometimes coincidence baffles explanation."

"If that's what it was." A trace of uncertainty shadowed her voice, but her lips went taut and she fired.

The bullet hit the pillow beside my head. I yelled, rolled aside and whipped out the Browning. I rolled over the far side, ducked down, and when I could aim, I squeezed the trigger and shot the Beretta from her hand. Impact slammed it into a mirror, shattering it. Yolanda yelped in pain and began sucking her fingers. I got up, walked over and unclenched her hand. The trigger finger was scraped, but no blood. I was breathing hard but I controlled myself and kissed the bruised finger. "Sorry," I said, "but your next shot could have been closer."

She stepped back, eyes glinting. "I wasn't going to kill you. You're not—mad, are you?"

"If I was, you'd be dead, bitch. What the hell got into you?" I thumbed on the safety and set the Browning on the night table.

She came over, circled my neck with her arms. "Will you forgive me?"

"I have. Because a woman in your line of work has to be careful. And I like the way you take care of yourself."

Her moist body pressed mine. "I like you even more than I did, Jack," she murmured.

"Strange way of showing it."

"Sometimes I do strange things—like going to bed with you."

"That was the part I liked," I told her, "not seeing that *mierda* in your hand."

"And you could so easily have hurt me—killed me," she crooned. Her head rolled back and her nipples pressed against me like flint. Danger and excitement were her aphrodisiac. From other women, I knew the syndrome. Poor Billy Joe, I thought, as I picked her up. Overmatched as never before in his criminal career.

I heaved her onto the bed. She bounced and sprawled there, gazing at me. Her tongue rimmed her lips until they were glistening. I said, "What about Freddy?"

"Later. I want you now."

I smiled. "Got a knife handy—to cut my throat?"

"*Chingado!*" One fist pounded the bed.

"*Puta*, I'm not your hired stud. Ask nicely."

"Damn you, come here!"

"Not good enough."

She sat up sulkily. "Please?"

I crawled over and slapped the side of her face. She gasped and was getting ready to claw me when I grasped her wrists and bore her backward. Abruptly her body went limp and from her throat came hoarse purring sounds. Like a jungle cat. Then her body enveloped me and her nails were raking my back. Her teeth nibbled my throat and neck as she moaned in passion. The strength of her body seemed enormous, then she collapsed, making small, happy sounds.

For a long time I held her, wishing she were Melody, and feeling semi-guilty that she wasn't. Then I bit her earlobe. "Freddy—remember?"

"Umm. Is that important?"

"I don't want trouble with him."

"You're afraid of him?"

"You know I'm not. But in my line of business I don't need more enemies. Or police curiosity."

"All right." She rolled over and reached for the telephone, dialed a call, and after a while someone answered. In Spanish she said, "Miguel? Federico is on the coast road south of the hotel. He needs a mechanic or a tow. I want you to take care of him."

There was some static until she said in a hard voice, "That doesn't matter. You do it now." No threats, just the tone of voice. She was accustomed to giving orders and being obeyed. She replaced the receiver and turned to me. "That's done."

"You're well connected here."

"A business associate. He's unimportant, but he has a boat."

"Sailboat?"

Her eyes narrowed. "Why?"

"I've done a good deal of bluewater sailing."

"Big boats?"

"Racing yawls. Seventy, eighty feet."

"Big enough. No, this man has a powerboat. For fishing—and other things."

"Sounds as though 'other things' could be interesting."

"Possibly. But you'd have to be working for me."

"Is that impossible?"

"It's something I'll have to think about."

"And ask Freddy."

"No! He's an employee, he has no power."

"But you do."

"Yes. With one other man—a relative." She reached for my hand. "I wish you could stay the night, but Freddy will be coming back."

"Another time, then," I said casually. "After all, we've just gotten acquainted."

Her smile was feline. "More than that, *mi amor*."

"Thanks. Well, I'm glad I just happened to be out driving. Where were you and Freddy headed, anyway?"

She raised on one elbow. "It happens I have a boat anchored down the coast. We were going there for a few drinks, some private swimming."

I knew that was a lie, but I said, "Maybe you'll take me—after Freddy leaves."

"Perhaps." Something was working in her mind. She had a sailboat, I could sail one. Maybe there was going to be a connection. All I wanted from her was the truth about Billy Joe, but so far nothing had developed, and I couldn't think of a way to get it out of her without revealing what my interest was. The old *Paz Paloma* seemed the only opening, but I couldn't push it.

I'd come to Mazatlán looking for Tara's father and ended up romancing his wife. And as I looked at her I didn't regret a minute of it. Too bad she was a Parra. Her face and figure could have taken her a long way, legitimately.

So I gave Yolanda a goodnight kiss and tucked her in bed. I picked up her Beretta from the mirror shards and shook off powdered glass. My bullet had entered the slide, making the pistol unserviceable. I told her so, and she said, "Freddy can get me another."

"Then I'll worry."

"Don't. That's behind us—and I'm satisfied."

I leered at her. "Me, too."

I got dressed and replaced the Browning next to my spine. Freddy would wonder about the shattered mirror, but Yolanda would have a plausible story, probably had one now.

Her eyes were closed, so I tiptoed from the bedroom and let myself out. Time: three o'clock. A lot of action in only four hours. I walked to Manny's next-door room and pressed the door buzzer, kept pressing until he opened up. I went in and saw his recorders turning. "She's down for the night," I told him. "No need to waste tape."

He ran fingers through dark, tousled hair. "Jesus, Jack, you got balls like an elephant."

"*Toujours l'audace,*" I said. "You weren't helping me, so I got into the thick of things myself."

"And when I heard that pistol shot I thought you were dead. When I heard the next one, I *knew* you were."

"Just keeping her humble," I told him. "Establishing the pecking order."

He slumped into a chair, yawned. "Find out what you came for?"

"No, and the way things are going, it won't be easy or brief. You could solve my problems by asking Freddy. Then I'll be gone, and out of your operational life."

He gestured at the wall. "Sure you want to leave—abandon that luscious *chocha*?"

"Hell, a little blanket drill doesn't mean lifetime bonding."

"All right," he sighed, "I suppose I could do that much." He looked up, smiling faintly. "How'd you gaff his wheels?"

"Sugared the tank." His yawning was catching. "If I had the strength I'd check out that jungle house, but I need sleep more than information. Freddy knows more than he's telling you, Manny. Shake him up. Make him come clean about the boat, the house and Billy Joe."

He said, "You seem to forget, Parra is my target."

"They're all connected," I said, "somehow. Freddy can draw the diagram. Squeeze him."

"All right," he said wearily, "since you're so damn sure. Now get the hell out of here—I need sleep too."

I found Rafe getting ready to leave, and returned the spare

key to him. Then I told him to take the TR from where I'd left it, back to storage.

"Everything work out, *jefe*?"

"Better than you could imagine," I told him, and got into a waiting taxi.

I was lying on the bed, wishing the overhead fan would move a little faster, when I heard vehicular clanking and rumbling from the street below. I slid off the bed and saw a tow truck hauling the orange Maserati. The front end was lifted and I saw Freddy Gomez on the passenger side. Behind the Maserati trailed a police car, and as the three vehicles drew nearer I noticed that Freddy's head was lolling at an awkward angle. Someone ran up to the Maserati and shined a light on Freddy's face.

Even at that distance I could see his shirtfront was covered with a dark stain. From a gap in his throat that ran from ear to ear.

I pulled on shoes and trousers and went down to the lobby phone to call Manny.

ELEVEN

"Damn it," Manny exploded, *"who killed my agent? Why?"*

We were sitting in a café at the north end of town, sharing a jug of boiled coffee. It was barely nine o'clock and both of us wore shades to protect sleep-deficient eyes. Half a mile offshore an island rose from the sea like a humpbacked whale.

The waiter brought over a plate of sliced papaya and some fried bread. I helped myself to the nourishing fruit, but my stomach wasn't ready for warm grease.

I said, "All I could pick up was that Freddy was dead when Miguel Ramirez found him. The machete nearly took off his head."

"If you believe Miguel."

I shrugged. "Yolanda told him to help Freddy, not kill him."

"I know, I know. And what will look so lousy on my report is I was *here* when my informant was wasted—not in Guadalajara where I belonged."

"Hell, if he had enemies—as apparently he did—it could have come any time."

Manny stirred the frothy coffee. "The motive coming to mind is that he was blown."

"Can't blame me for that," I said, and speared another papaya slice. "How's security in your office?"

"Sometimes I wonder—but you mixing in hasn't been helpful."

"Look at it this way. If Yolanda had been with him she'd be dead, too. So you've still got your opening to the Parra empire. All you have to do is run another *gavilán* against her."

"Yeah, but where to find one? Guys with brains and presence like Freddy don't come along every day. And when they do, they give you the Sicilian salute. I was months developing Freddy—now he's gone. *Shit!*" He pounded the table, and coffee jumped from the cup, spattering his trousers. "All I need," he said plaintively. "Any ideas, Jack?"

"The Parra operation's been functioning since long before you and I joined DEA. It'll be there while you scrounge up another penetration, so relax. Go back to Guadalajara and take care of business."

"How soon you going back to Miami?"

"I'll give this two days more." Before leaving the *posada* I'd knocked on Tara's door to make sure she was getting ready to leave. By now she should be at the airport, and the next plane overhead would be hers.

Manny dipped fried bread in coffee and munched away. Mouth half-full, he said, "Yolanda knows you didn't slice Freddy, but if one of her people did, she could frame you for it."

I thought it over. "That might occur to her," I admitted, "because she's a crafty creature. So I'm damn lucky she didn't check my billfold and learn my name ain't Reynolds. Around the Parra *estancia* the Novak name has a negative ring. So I'll be super-careful not to antagonize her until one of us leaves town."

"And then—? Not looking for work, are you?"

"No way. I'm in funds, thanks to Domingo Sanchez, and all I want is an inside look at that jungle house." I sipped coffee and ladled more sugar into it. "Know what I think goes on there?"

"Rolling phony Cuban cigars?"

"Maybe cockfighting or pit bulls. Setting's ideal for noisy goings-on."

"Except that it's a little hard to get to."

"Maybe they run busloads of customers out in the evening, return them at dawn. Like Everglades bingo."

"Yeah, anything's possible around these tourist traps."

"Or feelthy exhibitions."

"Feelthy mind," he grinned, and I was glad to see him getting over his depression.

"Just remember this," I said. "Freddy was holding stuff back from you, so it's not as though you lost a four-star informant."

"Dammit, when I think of all the shit I waded through with Freddy—" His teeth bared viciously.

"That's history, *amigo*. Rest up a few days at the Consulate and take another cut at it."

He sighed. "*Compadre*, you have a moral obligation to take Freddy's place."

I laughed hollowly. "Yolanda took a shot at me without knowing who I was. Imagine what she and her cousin would do if they ever found out."

"Yeah, but with the right alias documentation they'd never find out. Besides," he said, stretching back for a long yawn, "you've got a special advantage over Freddy. You can fly a plane."

"Who's got a plane that needs flying?"

"Yolanda. Freddy came in it to meet her. Pretty little Learjet 35, sunning itself at the airport."

"Do say. Well, that's too much plane for me. I haven't

flown jet since carrier days. The Seabee's about all I can handle."

"But you could fly the Learjet in a pinch."

"There's not going to be any pinch, Manny."

He ate a forkful of papaya and grimaced. "I don't know how Mexicans stand this—stinks like garbage." He laid down his fork. "Our government has spent millions and millions to get at Parra's plantations. And they'll spend millions more—unless the right man goes in and does a job."

I motioned over the waiter and asked for a Fernet-Branco and more coffee. The trend of conversation suggested I'd need it. I looked out over the ocean. Gulls and pelicans were diving gluttonously at a school of fry.

Manny said, "You listening?"

"Not **really**."

"What I mean is—maybe you're the right man—if I could get you a sizeable cut from the project appropriation."

I said nothing.

"How does a hundred thou sound?"

"Rattles like small change."

He snorted. "Two years' pay for me. Besides, as long as Omar Parra's alive and in business you need to keep looking over your shoulder. And when you and Melody have a family . . ." His voice trailed off.

A family, I thought suddenly. Three children, twelve years of college—two hundred thousand minimum, without inflation. "That'll be a while," I remarked, "seeing as how my intended won't have a degree for another two years." The coffee and *digestif* arrived, and I sipped them in turn.

Montijo squinted at the ocean. "How much, Jack?"

"How much—what?"

"Stop stalling."

"I haven't heard anything vaguely interesting."

"Two."

"Two what?"

"Hundred thousand—dollars."

"Tax free?"

"Has to be—confidential funds."

From the small glass jar I took three wooden toothpicks and laid them between us. Manny stared at them for a while. "Taxpayers' dough," he said, reached over and picked up the end toothpick. He broke it in half and laid the half beside the others. A quarter of a million dollars. Tax free.

I swallowed. "Win or lose?"

"I'll see that Melody gets your fee."

His word was better than an insurance policy. Besides, hazardous duty was uninsurable. "Plus expenses," I added.

"Naturally."

We didn't need to shake on it. I had his word, he had mine. "I'll need docs," I told him. "John Reynolds—Houston, plus regional pocket litter. Yolanda thinks I may be in the drug business."

He wrote it all down.

"How soon can you have it for me?"

He glanced at his watch. "By morning plane."

"One crucial thing—you have to keep it from Phil Corliss."

"Agreed." He got up. "I better make some calls, Jack. This time see if you can stay out of jail."

"I'll certainly try. That last Meskin jail damn near killed me."

"And I got you out alive."

"So I'm helping you now."

"For a quarter of a million I'd give Parra my sister—so it's not exactly in the favor category."

I grinned at him. "Now that I've got backing I may move into the Camino—to be near Yolanda, of course."

"Of course."

He strolled away and I turned my attention to the ocean.

Sharks were ripping into the fry, scaring off the gulls and pelicans. A hell of a feeding frenzy going on. I finished my libations and paid the score. Then I took a taxi to the Camino Real.

At a house phone I dialed Yolanda's suite. No answer. I wondered if she'd abruptly left town, and decided to look around before giving up.

I was glad Rafe didn't come on duty until later, because I didn't want to discuss last night's comings and goings with him. He might get the idea I'd planned Freddy's murder, and take it to the cops. On the other hand, I didn't evaluate him as overly endowed with public spirit, so I'd handle that problem if it arose.

I looked in bar and restaurant, and finally spotted Yolanda under a thatched *palapa* near the beach. She caught sight of me and gestured at a chair. Sitting down, I said, "Are condolences in order?"

"If you like."

"How soon they forget," I murmured. "What the hell happened?"

"Someone cut his throat."

"Robbery?"

She shook her head. "Not even hubcaps missing from the car. Billfold in his coat—with money."

"What do you make of it?"

"I don't know what to think." Her plate held the remains of *huevos rancheros*. Tragedy hadn't affected her appetite. From the waiter I asked for coffee and Añejo, and when he drifted off I said, "You implied the two of you were in a—ah, demanding business."

"Dangerous is a better word. Everyone has enemies, Jack. I guess one caught up with Freddy Gomez." She stirred her coffee and sipped unconcernedly.

"Leaving an opening in your organization?"

She looked away from me. "Perhaps. You can shoot and you can bullshit. What else can you do?"

"Hot-wire cars."

"Yes—I'd forgotten that." She eyed me levelly. "If you hadn't been with me, I might think you killed Freddy."

"Well, I could have arranged it without being there."

"I thought of that, too. Did you?"

"No reason. I was interested in you, not terminating him."

She sighed. "When I came here I didn't expect to be mixed up in murder."

"What about the fellow you sent for Freddy? Is he reliable?"

"Definitely. But—that's still a possibility." She pushed her plate aside. "Let's not talk about it any more. I'm on vacation, and I want to make the most of it. Death's a drag."

"It's all of that," I agreed. "So, what do we do today?"

"We?" She smiled invitingly.

"There's a bullring, and we could probably find some cockfights."

"Bloody. I'd be reminded of Freddy."

"Hire a boat—go off to one of the islands."

"Or take my boat—you said you could sail."

"Sure—how about you?"

"I came here on it. All the way from San—" Abruptly she stopped. "San Quintin."

"Don't know it."

"Baja."

I didn't need to board *Paz Paloma* again, or risk being recognized by Pedro Ramirez. So I said, "Sounds like more exercise than I'm up to today. Let's take it easy. Grab some rays and drinks on beach and pool."

"That's all I've been doing with Freddy." Her nose wrinkled. "I need more action than that. There's coke in the room."

"I don't indulge," I said, "on the principle that a merchant shouldn't consume what he sells."

"You sell the stuff?"

"When I can."

"Freddy snorted too much. I was thinking of getting rid of him anyway."

"Then you'll never find fault with me."

"You're beginning to make sense. You don't ask the wrong questions, and you don't brag. I like that in a man."

"And in a partner."

Her face stiffened. "I *have* a partner, Jack. Don't get pushy, you're doing fine."

"No harm in measuring boundaries," I remarked. "With Freddy gone, I think I'll check into the hotel. That okay?"

"I can't have you share my suite because I'll be making calls, seeing people."

"No problem."

The waiter brought me a short glass of cracked ice and poured a mini-bottle of Añejo. "*Salud,*" I said, and drank.

When I set down the glass she said, "Not too much of that. Don't want you falling asleep on me."

"Never fear, this is just an eye-opener for me, baby."

"And don't call me baby."

"Until you're paying my salary I'll call you whatever I want. Get bossy with me and I'll break your jaw." Tilting my glass, I drained the rest of the liquor. It made me think I could handle the balance of the day.

Her eyes smoldered. "Maybe I should have aimed better last night."

"Maybe. But you didn't, and that's history. Today, I don't like smartass broads with snotty mouths, so if we're going to get along, drop that act. Any more shit from you and I'll pull off your clothes and let you figure out what to do next. *Baby.*"

Her expression grew coy. "You mean—right here?"

I toed the sand. "Right here."

"You would, too, you *macho* bastard," she said with a pleased expression. "In Colombia I could have you killed for threatening me."

"But this isn't Colombia. Your nerves are on edge, baby. Maybe you need a little toot about now."

"I thought you'd never ask."

So we went up to her suite and got undressed, and she made a pilgrimage to Freddy's luggage and brought back a sandwich-size Ziploc bag bulging with the white stuff. She didn't bother to cut lines, just stuck a straw into it and snorted both nostrils. I could see the rush come. It hit her pupils, then her cheeks glowed. She licked her lips and her expression became dreamy. Seeing it reminded me too much of my late wife's addiction, so I went to the Servi-Bar and made myself a drink. When I came back to the bedroom she was stretched out on the bed, eyes closed. Her breathing was deep and regular. I could use a little rest myself, I reflected, so I lay down beside my quarter-million-dollar baby, adjusted the pillow comfortably and fell asleep.

She woke me, doing exciting things with her mouth and fingers. We made love for a while and then she fell asleep again.

The time was opportune to check out of the *posada*, so I got dressed and went down to the lobby. Rafe spotted me and came over. Drawing me aside, he said, "Sleep well?"

"Splendidly."

He glanced around. "What's it worth I don't say nothing about last night?"

"Clarify."

"What you did to the Maserati, then picked up his bimbo.

You had plenty time to cut his throat, *amigo*. What's it worth to you I don't tell the cops?"

I smiled. "What's it worth to you to stay alive, *pachuco*?"

He swallowed and his cheeks whitened. I said, "Sketch it out. If I wasted Freddy, and you can finger me, how long are you likely to enjoy living? Now, what was the question?"

He stepped back. "Ah—nothing. Me and my big mouth."

I nodded. "We'll overlook it for now, but you've been warned. I'm going to check in here—fifth-floor room, please, and I'll need a rental car. Can do?"

"*Sí*, no problem."

"Back in half an hour," I told him and moved past him toward the taxi line. A baggage caravan was entering, so I stepped aside and glanced back at where I'd left Rafe.

He was gone, but I saw a young woman walking along the pool edge, preparing to dive in. The bikini was new, but the face and figure were familiar.

Tara Vaill hadn't taken the morning plane, she'd just changed hotels. And if she and Yolanda connected, I could kiss the quarter-million goodbye.

TWELVE

By the time I'd collected my gear at the *posada*, paid my bill and taxied back to the hotel, Manny had checked out. So, I was given his room, which had a connecting door to Yolanda's suite. She was on the phone when I knocked, but opened her side in a few moments and I went in.

She was wearing a filmy peignoir, and her eyes looked baggy from too much or too little sleep. I said, "Feeling better?"

"Much. I'm glad you're nearby. Made any plans?" She shook out her long hair, then drew it back with a gold ribbon. The effect took five years from her face.

"Depends what you want, *querida*. Me, I'd like to get away from the hotel."

"My idea, too." She went over to the bureau and slipped on a thin bracelet loosely strung with small black, white and red beads. Then she laid crimson lipstick on her lips. I said, "That doesn't look like your kind of a bracelet. Local arts and crafts?"

"It's a good-luck charm, kind of. *Santería*. Ever hear of it?"

"Haiti?"

"Everywhere in the Caribbean."

"You a priestess or something?"

"I attend rituals now and then." She held up her forearm and the beads glinted as they slipped down. "Elegua's amulet."

"Elegua?"

"The trickster goddess."

"Ah," I said, "I'll remember that."

"The amulet is supposed to protect me against dirty tricks. Maybe it does—I need all the help I can find."

"Well, good luck," I said, "and too bad about the murdered goats and roosters."

"They'd die anyway. Shall we go?"

"Where?"

"My boat."

"Ummm. Not that I'm overly modest, but will we be alone? I mean, is your captain on board?"

She smiled briefly. "No captain, Jack."

"Watchman?"

"Only at night."

"Good idea," I said. "By the way, I traded the Triumph for one with a key."

"That's an improvement. Incidentally, I talked to the garage, and the Maserati would be usable tomorrow." She grabbed up towels and folded them into a beach bag. "Seems the fuel line was clogged. Don't suppose you'd know what it was?"

"Yeah. I pissed in his tank. Now, get off it, will you? I'd never seen Freddy's car until it stalled out on the road."

"Someone did," she said thoughtfully, "and set him up for killing." Taking my arm, she gazed at me. "If you hadn't picked me up, it could have been both of us with our throats cut."

"So stop complaining."

"You were adequately rewarded, weren't you?"

"More than adequately. Memorably."

She kissed the side of my face, quickly wiped off the bright stain. "*Adelante.*"

The rental car was a red VW Rabbit convertible with an impressive pickup. "At least," I said, "this will get us where we're going."

"Good—because I really don't want to stall out again."

We were driving south on the road I'd seen only at night. It was bad enough then, but under hot sunlight the potholes and chasms were alarming. A police team was working the area where the murder had taken place, crawling through undergrowth, sifting roadside dirt, looking for clues. We slowed and crept past. Yolanda averted her gaze, but otherwise didn't react to the location. So I speeded up and after a while she told me where to park the VW.

Because of darkness, I hadn't seen the railinged staircase leading down the cliff face. It was old and looked insecure, but it was better than clinging to roots and ledges. As we started down I scanned the boat's weather deck for Pedro— or anyone else—and tried to figure out what to do if he showed up. Dive deep, and not come up for air.

We were on the rocky beach in less than a minute, and walking to the skiff. Yolanda put her sandals inside, and together we shoved it from the sand into the water. I rowed to the ladder and tied up, steadying the little boat while Yolanda climbed on deck. I followed, noticing Pedro's shotgun on an outside rack.

She took me down through the untidy saloon and got ice from the galley's butane-run refrigerator. Scotch for her, white wine for me. Our glasses clinked, and I said, "Scuba tanks on deck. You dive?"

"Love it. You?"

"Been known to."

"I've only been down once in this anchorage, but there are

pargo and *huachinango*. There's some spears somewhere—Hawaiian slings."

"We might try our luck," I said. "Later."

We carried our drinks on deck. Yolanda squinted at the sun, laid cushions across the transom seat and took off her blouse and slacks. That was all she had on.

Face down, then, so I could cover her back with tanning oil. A beautifully contoured, well-nourished female. If properly manipulated, she could bring me a quarter of a million dollars. If not, I'd have had the considerable pleasure of her company. Which was more than I'd anticipated when I arrived in Mazatlán.

That thought turned my mind to Billy Joe and his daughter, who was blowing her Sanchez split at the Camino Real. Now I wished I hadn't been so generous with Tara. But, by deceiving me and staying on, she'd relieved me of obligation to search further for her missing father. She was on her own now, doing things her own way. Should I learn the Preacher's fate from Sister Grace, I'd let her know. In time.

Yolanda drained her glass and asked for a refill. I freshened both our drinks and came back into the cockpit. She sat up long enough to take her glass, then lay back on the cushions and oiled her body from toes to forehead. Eyes closed, she murmured, "I want to get as much sun as I can stand—then dive in and cool off."

"Can't argue with that, but you've got all the cushions."

"Look down in the front cabins. Should be some there—and pardon the mess. We had a rough trip sailing down from . . . San Quintin."

"Who was your captain?"

"What do you care?"

"Wondered if he was qualified to handle a big ketch like this."

"Said he was, but I didn't think much of his seamanship. Anyway, we got here."

"That's the bottom line," I agreed, and went below. I

111

rounded up three cushions where she'd suggested and picked up one of the church brochures. In the cockpit I dropped the cushions on deck and said, "What's this True Word Gospel Church? You a supporter?"

She jackknifed erect. "*Where*—?" She saw the folder in my hand, shrugged and lay back. "Complicated story, Jack. Look close at the photo of the preacher and Sister Grace."

I did, holding it to the sun and peering intently at the familiar faces. She said, "Well?"

"You don't mean—you're—?"

She laughed brassily. "That's me. Don't I look full of religion?"

"You look like a saint."

"That was the idea, and it brought in contributions. The preacher was working the suckers, while I was working him." She stretched her arms, lifting those magnificent globes. "A scam—all the way. Then the money slowed and I got restless, bored with the whole thing."

"And came here to rest up?"

"And reorganize my life. I—well, I had a hard time in the States and don't plan on going back." She laughed thinly. "You do what you have to do, right? I needed Billy Joe, and he found he needed me. For a while we made a good team."

"So, where's Billy Joe?"

Her eyes opened and she gave me a hard glance.

I dropped the folder and looked over the scuba tanks. Three valves were taped, indicating the bottles were charged with compressed air. The fourth's tape was missing, showing it had been used. Underwater fishing? I wondered.

Just forward of the tanks a bench-box held fins, snorkel masks, BCs, weight belts and regulators, several Hawaiian slings and long, thin spears. All commonplace on a pleasure craft.

I stripped, put on facemask and fins and dropped over the side.

The water was warm and clear, the sandy bottom littered

with rocks and boulders. The ketch floated in about twenty feet of water, its crescent keel knifing halfway down. I circled it slowly, looking for any anomaly, but before I'd completed inspection Yolanda was swimming toward me, naked but for fins and mask. Underwater we swam the length of the boat and surfaced for air at the stern. Pushing up our masks, we kissed, our bodies flowing together, tugged by the tide. Her thighs locked around my hips, her breasts pressed against my chest, and I clung to the rudder shaft while we made love.

Afterward we drifted back to the ladder and climbed on deck. Yolanda said, "I'm hungry."

"Any food in the galley?"

"Should be bread in the refrigerator, that's about all."

"Then I'll go hunting."

I put on scuba gear and leg knife, gripped a Hawaiian sling and spear, bit down on the regulator mouthpiece and went over the side.

From the bottom I looked upward and saw a small barracuda orbiting the keel. It was only about two feet long, but its razor jaws could mangle hand or foot. Keeping close to the bottom, I swam toward the mouth of the cove and deeper water. Blue parrotfish and triggerfish were nibbling along the sides of a reef. Striped grunts swam nearby. A pair of black margates fanned their egg-nest, wary of a spotted grouper. I could have speared him, but he was too small to feed us both.

Toward open water I saw a spine of coral running over dark volcanic rock, went deeper and noticed a sudden sand swirl near a crevice. Moray? I lay flat and poked with the spear. Current swept away the sand, and spindly antennae emerged. The spear pried out a blue-green spiny lobster, about two pounds, I estimated, and grasped him above the carapace. Swimming along, I found another lobster backing hurriedly into his hole, tickled him out and grabbed him too. This one was slightly larger. Carrying lobsters and spear, I kicked back to the boat, surfaced and tossed my prey on deck. Yolanda shrieked in surprise.

There was plenty of wine stashed around the saloon, so I filled a big kettle halfway with sea water, half with white wine, and set it on the butane range. When the mix was boiling I dropped the lobsters in, watched them turn pink.

Yolanda cleared the littered table, set it with forks, knives, bread, butter and wine. When the lobsters were crimson I extracted them, snapped off their carapaces and shucked the white meat on paper plates. As we ate I said, "Doesn't get any better than this, *mi amor*."

"You're right—it doesn't." She leaned forward and kissed my forehead. "You're quite a guy, Jack Reynolds. Anything you don't do?"

"Bet long shots."

Moisture glistened on her oiled skin. Her drying hair fell over her shoulders, nearly touching her breasts. She was a well-structured, desirable female, and I realized I'd have to keep reminding myself that she was also a criminal and possibly a murderess as well. Gazing at her face, I reflected that she was the potential key to my children's future education. The quarter-million would spare them from waiting table, give them junior years abroad in Rome, Paris or Madrid.

As she dabbed a lobster chunk into melting butter, she said, "Ever since we got here I've been thinking about you."

"I should hope so."

She smiled lazily. "Aside from pleasure—I mean, my business. How you might fit in."

I sipped iced wine. Let her do the talking. She said, "This boat will be going back to the States. With a certain cargo. Could you sail it there?"

"I'd need a mate or two."

"That could be arranged. You can navigate?"

"Loran or celestial—either way."

"There's no Loran gear, just a sextant and star tables. The other captain didn't know how to use them, so we were hardly ever out of sight of land." She drank from her glass and added more wine. "The trip I have in mind would take you far offshore."

"Away from Coast Guard boats."

She picked up her fork and stabbed the last chunk of lobster. After swallowing, she said, "You like the idea?"

"In principle. Frankly, my courage increases proportionately with the reward."

"What would you say to ten thousand dollars? For a few days at sea."

"If that's all it involved—but not against twenty-five years in the slammer." I chewed a piece of bread, washed it down with wine.

"The risk will be small. There's a place for cargo the Coast Guard would never find."

"I've heard that before," I told her, "and I'd estimate cargo value at twenty to thirty million dollars—right?"

She nodded.

"Since you trust me, why be stingy?"

"Good point. And since you mention it, I'm not sure *why* I trust you. But it's not up to me. My partner will have to okay you."

"Is he in Mazatlán?"

She shook her head. "Colombia. For now you don't need to know his name."

"Colombia's a long way from here."

"A few hours—in my plane."

"Ah," I said, "that makes a difference. When do we leave?"

"When the police release Freddy's body. It will go with us."

"In a casket, I hope."

"Of course. The plane crew is enjoying themselves around Mazatlán, but I can get them any time."

"Let's see. Two of them, you, me, and the casket. Must be a good-sized plane."

"It's a Lear," she told me. "Not big, but very fast. And it can get in and out of jungle strips."

"Will we be landing at a jungle strip?"

"After a fuel stop. Don't worry, the pilot knows the area."

"Like your captain knew the ocean?"

Irritably, she said, "You might as well know—Billy Joe was the captain."

"You don't say? Well, he was probably counting on divine guidance over the trackless sea."

She snorted. "The only thing divine was the way he got money from suckers. A con man, Jack, with a lot of prison years. And greedy—didn't want to split the money." She was working herself into enjoyable anger. "Had a daughter, too, blonde girl. She hated me. She was jealous of me."

"Jealous?"

"She and her father were close—too close, if you get my meaning."

"Not sure I do."

"Well, I never actually *saw* them in bed together, but . . ." Her head tossed angrily. "Enough of that, I don't want to talk about it any more."

"Fair enough. Sounds ugly."

She began clearing the table, tossing our paper plates in a trash bin, knives and forks in the small galley sink. When she came back we finished the wine bottle together.

Back on deck, then, we oiled each other's bodies. I'd had minimal sleep, a scuba dive and considerable wine, so I lay down on deck cushions and dozed in the sun.

I couldn't have been there more than a few minutes when a loud splash opened my eyes. I sat up thinking of gamefish jumping, then I saw a boulder carom down the cliff face and hit just off the beach.

Shielding my eyes, I glanced up at the top of the cliff and saw sun glinting on metal. Reflection came from a scope-mounted rifle held by a man who was taking aim at Yolanda—or me.

THIRTEEN

I grabbed her wrist and dragged her off the transom as a bullet whapped a cushion. The report echoed off the cliff. "Wha-what?" she blurted from her knees. "*Stay down*," I shouted, and tumbled her down the companionway.

The next shot slammed into cockpit decking near my feet. Another hard, intimidating echo, and I sprinted around the cabin, snatching Pedro's shotgun from its rack. A third shot splintered the cabin roof as I ducked down behind the windscreen. It wasn't much protection, but the mainmast stood between us, giving him a harder shot. I saw sunlight glinting from his scope lens, jacked a shell into the chamber and fired at it three times.

He was too far away for the pellets, but I thought it might discourage him. His two naked sleepers had suddenly become one dangerous man with a gun. I peered over the cowling for lens or barrel reflection, and saw nothing, but I fired again in his direction. Beyond the cliff escarpment an engine caught, roared, and tires spewed gravel. Whoever he was, he was gone.

I waited a few moments, came back in a crouch and went

down the ladder into the saloon. Yolanda was rubbing her knees. "Mother of Christ," she said hoarsely, "he meant to kill me."

"Or both of us." I cleared the shotgun's firing chamber and blew smoke from the barrel. Picking up the ejected shell case, I said, "Any live ones around?"

"Some—somewhere," she said unsteadily, "but I thought he was gone. Didn't you hear the car?"

"Maybe we heard what we were meant to hear. I want this shotgun loaded. Off your butt, and look."

"I hurt," she complained. "Did you have to be so rough?"

"You were disorganized, baby. No time to brief you."

She stood up, wincing. "Try that drawer at the end of the seat."

I pulled it open and found three boxes of shotgun shells. I reloaded from the open box. Four live shells in the tube, one in the chamber. I set the safety and looked at her. "I've been in shootouts before," I said, "but never naked."

She managed a smile, limped over and kissed my cheek. "You were wonderful, Jack. I—I'm—very grateful."

"I want more than that," I said in a hard voice. "Truth, baby. All of it."

She sat down and chewed her lower lip. I opened a bottle of rye and told her to drink. She swallowed, coughed and handed me the bottle. I don't like rye but I needed a tranquilizer. Otherwise, if she didn't come clean with me, I was going to tear off her head.

Glancing up, she said, "Some things I can't talk about."

"Bullshit. Freddy's dead, and you were today's target. I can't protect you if you don't level with me. And if you don't, lady, I'm off to Houston *mañana*." I swallowed more rye.

She lay back and rubbed a bruised elbow. "You can't do that," she murmured. "I need you."

I sat down by her feet, shotgun between my knees. "Talk."

With a grimace she said, "We've never actually spoken the words, but you know the business I'm in."

"Narcotics?"

She nodded. "I belong to a Colombian family with so much power you wouldn't believe—sometimes I don't believe it myself. No one dares challenge us. We do what we want. Anyone in the way gets killed. We control police and cabinet ministers, army generals. That takes money, incredible amounts of it. So we have to make big money to cover all the bribing and still have a profit."

I said nothing, while she stared at the overhead.

"My name isn't Marta, it's Yolanda. Yolanda Lopez."

"So?"

She swallowed. "My mother's name was Parra—mean anything to you?"

"No," I lied. "So you've got a big family connection in Colombia where men tremble at your glance. What's that got to do with Mazatlán and the hit man I just ran off?"

"It's—competition. We have a new lab here, and the Mexican organizations told us to close it down—or else."

I scratched the side of my face. "So Freddy's murder didn't surprise you."

She stared at the shotgun in my hands. "I was just—damn glad I wasn't killed too. Today—well, it's lucky you were here to save me."

"Me and Elegua."

She touched the amulet. "When I tell Omar all you've done, there's no question he'll want you working for us."

"Omar? The Tentmaker?"

"Omar Parra, my first cousin. He took over our organization after his brother, Luis, was killed. And I took Omar's place."

"Making you second in command."

"It's not that formal." She reached for my hand. "Jack, you'll be a very rich man. You won't believe how much money you'll have."

"I believe that—always have. So I don't spend money until I see it in front of me."

She said, "If you let my cousin know how much I've told you, he'll beat me up. You, too."

I touched the side of her face. "Couldn't have that happen."

We kissed lengthily, and she said, "I'm not up to making love, Jack. Those shots chilled me."

"No problem. How was it the killers happened to be around when Freddy's car stopped?"

"I don't know. Maybe they were driving to or from the lab and saw his car—only one like it in Mazatlán."

"You mean, the killers work in your lab?"

"No, no—but there are usually men watching. Ready to steal a load. So far we've only lost one."

"One load—and one Freddy."

"I'll miss him," she said. "He was fun for a while, and not bad in bed, but he knew the risks."

"Yeah—I've seen them too. So, the lab must be near the road."

"Freddy and I were going there last night, checking production. I need you to go with me tonight."

"In that case I'll borrow this shotgun." I lifted it and dropped the butt for emphasis.

She laid an arm over my shoulder and kissed me briefly. "We'll have dinner, leave the hotel around eleven."

"Sometime you must tell me how you became Sister Grace, then Yolanda Lopez again."

"Sometime. Now, let's go back to the hotel. I need a massage and a long, hot soak."

"We'll have dinner in your place."

She started to object, then touched her knees. "I like dancing—but I'd look awkward. Your idea is better."

I'd wanted to keep her out of view until I figured what to do about Tara, so I was glad I'd roughed her up pulling her from the gunsight. Providence takes care of us all—one way or another. And now that I had a clear idea of what went on at the jungle house I could hardly wait to get inside.

After we dressed I went topside with the shotgun and scanned the cliff very carefully, then the beach rocks and ocean, before rowing us in. I went up the staircase first, shotgun at port arms, ready to blast the first face I saw beyond the scarp.

Yolanda got into the Rabbit. I slid behind the wheel and was about to insert the ignition key when a thought occurred. "Out," I told Yolanda, "and don't close the door."

"What's the matter?" She glanced around, bewildered.

"Do as I say." I got out carefully, and had her stand thirty feet away. Then I walked slowly around the car and gently opened the hood. No trigger wires attached. I left the hood up and inspected the engine for foreign objects. Nothing visible. Tailpipe empty and clear. I lay down in the dirt and rolled under the chassis. Scanning the shadows would have been a lot easier with a flashlight—but I hadn't expected to be doing this. It took a while for my pupils to adjust, and then I covered every square foot of the underside, finally running my fingers over the invisible surface of the frame. My hand stopped against a metal object and I felt sweat roll down my face—not all of it from the heat of the day. I squirmed back on my shoulder blades until I could touch the object with both hands. Gently I pushed one end and felt it slide. It was held in place by a magnet. I wanted to wipe sweat from my eyes and face, but I had to keep going.

Gradually I slid it sideways until it was free of the frame's metal and I was gripping it with both hands. Keeping it horizontal, I lowered it to the ground and glanced at it before rolling out from under the car into sunlight.

Shakily I stood up, stiff from cramps and tension. I wiped face and neck and slumped against the car. Yolanda called, "Can I come now?"

"Not yet. In fact, don't move." When my breathing was regular I reached into the car and released the hand brake, then shoved the Rabbit a dozen feet ahead. Even at that distance I heard Yolanda gasp.

For what lay in the brilliant sunshine was a black sheet-metal box about ten inches long. I took a deep breath and went slowly to it. The case was big enough to hold four sticks of dynamite, or a bloc of C-4 plastic explosive. Wires ran into it from a nine-volt battery taped to the top surface; one wire fed into what looked like a glass spirit level—except that the tube was partly filled with mercury.

"What is it?" she called.

"Trembler bomb. You can get into the car."

"Are you sure it's safe now?"

"The car is, the bomb isn't."

She made a wide approach and got in, not closing the door. I slid in beside her and said, "Professional job, baby. First road bump and we'd have been hamburger in the jungle."

She shivered and looked away. "The gunman didn't have time to place it, did he?"

"He set it under the car first, because he had no way of knowing he'd get clear shots at us. So the bomb was a fallback. Fail-safe murder." I picked up the shotgun and thumbed off the safety, started the engine and drove fifty feet from the bomb. Then I laid the shotgun on the seatback and sighted on the black box. As I pulled the trigger I floored the accelerator and the car jumped ahead as the road behind exploded in sheets of orange flame.

Pebbles and metal fragments rattled against the Rabbit, but neither of us was hit. I slowed the car and glanced back. The smoking hole was at least three feet deep and just as wide. Yolanda gazed in awe. "*Ave María*, what that could have done to us! What made you think of a bomb?"

"The guy who shot at us was an executioner. So I tried to think like an executioner. If the contract had been mine, I'd have wanted to make absolutely sure of the kill." I licked dry lips. "As he did."

She clung to my arm and began whimpering. I patted her shoulder. "It's over now, nothing to worry about."

Tremulously she said, "What an extraordinary man. Where have you been all my life?"

"Trying to make a buck. Waiting for you to appear."

She licked the inside of my ear and laid her head on my shoulder. We rode that way all the way back to the hotel.

In her room Yolanda phoned for a masseuse and ran steaming water in the Olympic-size tub. I gave her a double scotch and went into my own room.

After a shower and a change of clothing, I locked my door and took an elevator to the lobby.

Looking for Miss Tara Vaill.

FOURTEEN

She wasn't hard to find. Lying in a poolside lounge with a Latino on either side. The plump one wore a Hitler mustache. The other was rib-skinny with a long, thin rat-tail mustache carefully curled like Dali's. Both seemed hypnotized by the blonde *gringa*, a syndrome common to Latin males.

A cooler stand held an inverted champagne bottle, while a convenient table held an opened magnum of Cordon Rouge. Clearly, Tara was beginning to live her fantasies. No telling how far she'd go with the two Aztecs.

Fatso filled their glasses from the magnum. Tara sipped and giggled. Ye gods, I thought, and returned to the lobby. From a house phone I had her paged at the pool, and after a while I saw her get up, frowning, and pad out of sight. Presently her voice said, "This is Tara Vaill. Who wants me?"

"I do, bitch. You crossed me. Why?"

"I—I decided I don't have to take orders from you."

"And I don't have to look for Dad. I thought Dom Sanchez demonstrated how unsafe it is for you in Mazatlán."

"Well, you took care of him, didn't you?"

125

"At some risk and effort. Who's the *macho* pair you're sunning with?"

"Orestes and Fausto? They're pilots—if it's any of your business."

"When I came here on your behalf a lot of things became my business. I told you I was working on answers to your Dad's disappearance. Well, for reasons I won't explain, it's crucial that you stay out of sight. I mean totally disappear, kid."

"Is—you've found my father?"

"I didn't say that. He may be alive, he may be dead. In the latter case I'll be able to tell you what happened. If the former, he can tell you himself."

I heard a quick intake of breath. "You're—serious?"

"Believe it." I glanced at my wristwatch. "You've got until six to check out of here. Stay at another hotel, and if you want whatever I come up with, be on that morning plane."

I heard an alcoholic wail. "Just when I was beginning to have fun."

"Why should you have fun and I none? And from the look in those brown Latino eyes, those pilots have got you qualifying for the mile-high club. Don't say you weren't warned."

"Mile—?" she blurted.

"Oh, forget it. Ask Melody." I was gritting my teeth. "Going to do the right thing this time?"

"Yes, but the boys are taking me to dinner. So—"

"Anywhere but this hotel," I snapped. "If I see you here after six, I'm off the case. Maybe your new pals will keep looking for Dad, but I've had enough hassling from you. Six o'clock, Tara."

I replaced the receiver, went over to the telephone office and placed a call to Miami. Melody took it by her pool, and said, "We keep missing each other."

"I certainly miss you."

"Shall I fly down, treasure?"

"No, pumpkin. Your friend is my main problem and I have to get her out of here and back to you."

"Is she trying to seduce you?"

"Honey, we can't stand each other. I'm making progress, but—" I went on to tell her about finding the boat and Sister Grace. "So, if they spot each other, forget Dad."

"You're doing marvelously, dear. When shall I expect Tara?"

"Tomorrow. Tell her nothing—absolutely nothing—and keep her occupied, okay?"

"I'll try," she sighed. "I'm on my way to the apartment now—it's a total mess, so I've hired new decorators. God knows how long they'll take."

"Love to Momma."

"Love you. 'Bye."

I strolled back to a point where I could scan the pool. Tara was gathering her things into a tote bag. The pilots seemed to be protesting, but she placated them, and I left the area hoping that everything was finally in train.

Rafe stopped me, saying, "The Rabbit run okay?"

"I thought it might blow up on me, but I found the source of the trouble. Otherwise, it's a good little heap."

"*Espléndido.* Anything else, *jefe?*"

I patted his shoulder. "I'll let you know." I began walking away and turned back. Pointing at the pool, I said, "Those two *cabrones* with the champagne claim they're pilots. Know anything about them?"

He grinned lasciviously. "Sure. They work for your girl-friend, fly her plane."

"She forgot to tell me," I muttered, and went back to my room.

At eight, Yolanda and I ordered dinner from a room service waiter. At nine it arrived, and by ten we were having coffee and Kahlua, and listening to music drift up from the dance floor below.

Through dinner, Yolanda had become progressively more businesslike. Massage, hot soak and drinks had dissipated aches and pains, and she seemed to have adjusted to the attempt on her life by not referring to it.

When she began talking about her family's immense land holdings with its marijuana and poppy plantations, the private army that guarded the Parra estate, I realized that she was beginning to regard me as a recruit. But she stopped short of describing specific smuggling routes, saying that would have to wait for Omar's approval. "After we get to the ranch."

"Which will be—when?"

"After Freddy's body is released." She stirred her coffee. "Maybe tomorrow."

"That's soon enough," I told her. "I need to cancel the arrangements that brought me here, and I don't expect the contacts to be happy about it. So, I have to cool the deal without closing the door—in case things don't work out in Colombia."

"I understand. And you must understand that once we're at the ranch, things can't be the same between us."

"You have a husband?"

"That's not important—Omar would not approve of anyone who works for us being my lover."

"What about Freddy?"

"That was here—not in front of Omar."

I drank from my cup, set it down. She wouldn't be expecting me to spend nights with her when I had other things to do. Reaching over, I held her hand. "I understand, *chula*. I'll be discreet."

She pushed the *santería* amulet above her watch and looked at the dial. "We can go whenever you like."

"I'm not crazy about going at all, but obviously you need someone to ride shotgun."

She smiled lazily. "You *gringos*—always cowboy talk."

"Standin' tall." I squared my shoulders. "This is all pretty exciting for you?"

"Once it was, no more. It's—too many people being killed. And now they're trying to kill me." She touched her amulet. "I'll be safer in Colombia."

"What about me?"

"You, too—if you don't break the rules. We don't kill each other, just traitors and informers."

I nodded approvingly. "Can't tolerate treason. But I was thinking, too bad you can't get lab protection here from the Mex police."

"They already work for Mexican organizations, so Omar says we must shut down. After enough is processed to cover our investment." She drained her cup. "I could have told him this was a bad idea, but I was—away." She looked quickly at me. "Working with the Reverend Billy Joe."

"What a circus that must have been."

She smiled reminiscently, but there was nothing pleasant about it. "He could have gone on for years working his con, bringing in big money and living well, but he had to have it all at once."

"Everyone's entitled to a mistake."

"If he'd been halfway sensible, I'd have stayed with him. Instead, he screwed up everything and I'm returning to the ranch. So, he changed my life—the wrong way."

"What did he do with his dough?"

"*Our* dough. Pissed it away gambling. Ran up big debts, and he'd be in jail now if I hadn't figured a way to get him out of the States."

"How'd you manage that?"

"Another time." She rose from the table in a graceful serpentine uncoiling. "Funny the way things come apart—never slowly so you have time to prepare. Like a building falling down, everything together."

"His daughter clear out too?"

"She wasn't involved." Yolanda laughed shortly. "Billy Joe wasn't even sure Tara was his child—thought she was, but her mother was a swinger. Anyway, he adored the kid, kept her away from trouble while he did his thing."

"Normal for a father." I got up and put away our chairs.

"But the way Tara watched him wasn't normal. Never taking her eyes off him, afraid he'd show me affection. I told you she was jealous. All so damn weird." She shook her head. "Ready?"

I went into my room, fitted the Browning pistol into my belt and pocketed Domingo's switchblade knife. Also the small flash I'd borrowed from Tara. Then I was ready to go.

For protection I drove with the Rabbit's top up and locked in place; if there were roadside snipers, we'd be a little harder to hit. Yolanda steadied the shotgun between us as I followed the treacherous road.

It was a night like any other night in Mazatlán. Clear air with windborne jungle scents and plenty of moon. Phosphorescent breakers below, and fishing boats winking off at sea. Tranquility prevailed—except that twice today we'd escaped death, and the memory weighted me like ballast.

We didn't talk much, and I began wondering if Tara was holed up as agreed. A strange girl, whose demanding friendship Melody didn't need. Anyway, she and her Dad had dropped down on my priority list since I'd accepted Manny's offer. And from things Yolanda was letting drop, Billy Joe was sounding like a head case, his daughter as well.

Melody, I reasoned, had an exaggerated sense of responsibility for wounded birds, whereas I'd always lived on the self-help principle and expected others to do likewise.

Yolanda said, "We're close to where the Maserati stalled, so don't slow down."

"No way. How much farther to go?"

"Couple of miles, and the road gets worse."

I knew that, but this was supposed to be my first time out, so I concentrated on steering, using high beams to lead the way.

After a while she said, "There'll be a small road off to the left. It's so narrow and rutted we practically have to crawl."

"Sounds like a great place to pick us off."

"It's been tried," she said unconcernedly, "so about now my men will start running off anyone who shouldn't be there. Besides, you're armed." She tapped the shotgun.

"I do better when I can see a target. This jungle reminds me of Nam."

"I suspected you'd been there. That's one reason I have confidence you'll fit in with us."

"Well, I'd prefer an opportunity to use my brains, not just my trigger finger."

"You'll use both—if you want to survive."

"It's paramount in my thoughts." As were Manny's quarter-million bucks, and to collect them I'd have to live.

So I continued driving, and the access road was so well concealed that I overshot it and had to back around and return. As I entered it Yolanda reached over and blinked the headlights off and on in a recognition sequence. "Keep going," she said, "they'll let us through."

The narrow road—no better than a cowpath—was rutted from heavy trucks, and so overgrown that shrubs and branches scraped the top and sides of the car. After dipping down into a soggy gully, the trail slanted upward toward the mountainside. I knew what was at the end of it.

Finally, headlights picked up iron grill gates set into solid-looking posterns from which whitewash was peeling. Two men in straw hats, wearing loose peasant garb, stepped out of the jungle, holding not rifles but short-barreled submachine guns, extra clips around their hips. Each had a machete scabbard looped around his thigh by a leather thong.

131

Yolanda rolled down her window and called to open the gates. One man touched his hat respectfully and helped the other move the heavy, rusted iron.

When the opening was wide enough I drove through and found the approach cobbled. Yolanda said, "Pull around to the side, and don't get out."

"Why not?"

"You'll see."

Up close, the old mansion looked even more ominous than from the road, the concrete patched with moss and lichens, window bars covered with tendrils. Someone's dream house half-devoured by the ravenous jungle, now partly resurrected to serve the Parra family's needs.

I heard a man yelling, then two large hounds slammed up against my car, clawing paint and windows, barking viciously. They were Rottweilers, and they looked capable of taking down an elephant.

My grip tightened around the shotgun but Yolanda said, "Not necessary, Jack. Be patient."

Finally the handler appeared, leashed the hounds and half-dragged them off. He was somewhat better dressed than the *campesinos* at the gate, and wore an old Mauser pistol in a long wooden holster that was usable as a shoulder stock. Almost a collector's item, I thought, but I hadn't come to evaluate weaponry. The faint scent of ether was what my mission was all about.

Yolanda said, "We can get out now—leave the shotgun here."

Out behind the building the hounds were snarling and baying. A bullwhip cracked, the hounds yelped and whimpered, then nothing but the harsh croaking of tree toads and gecko lizards in the humid air.

As we walked toward a steel-shod door I became aware of generator hum. That explained electric lighting this far from civilization. And of course electricity was essential in processing narcotics. Yolanda clanged a ship's bell, and presently the door opened a crack. I could see an eye peering at us until Yolanda said, "All the way, Carlos."

A snub chain rattled free and the door opened, drawn inward by a man in blue pantaloons and denim work shirt. A foreign-made machine gun hung from his shoulder. He locked the door after us, and the inside air was redolent of mildew and ether.

"Good security," I remarked.

"You better believe it—and necessary." She walked imperiously through the cavernous first-floor room, stopping short of a messy-looking kitchen and punching a sequential lock on the jamb beside another iron-plated door. The electronic lock opened and I saw a heavy wooden staircase leading down into a cavernous basement. From a wall rack she handed me a protective mask and put on another. "Don't take it off," she told me, "or you'll have the high of your life—and the last."

Docilely I followed her down the staircase, glad the mask filter was letting me breathe uncontaminated air.

The chief chemist, operations foreman, or whatever his title was, hurried over to Yolanda, mask bobbing like a tapir's snout. They talked for a few moments, then he led us into the lab area.

Yolanda checked boxes and bags of raw materials, moved on to the stainless-steel cooking vats, examined the hotter drying area where chunks of cocaine cured under thermal lamps.

On to the pulverizing machine, where the stuff became white powder poured into kilo-sized plastic bags. I'd seen it all before during busts, but I pretended interest and stayed at her side.

A thick masonry wall separated drums of ether and acetone from the processing area, and toward the rear of the lab a machine was stamping out Lude tablets.

All told, there were about a dozen workers, anonymous behind their protective masks, working like robots at their assigned tasks. They wore surgical gloves to prevent dermal absorption of the chemicals and consequent addiction.

In a cooler section, under overhead fans, bags of cocaine were being packed into a variety of shipping containers: duffel bags, plastic garbage bags, laid in floral boxes and fitted into an assortment of simulated fruits and vegetables molded from fiberglass and realistically painted to resemble pineapples, mangoes and yams. I tapped Yolanda's shoulder and said, "That what I'll be delivering?"

She shook her head.

"How big a cargo?"

"You don't need to know."

She put a tally sheet on a clipboard and began going over figures. That was going to take her a while, so I wandered away from the active area and came to a heavy wooden door with a lift bar. No one was watching me, so I opened the door and slipped inside.

Overhead light came from a single low-wattage bulb hanging from a double wire. Dim orange light showed a packed-dirt floor separating the stone foundation wall from what looked like three monks' cells. The area was cool and damp. I lifted my mask and sniffed—no ether in the air. I wiped perspiration from my face and peered into the barred opening of the nearest door. It was face-high, but the inside was dark. Second cell the same. I was about to turn back when I heard the faint sound of a radio, and walked to the third door.

Through the bars I could see light in the cell. There was a rough wooden chair and a table on which lay a small portable radio. There was a water bowl, a slop bucket and a metal cot. On the striped, stained mattress lay a man in skivvy shirt and faded bluejeans. His hands were folded over his chest and his eyes were partly closed as though he was dozing. His long hair was dark and a heavy beard covered his face.

Some poor slob in the brig for violating house rules, I was

thinking, when the prisoner sat up and reached for his radio. He held it toward the light bulb to read the dial, and though the beard exaggerated the fullness of his face, I made out the high cheekbones and deep-set eyes.

Of Billy Joe Vaill.

FIFTEEN

I could have walked away without a word—and should have—but in the moments I stared at him I remembered Tara and Melody and why I'd come to Mazatlán. He was a sinner and a career criminal, but one person in the world loved him—his daughter—so I couldn't hold him irredeemable. Besides—the thought flashed through my mind—he'd run afoul of Yolanda, one of the Parra tribe, and the enemy of my enemy was my friend.

If I left him my Browning, Yolanda could recognize it. So I fished out Dom's switchblade and tossed it through the bars. He glanced up for a moment, then grabbed the knife and tucked it away.

I hissed, "Your daughter's in Mazatlán."

"Who . . . are . . . you?"

I shoved all my loose pesos through the bars. "Get to the *posada* Gran Camarón, and wait."

"Bless you, stranger," he said huskily, snatching up the pesos as I turned away. I was walking back along the passageway when the door suddenly opened and Yolanda, in facemask, snapped, "Get back here. What are you up to?"

136

"A few breaths of pure air," I told her, and slid down the mask.

"Stay out of places that don't concern you."

I pushed past her and she closed the door, lowering the bar in place. If the prisoner could get out of his cell, the switchblade was long enough to lift the bar. And a facemask would give him anonymity among the drones, busy with their deadly work.

In mask-muffled voice Yolanda said, "Stay close to me, Jack."

"Like a puppy on a leash? This may fascinate you, but I can think of better ways to spend an evening."

"This has to be done." Irritably she walked ahead of me and picked up her clipboard. "Did you talk to anyone back there?"

"Sure—three spiders, two mice and a roach. How much longer we staying here? I need a drink, not a fix."

I eased onto a stack of sealed cartons, folded my arms and shook my head impatiently. She said, "Another hour."

"I didn't ask to come here," I reminded her, "so speed it up."

"You're working for me, and—"

"Am I? I haven't seen the color of your money, just heard how powerful you and Omar are—in a distant country. I'm real impressed."

Her hand touched my arm. "You will be—I promise you. So for now, be a good boy and be patient while I do what I have to do."

"You asking me or telling me?"

She hesitated. "Asking, Jack."

"That's different."

She went back to her tally sheet, and I to my thoughts.

From all his prison years Billy Joe should be able to figure out how to conceal knife and money until breakout time. He moved normally, so he hadn't been beaten or starved. What had set him crossways with his wife? That answer was unimportant, unless it bore on the Parra plantation, but I didn't expect to know. If he made it outside the guarded house, he'd still have those bloodthirsty Rottweilers to deal with. Billy Joe knew they were there, so if smart he'd pick up firearms along the way.

And if he was captured during the attempt he couldn't implicate me because he hadn't seen my face. The only person who might suspect me was Yolanda, having seen me near his cell.

Even if Billy Joe managed to get free, he'd still be broke and illegally in Mexico—an alien the cops could hustle across the border to grateful U.S. authorities. So his future seemed far from bright.

Necessarily, Tara would figure in his future, but I hoped to discourage Melody from providing further aid. Having found Billy Joe, I'd fulfilled my verbal contract with the girls. Now I could focus on Yolanda, her family ties and business.

She was walking around, mechanical counter in one hand, inventorying and double-checking all stock on hand. I had an idea where my portion of it would be concealed on the boat, but no sense letting her know that I was figuring ahead.

Perspiration dripped down my face, the glass eyeholes were foggy. I listened to the rumble of the mixing vats, the clacking of pill stampers, and wondered how the crew could work there hour after hour without relief. Probably because they were being paid beyond their wildest dreams to perform like mechanical parts.

I spotted several excellent points for sabotage—tanks of butane gas that heated the cooking vats; the intricate arms and levers of the stamping and pulverizing machines; the drums of acetone and ether; the generator itself. But the Parras were closing down this lab, and I was far more interested in what they were running on their isolated sanctuary.

Still, this basement set-up probably resembled what I'd find in Colombia in larger multiples, so the preview wasn't wasted.

My gaze strayed to the door that blocked off Billy Joe's prison area. Improvising, in limited time, I'd told him to go to the *posada*, so unless I could locate his daughter before morning, there'd be no one to greet him if, despite odds, he made it out of the jungle.

Tara could be overnighting in any of Mazatlán's many hotels, but how to find her? A last resort would be to intercept her at the airport . . . Ahhhhh. Maybe Rafe could help. The thought improved my outlook, and the prospect of finally being rid of both Vaills made me smile.

Yolanda touched my arm. "A few more minutes, *querido*."

"I'm fading fast."

As she strolled off I found myself wondering what her plans were for Billy Joe. Disposing of him at sea or in the nearby jungle was easy enough—why keep him around as a prisoner? Perhaps some lingering affection, or gratitude for her parole from Tehachapi. No accounting for female motives, and I wasn't about to query hers.

Finally, Yolanda finished what she was doing, spoke with the lab chief and shook his hand, goodbye. Then she beckoned to me, and we went up the stairs to the main floor, hung our masks on the rack and walked to the front entrance, where we waited until the guard dogs were secured.

Into the Rabbit, then, and down the muddy trail through the barrier gates and onto the coastal road. As I wheeled toward town she said, "What do you think of it?"

"The lab? Too bad you're shutting it down."

"Yes, but there's already enough coke for your voyage."

"Good. I hate waiting once a decision's made."

"Me, too." She kissed the corner of my mouth. "Wish I were going with you, Jack—a holiday cruise for us both."

"After Omar's okayed me."

"That won't take long. And the Lear will fly you back here with a crew."

I glanced at her, then back to the road. Under that sensuous tropical beauty functioned a steely, masculine mind, and I admired it despite her heritage. Billy Joe was no match for her, much less Tara, and I could think of no woman I knew who could make a serious challenge. Delores Diehl was fascinated by money and intrigue, but shrank from violence. She was soft where Yolanda was tough and uncompromising; a nestling versus a falcon.

And the contrasts reminded me how dangerous Yolanda could be. In Colombia she'd turn on me instantly if I made a false move, denounce me and save herself. Well, that was one of the risks I assumed from Manny Montijo. One of the many.

At the hotel entrance I turned the Rabbit over to the parking valet and told Yolanda I'd be up shortly.

"Don't be long, I might fall asleep."

"I'll wake you."

She squeezed my hand and walked away.

Rafe was dozing in his cubbyhole. Rousing him, I asked where Tara Vaill had gone.

"Easy. Those *chingado* pilots carried her bag and screwed me out of a tip. They were taking her to—" He grimaced, stared up at the ceiling. "Uh . . ."

I got out my wallet and handed over ten thousand pesos. "This help?"

"Puesta del Sol," he finished, and pocketed the money.

"Why there?"

"That's where the fly-boys are staying."

"Makes sense. See you *mañana*." I went up to my room, peeled off my coke-scented clothing and took a long, soapy shower. Then I opened the connecting door and joined Yolanda in bed.

As we kissed, I could smell cocaine in her nostrils—she'd had a preliminary snort—and after we'd made love I encouraged her to repeat. As before, she didn't bother with mirror and razor, just stuck a straw into her coke bag and inhaled. I left her long enough to make myself a drink, and when I returned to the bed she was lying back, eyes half-closed and slipping away. We held hands for a few minutes, until I felt her grip relax, and when her fingers were slack and her eyes closed, I went back to my room and closed the connecting door.

After pulling on clothes I took a taxi to the Puesta del Sol hotel and called Tara's room from a lobby phone. It was a while before she answered, and her voice sounded terrified. "Thank God it's you, Jack. Those two bastards who picked me up have done everything but rape me."

"Well, I warned you," I said. "Get a handle on *machismo* and conduct yourself accordingly. Where are they now?"

"In the hall. Can't you hear them pounding my door?"

I listened, and sure enough, I could hear dull, arrhythmic beating. "Don't let them in," I told her, "and I'll see what I can do. Meanwhile, pack your bag."

"I haven't even unpacked it."

"Don't panic. I'm taking you out of here."

Her room was on the third floor. I took an elevator to the second and climbed the fire stairs to the third. As I opened the hall door I could hear Fausto and Orestes snickering and beating away, yelling at Tara to open up. They sounded drunk enough to be easy marks.

Nobody else in the hallway. I made a triangular mask from my handkerchief and tied it over my face. Then I got out my Browning and carried it beside my thigh until I was behind them.

Both pilots were leaning on the door, beating it and

mouthing Spanish obscenities. They'd bought her champagne and dinner, been nice to her, and now they wanted the payoff.

Grasping the pistol by its barrel, I swung against the nearest skull, and before he dropped I whacked the other. Both were out of action for a while.

Tara let me in, staring goggle-eyed at her unconscious admirers. "Grab your bag," I said, and dragged them into her room. I shut the door and knelt beside them, took out their billfolds and stripped the cash, then slid off their gold necklaces and Rolex watches.

"This has to look like robbery with no connection to you, so don't try selling the gold until you're far away." I opened her bag and put in everything I'd taken from the pilots.

"There's been a change of plans," I told her as we walked down the corridor, "and you'll be staying at the *posada* for the next few days."

"I'm beyond wondering why."

"Pay your bill and I'll rustle up a taxi."

In the lobby she walked off to the cashier, and I carried her bag outside. Same taxi I'd used earlier, and the driver was glad of the return trip. I didn't want her traced to the *posada*, so we got out on the waterfront and walked down the nearest pier, kept walking until the taxi was out of sight. Then we went back to the *posada*. Different clerk, so she signed for the same room, whose bed was still unmade. I locked the door and said, "Sit down. I have something to tell you."

"My—father . . . he's dead, isn't he?" Her eyes closed and her fists tightened.

"On the contrary. He's alive, and with luck he'll be able to get here. Give him forty-eight hours—during which time I don't want you on the street. Those damn pilots might spot you and make things unpleasant."

She was sobbing almost silently. "Alive," she choked.

"*Alive.* Oh, Jack, I'm so glad, so *happy*. How can I ever thank you?"

"By getting your life organized—your Dad's, too, if that's still possible."

"Where is he?"

"He's safe, and he hasn't been harmed. That's all I'm going to tell you."

"You—actually spoke with him?"

"That I did. Gave him money and a weapon, and that's all I could do. How he gets here is up to his own resourcefulness." I cleared my throat. "If he makes it, both of you get out of Mazatlán as soon as you can. Head for Mexico City, or some other place you can melt into. Get false documentation for him, but whatever you do, don't let him go back to the States. Okay?"

She nodded, wiped away tears.

"Finally," I said, "and most important—don't tell him about me. Not my name, description, nothing. I was just a casual stranger who helped out and vanished. After you've gone I'll tell Melody all she needs to know, because you won't be contacting her. Understood?"

Again she nodded. "Only I don't understand why."

"Because that's how we're playing it and it's all you need to know." I started walking to the door and halted. "He's wearing bluejeans and a heavy beard. Get him a change of clothing, a shave and a close haircut. Then, get the hell out of town." I reached for the bolt, but she dashed up and flung her arms around my neck, kissed my face wildly until I pulled her arms away. "I can't help you any more, Tara, and it will be a lot safer for both of us if we don't meet again. I'm depending on you to keep your promises and follow my instructions. Will you?"

"I—I will."

"Even if Dad doesn't show?"

"Yes."

I kissed her forehead, said goodnight and went down to the street.

Except for music from some of the harbor boats, the town was as quiet as though a blanket had been thrown over it. I liked things that way, the boats riding gently on the water, the moon on its silent journey to the dark horizon, and the breeze bearing scents of wildflowers and the sea. Moodily I walked toward the Camino Real, hoping that Billy Joe would break out of captivity and go directly to the Gran Camarón, per instructions. Because if he decided to check out the *Paz Paloma*—assuming he knew where it was—he would likely find Pedro Ramirez in an ugly mood. I'd done what I could for Dad, and if he fouled things up, the fault was his, not mine.

Cur dogs snarled at a garbage heap. One snatched up a mess of fish guts and scuttled away, the pack barking and yelping in pursuit. Not unlike human behavior, I reflected, and walked on until I was at the hotel.

In my room I undressed quietly, took a quick shower to get rid of perspiration, and found Yolanda still deeply asleep. Only an arm had moved, so I lay down beside her, pulled up the covers and closed my eyes.

A door buzzer woke me. I sat up, dazed, and looked around. Light through cracks in the blinds. The buzzer again. Not Yolanda's, mine. As I got off the bed she stirred, opened her eyes. The buzzer sounded and I went into my room, closing the connecting door. Towel draped around my hips, I opened the door on its chain and said, "*Quién es?*"

A pleasant-faced young man in a tan suit and leisure shirt stood there, a brown envelope in his hands. "Mr.—?" he began, but I said, "Something from Manny?"

He shoved the envelope into my hand. "Hope it's in time."

144

"It is. Have a good flight back." I closed the door and opened the envelope. The ID was all there— driving license, SS card, bank and credit cards, pocket litter—all in the name of John C. Reynolds of Houston, Texas. Plus a new billfold to hold it all.

I transferred money from my wallet and sealed the wallet in a hotel envelope for mailing to Melody. Then I laid the alias documentation on the table and looked it over carefully, signing my new name here and there before slipping everything into the billfold.

Yolanda rapped on the connecting door. "Jack, you okay?"

"Never better," I said, and walked over to unlock it.

She came in, naked, and glanced around. "Who was that?"

"A disappointed supplier."

"It's only nine-forty—why don't you come back to bed?"

"I'll do just that," I said. "That was a heavy night you put me through. Then you blasted off where I couldn't find you."

"I know." Turning, she padded off to the big nuptial bed. "I shouldn't have taken so much. Don't let me do that again."

"You're the risk-taker. Don't involve me."

She made a face and plopped down on the bed.

Before returning to her bedroom I glanced back at my just-delivered ID, and thought that, along with Yolanda, it was going to be my passport to the fields and labs of old Colombia.

SIXTEEN

We shared late breakfast beside the pool, plenty of fruit and coffee, *pan dulce*, and a bottle of Añejo beside my plate. Yolanda was wearing a loose turquoise tunic over her Brazilian lace bikini, and designer shades shielded her eyes. Both of us were pleasantly relaxed, and as I ate a slice of mango I reflected that with Daddy Vaill found and Tara out of sight, I could finally concentrate on Manny's op. And with the alias ID at hand, I was eager to leave Mazatlán.

Yolanda left our table to make phone calls, and after a third cup of coffee, she decided to relieve my latent curiosity.

"The police," she said, "have sent Freddy's body to a mortuary, so I've put the pilots on alert."

"We leave today?"

She shook her head. "Tonight we'll load the boat so it will be ready for you to sail when you return from Parraland."

I dribbled rum into my coffee. "You've told me a good deal, *chula*, but two things you've avoided. Where the

146

cargo's to be concealed, and how much all this is going to enrich me."

She smiled. "You'll learn about the cargo tonight. As for payment, what do you say to seventy-five thou?"

"For an even hundred I'll almost guarantee delivery."

"Don't get greedy, Jack."

"I'm not starving," I said, "and that's my bottom line. Half in Colombia, half when I deliver Stateside."

She thought it over. "That's fair—if Omar agrees."

"Old bills, not new currency that could be queer."

She gestured at the lobby doorway. "Here come my pilots. I won't introduce you, and don't say anything."

Turning, I saw Fausto and Orestes looking the worse for wear. The back of Fausto's head was bandaged, but not Orestes', so he did all the talking, blurting that they'd been attacked last night, robbed of all their money and jewelry. Yolanda listened without reacting other than to cross her well-tanned legs. Finally she said, "You should have expected that—in a Mexican whorehouse."

"But, señora, it was in our hotel, I swear it."

Fausto glanced at me, wondering where I fitted in. I poured more coffee from the glazed Oaxaca jug and looked innocent.

"You're lying," she told them, "but I'm stuck with you two assholes." Her face was stern. "And now you can't pay your hotel bill?"

"No, señora, unfortunately that is the case."

"Cretinos," she spat. "Well, I have to lend you the money so we can fly home tomorrow."

Orestes looked relieved, and Fausto sighed.

"Meanwhile," she said, "make arrangements to transfer the casket to the plane. If you can do so without being attacked."

"Sí, señora," Orestes said gratefully. "I have confidence there will be no problem." He glanced at Fausto, who nodded.

"And my friend here will be flying with us."

They looked at me with instant respect.

Fausto said, "At what time, more or less, do you care to depart tomorrow?"

"When it pleases me."

"Of course, *señora*—ah, could you supply some money for food?"

"Eat in your room where you belong. Go." Peremptorily she waved them off, and after servile bowing they went away.

A partial smile on her lips, she said, "Well?"

"Well what? Maybe you could use a labor relations refresher, but, ah, what the hell—your system works. Anyway, those *cabrones* act like Laurel and Hardy."

Her hand smothered laughter. "*El Flaco y El Gordo,*" she gasped. "Perfect—and I never thought of it."

"Two comedians," I muttered. "They can fly jet planes?"

She laughed again. "Jack, you're too much. Now, what were we talking about?"

"Logistics, money—and the sooner we leave Mazatlán the safer we'll be. That sniper-bomber could be waiting for another try."

Her face sobered. "That's true. But I feel safe when you're with me."

"I wasn't planning to desert." Not, I thought, with a quarter-million at stake.

So, we swam and sunned, lunched at poolside and went back to bed for *siesta*. After Yolanda was asleep I got dressed and taxied to the *posada*. Cautiously, Tara let me in, and said, "I'd hoped you were my father. I couldn't sleep last night, waiting for him. Then I began thinking you were putting me on."

"Why would I do that?"

"I dunno—get rid of me, probably. Anyway, you bothered to come, so I know you were serious."

"Don't give up hope. This could be the night."

She sighed. "You didn't mention Graciela—Sister Grace."

"You weren't interested in her. Anyway, she's undergone a sea-change."

"What?"

"Into something rich and strange."

She shrugged. "Whatever that means."

"Shakespeare," I told her, "so let's hope Dad arrives. I'll try to check later."

She thanked me for coming, and I went down to the water-front.

At one of the café tables a very large man was working on a big bowl of shrimp. He had blunt, broken features and a shaved skull. He looked as though he should be wearing a Mohawk and a bear-claw necklace. His presence gave me bad vibes, so I beckoned over my helpful waiter and asked about the big stud.

"He came yesterday," the waiter said, "asking questions about the same boat captain you asked about."

"What did you tell him?"

"Nothing, *señor*. He offered no gratification and his manner was unpleasant."

"Maintain silence," I said, and gave him ten thousand pesos for the information. The nosey stranger was as large as Too Tall Jones and much uglier. Not a man to get cross-wise with.

As I rode back to the hotel I considered phoning Melody, and decided against it. If I told her I was headed for Colombia she'd get terribly upset, and because my policy was not to lie, better to say nothing. Anyway, I rationalized, chances of finding Melody at home were slim. Either she'd be battling the new decorators or studying at the U-M libe, and didn't need a load of grief from me. Besides, what I was doing was in a good cause: narcotics suppression, plus col-

lege bucks for our progeny. If I returned home from the
Guajira, we'd celebrate; if not, she'd get the money. How
could she reasonably complain?

As for the shrimp-feeding hulk, Tara would become
frightened if she knew he was asking questions about the
Preacher. Billy Joe might or might not know him, but in
either case, Dad was on his own.

I tried to analyze why I felt optimistic he'd make it out
of his cell and through the jungle, realizing finally that it
had to do with prison smarts. I didn't overvalue them, but
convicts with smaller shanks, under heavier guard, had broken out of Leavenworth. And compared to federal maxi-
mum security, the jungle manse was a gingerbread hut.

So I went back to my room and stretched out, and when
Yolanda wakened me it was time to go down for dinner
dancing—before we headed for the boat.

We left the hotel a little after moonrise, while the sky was
deep indigo and only a few twinkling stars showed through.
Yolanda was wearing dark designer coveralls and Italian
sandals, and she held the shotgun vertically so I could get
it fast, if necessary. Looking at her watch, she said, "No
hurry, Jack, loading takes a while."

"How much junk will I be sailing to the land of the Big
PX?"

"More than five hundred kilos."

"And the Ludes?"

"By mules." She used the *narcotraficante* term for human
smugglers—kids, mostly, eager to cross the border for a
plane ticket back to Smalltown, USA.

I said, "What's my destination?"

"Omar will tell you."

"Hail Colombia, land of unfettered enterprise." Gripping
the wheel, I stared at the pocked, unsurfaced road.

"Omar has no sense of humor," she said thinly. "Fortunately for you, I do."

"Fortunately for you, I'm available to make the run to Southern Cal," I told her. "But I don't have to like what I'm doing. What happens when I make delivery? Some wise guy blows off my head to save Omar fifty large?"

"We don't cheat our men," she said stiffly, "we deal straight. If we didn't we wouldn't have the organization we have."

"I'll want to hear more about that," I said. "In Colombia, of course."

"And you will."

Nothing more was said until I saw dimmed headlights well down the road. Yolanda saw them, too, and said, "Slow down, don't come up on them too fast."

As she spoke I saw other lights, horizontal streaks I'd become familiar with in Nam. "There's firing," I said, and she gripped my arm. "*Carajo!*" she swore, and I rolled down my window to hear the *pock-pock* of pistols and the flat stuttering of automatic weapons. Pulling over to roadside, I turned off lights and engine. "We'll bide our time," I said, "until there's a clear winner."

A star shell would have shown me what was going on, but as I watched, the firing began to diminish. I didn't care which side won, as long as they didn't shoot me.

Yolanda wiped perspiration from her forehead. "I expected this," she said, "so I sent along extra gunmen."

"Hijack?"

Silently, she nodded.

No more pistol shots. Then, short bursts from what sounded like AR-16s, ending in an agonized scream. I looked at Yolanda, and her face was set. Like a regimental commander, she'd given orders—had they been carried out?

She said, "I think it's safe to go, now."

"What makes you think so?"

"Those headlights."

They were on high beam. Through the night's stillness I could hear men's voices on the sea wind. Then, a single pistol shot. Coup de grace? I wondered.

Mouth dry, I started the engine, set the headlights on low beam and crawled ahead. We followed a curve and the far lights were hidden from sight. When I could see them again we were much closer. Yolanda said, "Stay to the center of the road, and stop when I tell you. Then turn your lights on high."

"Yes, ma'am." Her men, her arrangements.

When we were thirty or forty yards from the headlights she told me to stop, and I braked, but kept the engine running. Without a word she got out, slammed the door and walked in the bright headlight glare, arms upraised and waving. One brave woman, I told myself; too bad she was going to have to go down.

As I watched, she lowered her arms and a man came out of the darkness to greet her, automatic rifle slung over his shoulder. He gestured behind him, and she waved me ahead. I pulled over to the edge of the road, turned off lights and engine and got out. Below, the white ketch lay still as a painting.

Arms raised, I walked toward Yolanda, who said, "It's all right, Jack. Two of my men are wounded, but four Mexicans are dead."

I passed the headlights and found a panel truck with rear doors open. Stolidly, two armed peasants lugged a body from the road shoulder toward the truck, tossed it inside like a sack of grain. She said, "Humberto thinks we killed them all."

"Let's hope. Don't want no straggler looking for revenge."

The four corpses wore parts and pieces of Mexican army uniforms; two had machete scabbards dangling from their belts. *Adios, muchachos,* I thought. Tough on the widows and kids, with no insurance.

Yolanda's men searched the grass and scrub, brought back an assortment of weapons. They loaded them into the truck with considerably more care than the bodies. The man called Humberto motioned his men inside the truck and came back to Yolanda. Touching his cap, he said, "*Señora*, I regret to inform you that the prisoner escaped."

"What?"

"*Sí*—at feeding time. With a knife he took the guard's gun."

"*Pendejo!*" She slapped his face. Both cheeks. Slowly and deliberately Humberto took it as though prepared for punishment. Wetting his lips, he said, "I doubt he can get through the jungle."

"And the dogs?"

He shrugged. "Dead, *señora* Yolanda. We would be searching for him now, but for this." He gestured at the yacht. "Now we are free to begin."

"And leave the house unguarded? *Cretino*, go back and resume your duties. Is everything on board?"

"*Sí, señora*. All of it."

"Then go."

He touched his cap again and got into the truck. It backed around and rumbled down the road. When its lights were out of sight I said, "Bad news?"

"Oh, a troublemaker got out of detention." She spoke casually, but her face was strained.

"No big deal, then?"

"No big deal. I'll start down to the beach."

I went back to the Rabbit and parked where the truck had been, then got out the shotgun and followed Yolanda down the rickety stairs.

As we rowed out to the yacht I worried about Pedro recognizing me. Still, I had his shotgun and I could make him eat it. We climbed aboard and I looked around, half-expecting Pedro to emerge from the shadows, but we were alone. "Where's the watchman?" I asked Yolanda.

"Elsewhere—didn't I tell you? I don't want him to know about this."

I laid the shotgun on transom cushions near yesterday's bullet hole. "What now?"

She pointed to a dark part of the cockpit. There lay a row of oval-shaped pods that reminded me of what alien life forms are supposed to reach earth in. Each was about three feet long and half that in diameter. I rapped the nearest. Molded fiberglass, light, and nearly as tough as metal. Yolanda said, "They're waterproof."

"What do I do? Tow them behind the boat?"

She smiled tolerantly. "What you'll do with them is load them into the keel."

So, that was it. And that was why we were loading under cover of darkness. I hefted a pod and judged its weight as about that of an air tank. Fourteen pods in all. Standing, I said, "How do we get into the keel?"

"Underwater." She was pulling off her coveralls and presently all she wore was the lace Ipanema bottom. God, what buns! She went down into the saloon and came up with two underwater halogen lamps and a large Phillips screwdriver. I said, "If you hadn't heard, light attracts fish. Sometimes big ones. Got a bang stick?" When she didn't react, I said, "Long metal tube with a shotgun shell. For sharks."

"No, but we'll have a knife and a spear."

"And I'll be wrestling those pods." I shook my head. "Night diving is dangerous, even when you're used to it— as I am, and you're not. I'll do the labor, but you'll have to pull guard duty."

She nodded, so I rigged two unused tanks with regulators, got out the rest of the scuba gear and made sure we each had a dive knife strapped to a leg. There were sharks and barracuda in the neighborhood and we were intruders in their world. She told me where to find the keel plate, and I decided to dump all the pods over the side. Then I could bring them up from the bottom and push them into the open keel. Careening the ketch would have made more sense, but we'd need help for that, plus just the right tides.

So I began shoving pods over the railing, and when the cockpit was empty I stripped to my shorts, fitted on Yolanda's back pack and buoyancy compensator and handed her the spear and light. Then she went backward, over the side.

I could see her light all the way down to where the pods lay, and reflected that I was starting to earn my money tonight. I checked tank pressure—2800 psi—purged the regulator, and with the screwdriver in my weight belt and the rubber-covered lantern in hand, I dropped into the water.

I had to blow air into the BC for neutral buoyancy, and after that I swam up to where Yolanda was holding her light on the keel. A plate had been finely cut from the metal, and secured by large Phillips screws. I began unscrewing them, and water rushed into the void. I stuck the screws into my fins and laid the plate on the bottom near the fiberglass pods. This was a hell of a mode of concealment, I thought, and wondered how often it had been used before. A Coast Guard boarding party would have to dive down to inspect the keel, and I'd never heard of that happening in the annals of drug interdiction. This could be a first for everyone.

The pods were nearly weightless, so it was easy to maneuver them up from the bottom and into the hollow keel. Yolanda stayed nearby with illumination, and I was glad to see the spear in her hand. I might have questioned some women's courage, but not hers.

Fins planted on the bottom, I was lifting a pod when unexpected motion made me glance up.

A long silver streak flashed above me, heading straight for Yolanda. When it struck, the lamp tore loose from her hand and dropped bottomward, spinning end over end. I couldn't see Yolanda, just the glistening body of a six-foot barracuda as it swirled around to strike again.

SEVENTEEN

I snatched my lamp from the bottom and shined it on the savage fish while I jerked my leg knife from its sheath. I thought the light might distract him, or at least show Yolanda where he was. I couldn't see her body, only the shiny tip of her Hawaiian spear. And it pointed directly at the 'cuda.

I thrust upward, hoping to gut him before he charged, but he had his prey in view, and I never got a chance. With a powerful, open-jawed lunge he surged toward her, and my knife slashed only water.

I saw her go down before the predator's violent rush, tumbling toward the bottom as the 'cuda vanished in darkness. The spear was no longer in her hands as she leaned against a coral head, but her right hand gripped a knife. A red cloud bloomed from her forearm, and I knew the smell of blood would quickly attract other flesh-eating fish.

I was hovering between Yolanda and the surface when her attacker suddenly appeared. It came on a crazy, downward-slanting course, whirling and thrashing, speeding fast, then slowing, and as I shined the light on its menacing snout I

156

saw a foot of spear shaft protruding from its jaws. She'd rammed it down his throat, penetrating guts and air sac, and the big fish was dying. As it began another lunge at Yolanda, I kicked toward it and buried my knife in its eye, the shortest route to the walnut-size brain. Rolling over, the fish's muscular weight tore the hilt from my hand, and I watched the body spin downward until the spear shaft buried in the sand.

The great body sagged, then, and its weight pried the shaft from the bottom. Still turning slowly, the 'cuda swirled clouds of sand as it died, then with a convulsive shudder it lay still except for fluttering gills.

I kicked down to Yolanda, signaled Up and brought her to the surface. I helped her swim to the ladder, unsnapped her heavy tank and boosted her up on deck. I hung my tank on the gunwale and went to her.

Moonlight showed a red patch on her forearm, about four inches long and two inches wide. The 'cuda's lateral teeth must have grazed her as it knocked her aside, without taking off much meat. Scale-slime glinted on and around the wound, so I went into the saloon, groped around for a sheet and tore off enough for a torniquet. Her teeth were chattering as I twisted the tourniquet below her elbow and told her to hold it tight. I went below again, found a wine bottle and knocked off the neck. "Drink," I told her, "before you go into shock."

I arranged pillows on the cockpit deck and laid her down, brought back a blanket and covered her body. "I'm going to soap the wound," I said, "and scrape it to get off that slime."

"Why?"

"You'll get an infection you won't believe." I lifted her head so she could drink more wine, and after swallowing, she said, "Thanks—for all you did." Her voice was husky and I noted a tremor, but what the hell, we all go slack after battle. And she'd been a damned stalwart woman to ram that spear down the 'cuda's throat.

I found soap and clean rags in the galley, cleansed her flesh wound and rinsed it with wine. The pain made her gasp, but she didn't whimper, and my admiration for her increased. Then I loosened the tourniquet so bleeding could flush the raw part even more. Finally, I wrapped the tourniquet as a bandage around her forearm, swallowed a mouthful of wine and stood up.

She said, "Don't go down again, Jack."

"I have to. Pods to load and panel to replace. Has to be now, because your blood and the 'cuda's are going to bring visitors—if they're not already there."

I got my tank on again and dropped down to the bottom. A few small fish were nosing around the 'cuda's open jaws, but I saw no other menace, so I pried my knife from the barracuda's eye socket and got to work. The two lanterns on the bottom gave more illumination than I needed, and I worked desperately fast.

On my last trip down I saw that a brown moray eel had slithered out from somewhere and was tearing at the 'cuda's soft belly. Tiny fish gathered for bloody morsels as the moray shook and chewed away. And they were just the first of the nocturnal feasters.

It was hard to hold the plate in place while I screwed it back into the keel, but I managed it, with fear as my spur.

Then I surfaced, swimming wearily to the ladder. Too tired to haul the tank aboard, I freed and let it drop below. From the deck I leaned over the gunwale and saw dark shapes occulting the lantern beams on the bottom—but I was safe.

I crawled over to Yolanda and pulled the blanket over us. Almost asleep, she turned against me for warmth and comfort, and I was glad that we were both alive.

After a while I got up and pulled on my clothing and fitted the remaining scuba gear in its box. When I woke Yolanda she sat up, frightened, until I said, "It's okay, *chica*. Job's done. We can go now."

"I'd rather stay—you have no idea how exhausted I feel."

"All the more reason to leave. And the wound needs treating." I tossed over her coveralls, and as she peeled away the blanket I said, "You did damn well down there, all the right things."

"Coming from you, that means a lot, Jack. But you killed the creature, got me safely back." Carefully, she pulled the sleeve over her damaged arm, gasped and pointed at her wrist. "Gone—my amulet's gone!"

"Elegua? Snagged by the 'cuda. Could have been your arm."

She shivered. "Let's go."

So I rowed her back to the beach and hauled the dinghy well up on the sand, then steadied her as we climbed the sagging stairs. At the top I peered over the rim of the cliff, scanning for anything hostile, then checked the car. Finally I told her she could get in, and positioned the shotgun between us. I drove toward Mazatlán with high beams, wishing I had a few frag grenades to clear road obstacles, human or otherwise, but there was no ambush, so Humberto's platoon had worked efficiently.

I drove through quiet streets until I glimpsed an illuminated sign with a green cross and took Yolanda inside. I woke the young Mexican doctor, explained what had happened to Yolanda's arm and helped unpeel the crude bandage in the examination room. He trimmed loose flesh from the borders, sprayed the crusting wound with something that made her wince and dusted it with antibiotic powder. Then he bandaged it with sterile gauze and gave her antibiotic capsules to take. She hadn't lost much blood, but her nervous energy was drained, and she almost fell asleep lying on the steel table.

"Keep the bandage on for two days," he said, "and come back if there is any infection."

I paid him a few thousand pesos, which he duly entered in his ledger, and told Yolanda that rest was the best curative of all. For a young Mexican physician doing forced labor in the provinces, he was responsive and amiable, unlike so many who resented repaying the government for their free education.

She clung to my arm all the way to the hotel, and in the elevator fatigue made her slump against my body. So I put her to bed and went to my adjoining room.

There I turned on the lights, opened my pint of Añejo for a nightcap and noticed a folded piece of paper on the carpet by the door.

I picked it up and read: *Please come as soon as you can.* The message was signed with the initial *T.*

Tara, of course, and with no room phone she had to put things in writing. I tossed the message into a wastebasket and swallowed a good slug of sleep-inducing rum. If I hadn't learned through Humberto that Billy Joe had escaped, I might have been more curious over what Tara wanted to convey. But I was stressed-out from the night's labors, and Tara and her dad could wait until I was rested and in a better mood.

Because I was having mixed emotions about Yolanda. As they said in Latin America, she was one *pedazo de mujer*— a *real* woman—and there hadn't been many in my life. Sarita Rojas had been one—until her death—but Melody was still in the learning/maturation stage of life, so comparing her with Yolanda wasn't fair. Moreover, Yolanda was part of a vicious criminal conspiracy that had to be stopped. She liked me and was grateful to me, but that wasn't enough to turn her against her cousin Omar. And if she ever learned the part I'd played in Luis's death, she would have me roasted over glowing coals while she danced a mambo. So, I couldn't let admiration stand in the way of duty, and the only way to handle it was deal with her on two levels: lover and criminal target.

The Añejo was taking hold, lights began to blur. I turned them off and lay back, gratefully, on my bed. It seemed only minutes later that I woke, but there was daylight beyond the blinds, and Yolanda was creeping under the covers beside me.

After lunch, I insisted on dropping her off at the hospital for further examination and treatment, telling her that unless her wound was expertly treated she'd have an ugly scar for the rest of her life.

That wasn't necessarily true, but I wanted free time for my own purposes. So, while she waited for a dermatologist I drove to the *posada* El Gran Camarón and went up to Tara's room.

Knocking, I called her name. No answer. I knocked again. Suddenly, the door opened, and through a three-inch crack I was looking at Preacher Billy Joe.

EIGHTEEN

The heavy beard was gone, leaving his skin bone-white. The long shaggy hair had been roughly cut, making him look less like an animal and more like a member of the human race.

There was a knife in his hand. Gripping it, he said hoarsely, "Tara's not here. Who are you?"

I pointed at the stiletto. "That's my shank."

His mouth opened. He stepped back and I went in. "Where's Tara?"

"Gone out for food and clothing." He was wearing the same shirt and jeans, now torn and muddy. I said, "I don't know how much Tara told you, but I recommend you get out of Mazatlán right after dark. Bus, boat, any way you can make it."

He folded the switchblade, shoved it into a pocket. "First I got a score to settle."

"Sister Grace? Forget it."

"That bitch—you don't know what she done to me, brother. I'm gonna cut her fuckin' throat."

"No you're not. I want her alive."

162

His thin smile was deadly. "Got you hooked too, has she? Well, get yourself another lay."

"She's a prospective federal witness, under my protection."

"Witness against *me*?" The switchblade reappeared.

"The Parra operation." I sat down. "You grabbed the chance I gave you and so far you're doing fine. Settle for that, and get the hell away from here. Fast."

He sat down on the bed edge and put away the knife. "You a narc?"

"Preacher, I'm not interested in you. Just take care of yourself—and Tara."

He sighed heavily, glanced up at the ceiling. "Makes sense. But what kept me alive was thoughts of killing Grace."

"You owe me that," I told him, "and if I were you, I'd trade that shank for a handgun. The people looking for you are very heavy types."

He nodded. "Thanks for all you done. I know it was for Tara, not me, but it comes out the same."

"Whose idea was it to broadcast the SOS?"

"Graciela's—and part of it was true. The Ramirez brothers were on board. With guns."

"What put you crossways with her?"

He shook his head slowly. "She wanted to pick up a load of dope here and have me run it back to California. I figured it was too dangerous, and dope is one thing I never touched. No way. I have a daughter—couldn't sleep right thinking of what that shit would do to other men's daughters. So—"

The door opened noisily. I thought it must be Tara returning until I noticed Billy Joe's eyes. They were staring in horror.

I looked around and saw—not Tara, but a man.

I'd seen him once before, demolishing shrimp at the waterfront café, and he hadn't grown any smaller.

He was a big man. So big that when he came through the doorway his frame blotted out the hallway light. His skull was shaved, and below the big, broken nose a handlebar mustache stretched across his ugly, damaged face.

In his ham-sized hand the double-barreled sawed-off looked as big and deadly as a bazooka. He waved it around like a feather, pointing it, finally, at the Preacher. "You," he boomed, "on your feet. We got travelin' to do. Miles to go before I sleep."

The Preacher got up slowly, face white and strained. Corpses have looked healthier.

The big man turned to me, smiling nastily, as Mean Muthas do. "You got objections, boy?"

I'd been considering counter-action, but even if I could hit him before he blew my head off, the effect would be like a fly landing on Mount Rushmore. So, I shrugged. "Not me, friend. You got a beef with the Preacher, it's between the two of you."

With a grunt like a bull moose he collared the Preacher and dragged him away like a naughty child. When I closed the door I didn't feel heroic, just alive.

And grateful.

There was a bottle of José Cuervo on the basin, and as I swallowed a bracer I reflected that the Preacher now faced a real challenge. Converting his captor to pacifism and brotherly love was going to require all the Preacher's extraordinary talents. And resourcefulness.

Swallowing more tequila, I shivered and wished him well.

Tara was going to be confused and distraught, but I couldn't handle further Vaill problems. The Mean Mutha didn't wear federal marshal uniform—three-piece Monkey Ward suit—so what was his interest in the Preacher? He could be a casino enforcer, but unlike Dom Sanchez, he was upfront and forthright, so I figured he was looking to repossess the stolen *Paz Paloma* and sail it back to Dago.

With the forced assistance of Billy Joe.

First, though, he'd have to find it, and that might keep him around long enough for Tara to make a deal.

I didn't feel up to explaining matters to Tara just then, and besides, it was time to pick up Yolanda. The Vaills would have to solve their own problems from now on.

So I left the *posada*, and as I passed the waterfront café, the waiter hurried up to me. "I saw them," he said excitedly. "The big man and the boat captain."

"Where did they go?"

"In a gray truck."

"Well," I said, "that ends that."

He fished in his pocket and brought out a crumpled business card. "Yesterday the big man gave me this."

The card was beige and on it was printed:

AAA Ace Acme Bail Bonds
Axel Jorgensen
REPRESENTATIVE

Below, a San Diego address and phone number. "Interesting," I told him, and returned the card. "When you see my blonde *amiga*, the *señorita*, give her this and tell her about the two men."

"*Sí, señor.*" He put away the card and the five-thousand-peso bill I gave him.

Alive, and on the hoof in court, the Reverend Billy Joe Vaill was worth eighty thousand dollars to AAA Ace Acme Bail Bonds. To me the Preacher wasn't worth a pinch of piss in a high gale.

I got into the Rabbit and drove back to the hospital, where Yolanda impatiently waited.

A message for her at the hotel desk said that Freddy's casket had been cleared for export. The Lear was fueled and ready to go.

Yolanda smiled. "Nothing to keep us here. Next stop, Jamaica."

To load the casket into the Lear's narrow fuselage meant removing rear cabin seats and replacing them after the wooden casket was secured. I followed the pilots' pre-flight checkoff, not being fully confident of their abilities, but once in their seats they seemed to know what they were doing. It had been years since I'd flown an F-16 fighter, and I'd never piloted a turbofan Lear, so after the clamshell door closed I watched attentively.

Battery switches and inverter On. Flaps at 20°. One engine flamed, then the other. Pilot heat switches On. Auto Pilot Master, Emergency Attitude Indicator and Radio Altimeter On.

The plane began moving toward the takeoff line.

Fausto, the co-pilot, activated the stall warning and generator switches, and Yolanda tapped my shoulder. "Better buckle in, Jack. This thing takes off in a hurry."

Reluctantly I moved into the seat beside her, not having seen the full start-up sequence. Orestes throttled ahead, the plane accelerated rapidly and field and buildings blurred. Just after liftoff, Fausto retracted wheels and flaps, and I felt heavy Gs as the Lear shot steeply into the clouds.

At thirty thousand feet we leveled off. Orestes set a southeast course, locked the controls on auto pilot and came back to us. "Should be good weather all the way to Kingston," he said. "Touchdown in about three hours."

Yolanda looked at her watch. "We'll overnight at the airport, leave early in the morning."

I said, "Why the delay?"

She said, "We need daylight to land at the plantation. It's not an authorized field."

"Got it," I said brightly, and asked Orestes where the drinks were cached.

I poured scotch for Yolanda, rum for myself, and watched the clouds roll by. I'd left Mazatlán and its complications, the cocaine-loaded yacht, the recaptured fugitive and the abandoned daughter, and for the rest of the flight to Parraland I could relax. But once I was on the ground, real problems would begin.

For a while I could count on Yolanda's good will, but suppose one of their workers recognized me from an old DEA bust?

Bad joss. And me thousands of miles from home.

Well, no point in buying trouble beforehand. I drank from my glass and settled back for a snooze.

The pilots brought the Lear into Kingston's Manley Airport without incident, though I felt the landing could have been lighter than a carrier touchdown.

While Fausto saw to plane maintenance, Orestes booked rooms at the airport hotel. Yolanda and I shared a welcome shower, changed clothing and went down for dinner at a table distant from Laurel and Hardy.

Seeing them reminded me of how they'd fawned over Tara at poolside, and how fast they'd dropped when I whacked their skulls at her doorway. A pair of no-goodnicks.

Tara Vaill. I considered all the needless trouble she'd caused me by coming to Mazatlán. At least I wasn't there to be clutched at and pleaded to. I'd done all I could for her dad, but it hadn't been enough. And trying to pry him loose from Axel Jorgensen would have been the ultimate in folly for a man of normal size and strength, like me. So it was up to Tara to pick up the burden if she expected to see the Preacher again this side of prison bars. She had a few thousand dollars in cash and convertible jewelry, but I doubted if Axel could be bribed with that. The Mean Mutha had impressed me as a man of determination, eager to please his employers and the California courts. Title aside, he was a bounty hunter, a profession that defied normal limitations on enterprise and violence.

Yolanda said, "You've got a faraway look in your eyes, Jack."

"Those business contacts in Mazatlán were none too happy about me backing out, and I won't be welcome again for quite a while." I looked at her. "So, I hope this deal of yours produces some spendable revenue to compensate me for losses incurred."

"*Mi amor*," she murmured, "I'm sure there'll be no problem with Omar," and touched her bandaged arm. "Only think of all you've done for me."

I smiled lecherously. "I'm thinking of all you've done for *me*."

Her expression sobered. "After tomorrow things will have to be different between us."

"So you told me."

"But that doesn't mean we can't be together again. When you come back from the boat trip I can meet you any place you like." Her hand swept broadly around the room. "Jamaica, Monaco, Nassau—just so it isn't the States."

"I'll bear that in mind. While shooting the stars I'll be thinking of an ideal spot for reunion."

Her hand pressed mine. "We still have tonight."

"A short night, too. More wine?"

"Do you really need to ask?"

So we shared harmless banter and a fresh bottle of Bordeaux, lingering long after her flight crew had left their table. As Yolanda signed our check I thought of Freddy's coffin in the Lear fuselage, and tried to convince myself that I wasn't responsible for his slaying. Meskin assassins had also tried to eliminate Yolanda and me, so all three of us had been targets. And kismet caught up with Freddy Gomez sooner rather than later.

Too bad for Freddy, I thought, but I wasn't prepared to grow morose over the death of a *narcotraficante*. Instead, I enjoyed an hour of Yolanda's caresses before sleep claimed us, and the wake-up call came at dawn.

*   *   *

During pre-flight and takeoff, I watched cockpit procedures without appearing unduly interested. Part was professional interest in a hot aircraft, the other concerned the possibility of having to take over the controls in an emergency. A roving condor crashing through the windshield could disable the flight crew.

In less than two hours we made landfall on Colombia's northeast coast, and as we closed with the outthrust head of the Guajira peninsula I could see the wide mouth of the Gulf of Venezuela beyond. Maracaibo was out of sight, but I knew it lay at the gulf's choke point where oil seepage tinted pearls a lustrous golden hue.

Descent procedures began, the plane turning southwest above the coast, flying over thick jungle with a jagged mountain range distantly visible. Gradually we lost altitude, and soon I was able to make out thatch-topped jungle villages and bullock carts on deeply rutted roads. As we approached, I saw an old C-54 lifting heavily toward the Caribbean and wondered where in the States it would put down—if it made the full journey without crashing into the sea.

Below, the jungle was pocked with crash sites, some partly overgrown, others still charred by recent flames. A hazardous occupation, I mused, getting max loads off soggy runways in antiquated planes. And the waters off the Guajira were infamous as an aircraft graveyard. On a clear day you could see dozens of wrecked planes on the bottom.

But that, I reflected, was not to be my fate. My problem would be making it out of the jungle on foot, across the mountain range and down to safe-haven in Venezuela. A survival journey of fifty to a hundred miles, depending on where I crossed the border. Through jungles filled with vipers and anacondas, jaguars and other predatory beasts. If I could get to Maracaibo and the Consulate, a plane would take me home.

A large If.

Yolanda clasped my hand. "Almost there," she said. "I'm going to miss being with you, Jack."

I kissed her cheek and looked down.

Ahead, like a rift in the jungle walls, thrust a black macadam landing strip. I could see a wind sock above a small control tower, transmitter antennae and aircraft hangars. Orestes fishtailed down, and I estimated the strip at no more than three thousand feet long. Still, it was longer and better-surfaced than I'd thought, giving Parra cargo planes a better chance of liftoff—a clear advantage over rival operators.

Between hangars stood olive-drab jeeps, some mounting light machine guns. Behind the hangars was a long, low building, whose laundry lines suggested barracks use, and I saw uniformed personnel lounging in the shade.

Then we touched down, rolled for a while until Fausto released the drag chute that slowed us to a halt near runway's end. As Orestes turned the plane around, a troop carrier sped out to meet us, and Yolanda gave me a final kiss. "Don't be intimidated," she whispered, "regardless of what Omar does."

"In other words, pecker up, as the British say." I nuzzled her earlobe as the clamshell door opened and unfolded into steps.

I followed her to the doorway and started down the steps before I saw the reception committee.

A thin man with scimitar sideburns and narrow mustache stood at the apex of a semicircle formed by six uniformed men. His brown skin was pockmarked, and sunken cheeks gave his face a lupine appearance. Below his starched white guayabera hung a braided holster and a large gold-plated revolver. His men were armed with Uzi submachine guns, and all six barrels pointed at me.

I couldn't see his eyes behind dark sunglasses, but I saw his lips move as he snapped, "You, *gringo*. Hands up, don't move."

NINETEEN

Runway heat enveloped me like sauna vapor as I raised my arms. Squinting at the sunlight, I grumbled, "What's the problem, *jefe*? Think I'm a stowaway?"

Pockmarks glanced sideways, then back at me. "Tell us who you are, why you're here."

"Jack Reynolds," I said. "Houston's my base, and as to why I'm here, that's something for your ears alone—if you're Omar." I grinned bleakly.

Yolanda had drifted out of my peripheral vision, but now she appeared, a smile on her lips I didn't care for.

Pockmarks said, "Who I am is not your affair, *gringo*. Keep talking."

"If the *Señora* permits." I glanced at Yolanda, who walked toward him and said, "He is my guest, cousin, so stop this nonsense. Is this how you greet me after two years?"

The cavernous face relaxed. With a gesture, he dismissed the guards, who slung their weapons and stepped back against the vehicle. Yolanda put her arms around Omar's shoulders and kissed his ugly cheek. He responded with an *abrazo* and looked up at me. "You can lower your hands."

"Thanks," I said acidly, and shuffled onto the tarmac.

Yolanda said, "Jack, this is my cousin, Omar Parra. Omar, Jack Reynolds. Twice he saved my life, so try to be hospitable."

Unenthusiastically he shook my hand. "Welcome to my *estancia*. The pilot radioed he did not know who you were, only that you were aboard the plane. What was I to think?" He shrugged semi-apologetically.

"What, indeed. Now I understand, Señor Parra. You were doing the prudent thing."

"In my business it is necessary," he said shortly and turned to Yolanda. "So you brought back Federico Gomez?"

She nodded. "His family is in Baranquilla. Let the plane take the casket there."

"Yes. And you have much to tell me—not only about Gomez's death, but how you passed the last two years, and why this guest is here."

"Over a drink, Omar, *por Dios*! The sun is melting me." She dabbed at her forehead and I saw that Omar was staring at her bandaged arm. Suddenly he pulled out his golden gun and fired two shots in the air.

From one of the hangars sped a white Mercedes stretch limousine. It accelerated down the runway, pulling up beside us with a raw screech of tires. A driver got out and quickly opened the rear doors. Yolanda got in, and Omar gestured me next. In the air-cooled interior he sat facing us as the car headed toward the end of the runway.

His teeth had gleaming porcelain caps, but aside from that improvement, Omar's resemblance to Luis was eerie—and Luis had perished at my hands during a blazing night at Melody's estate. The killings were etched in my mind—as undoubtedly was his brother's death in Omar's. But this was another time, another place, and there were new cards to play.

The black asphalt road that led into the jungle was striped with Day-Glo for night visibility, and the guides were al-

172

most needed now, for tall trees arching above obscured all but a little filtering light.

Omar gave his cousin a Marlboro cigarette and lighted one for himself. As he inhaled I checked his nose to see if the nostril membranes were decayed from cocaine, the immutable sign of addiction, but saw no indication. At Omar's exalted level in the international narcotics trade it was unusual to find a habitual user—the business was too demanding of successful practitioners.

We'd gone a quarter mile before Omar spoke. "Houston, eh? We had a contact there once—a very useful one. Ever hear of Vernon Saunders?"

"Who hasn't? Gave a lot of money to charities and to the symphony."

"But you never knew him?"

"Hey, he was on the mountain peak—I was down in the mines."

His smile was sardonic. "Saunders had woman trouble—some say he went to Brazil just ahead of the Feds."

"That's more than woman trouble," I observed.

"Others say he died the night my brother was killed."

I could confirm it, but I said nothing.

Parra said, "My brother, Luis. You heard of Luis Parra?"

"Sorry."

"A *gringo* killed him—one reason I don't like *gringos*."

"Omar," Yolanda said in exasperation, "play a new record, will you? I didn't bring Jack here to listen to you moan over Luis."

His face set. "Then tell me why he's here."

"I said—over a drink."

Parra gave her a sullen glance, then jerked out his gold-plated revolver. I tensed, half-expecting him to shoot one of us for kicks, but instead he held it by the barrel and passed it to me. The grip was knurled ivory inlaid with gold. Great balance for an eight-inch barrel, and a beautiful piece of workmanship. I said, "Looks like a Colt .45."

"It's a Dragoon, and made of better steel than those old Colts. You know guns?"

"I know which end to stay away from."

He smiled condescendingly as I returned his weapon. "You been in the Army?"

"Peace Corps."

Omar guffawed and slapped my knee familiarly. To Yolanda he said, "That true, cousin?"

Turning to gaze out the window, she said, "I wouldn't know."

Casually, I studied Omar Parra's face. It was uglier than his late brother's, with an additional layer of brutality, and I remembered with revulsion that DEA had freed him in return for my release from a Mexican jail. Behind the scenes, Manny Montijo had negotiated with three nations to arrange the trade, and now, for the first time, both principals were together.

Undoubtedly Omar Parra knew that Jack Novak had been his trading counterpart, making it all the more important he not learn who I really was. And because I was responsible for his return to Colombia, my obligation to put him out of business transcended my deal with Manny.

Presently the access road left the jungle and the big Mercedes entered a broad cleared area.

Where once there had been only forest there were now cultivated flower gardens and plantings, topiary shrubs, even a smooth lawn for croquet. Beyond it, a high grillwork fence surrounded what looked like a castle.

Parra said, "Welcome to Casa Dorada, Señor Reynolds. For three centuries this chateau stood in southern France. My brother and I had it dismantled stone by stone and reassembled here."

"I'm impressed," I said, and I was, as I scanned it.

The center section was thicker than its two extending wings. Four storeys high, the huge building was of buff sandstone and resembled what I could recall of Churchill's "Chartwell."

Uniformed guards presented arms as the Mercedes passed through wide, grilled gates and drew up in front of the main entrance. As I got out I could see peons working in the garden, wearing wide-brimmed straw hats and loose white clothes. Just visible beyond the left wing was a tennis court, and offset behind the right rose the tall enclosure of a jai alai fronton. Yolanda said, "Come on in, they'll take your bag to your room."

Servants bowed as we crossed through the hallway and went out onto a patio that faced a huge swimming pool. There were *cabañas* at both ends, an enclosed bar, and large *parillas* for barbecuing sides of beef.

As we seated ourselves at a shaded table two Indian servants appeared and took our orders. White wine for Yolanda, anis for Parra and rum-and-coke for me. Parra lighted a Marlboro for his cousin and a thin cigar for himself before saying, "All right, Yolanda, you can begin any time."

So she told the story of our chance encounter on the road, Freddy's death, the clifftop sniper, the car bomb, and our nocturnal brush with the barracuda while loading the yacht. Drinks arrived during the telling, and when Yolanda fell silent, Parra drained his glass and said, "So you trust this man, cousin?"

"Obviously. Or I would not have brought him here."

He turned to me. "I thank you for protecting my cousin, but how do I know you are the man to take the boat to California?"

"You don't," I said. "I could use the money, but if you don't feel easy with me, I'll be on my way."

He rubbed chin stubble and gazed out over the shimmering pool. "The problem," he said musingly, "is that you know much that would be valuable to my enemies."

"*Our* enemies," Yolanda corrected.

"But by bringing Reynolds here you force a decision on me. If I decide it is not wise to employ him, then I must shut his mouth." He shrugged. "You would be responsible for his death."

I sat forward. "Without a trial?"

He smirked. "You could have as much trial as you wanted—before we shot you."

Yolanda smashed her glass on the table. "Have you gone crazy, Omar? This man saved my *life*—and you threaten him with death. Is that all you can think about? It was my decision—yes, *mine*—to offer him the boat job. If you don't agree, then I demand he leave here in safety."

Omar wiped wine spatters from his face. The brown flesh over his cheekbones was splotched with white. Controlling himself, he said, "While you were gone, I managed without you, cousin. Don't think you can run things now—alone."

In a steely voice she said, "You know that's not my intention, but ever since we arrived you've been acting like a *culo*—someone I don't know. Now, listen to me—in Mazatlán I told Jack the final decision was yours, and it is. We've always dealt fairly with our men—at least while I was here—and if you've changed that, say so. If I'd known how much you've changed I don't think I would have come back."

Omar looked away from her. "I've been under pressure, great pressure, Yolanda—from the government, from traitors, from *chivatos* the DEA sends here. I don't want to offend you, but it's not been easy for me."

She sat back, partly mollified, and I realized that was as much apology as she was likely to get from Omar.

I said, "While you two get reacquainted, I'll go to my room, unpack and have a bath."

Yolanda gestured at the pool. "Then a swim."

I finished my drink and walked back into the seat of the Parra empire. A servant escorted me to a room on the third

floor of the east wing, and after locking the door I hung up
my clothing and bathed in a marble tub with gold faucets.
In swim trunks, I made my way down through a building
that was eerily empty considering the number of attending
servants.

Where was Parra's wife? I wondered. His children? Who
else lived in the enormous chateau?

I dived into the pool, swam a few lengths, and while
recovering my breath I saw Yolanda coming toward me in
a beach robe and sandals. She slipped into the pool beside
me and said, "I finally got it out of him. Omar's wife—
María—took the four children to Bogotá, and won't come
back. That's why he's in such a bad humor."

"Don't know as I blame him."

"María hated the isolation, but this is where she should
be."

"So he was going to kill me to cheer himself up? Terrific.
I'd better haul back to Houston before things get worse."

"They won't—I promise you." Underwater she gripped
my hand tightly, and I remembered that we couldn't be
openly affectionate. "Also," she said, "he agreed to your
price. Fifty thousand before you leave here—another fifty
at the other end."

"Then I'm hired?"

"I think so—but let him tell you himself." One of her
knees touched mine. "Is your room satisfactory?"

"Palatial."

"Maybe I'll visit tonight."

"That would be more than agreeable. The door will be
unlocked."

"I'll come when it's safe."

We played toesies underwater for a few moments, then
swam in a relaxed way until a servant invited us to lunch.

The buffet table offered pâté, shrimp salad, cold lobsters
and a choice of French white wines. For a light, midday

repast the spread was more than adequate—and, in the heart of the Guajira jungle, astonishing. Yolanda said one of their planes regularly ferried in delicacies for the chateau, and staples for the guards and soldiers, who supplemented their diet by fishing and hunting in the jungle.

"For a while," I remarked, "that's probably good fun, but I'll bet it gets old pretty fast."

She smiled. "I've never heard any complaints."

I smiled back. "That doesn't surprise me. Where's Cousin Omar?"

She shrugged. "Checking things, worrying about security."

"He looks like a worrier. But now you're back, he can relax and delegate responsibilities to you."

"Relax? He'll just find other things to worry about."

I refilled our wineglasses, sipped mine, and developed a faraway look. After a while I said, "My guess is this operation doesn't need two heads, that you could manage very nicely on your own."

She didn't meet my gaze. "Perhaps. But there *are* two of us."

"Suppose there was only you . . . ?"

"I don't . . . know," she said vaguely.

"But you must have thought about it. What life would be like for you if all this were yours. Nothing you couldn't buy, nothing you couldn't do."

"I suppose so, but—let's change the subject, okay?"

"Okay."

Presently a servant brought her a portable phone. While she spoke I busied myself with my plate and looked around the premises. Set back beyond the fronton was a white-painted satellite dish, large enough to bring in the sound of ice melting on Mars. Parra probably had excellent radio communications with his far-flung empire. But so far I'd seen no transceiver antennae, just a few short-range walkie-talkies.

Yolanda returned the phone and said, "Omar is sending a jeep for you."

"That good or bad?"

"I feel he wants to make up for his crudeness, show he's coming to trust you."

"How do I play it?"

"Pay attention, and don't ask questions he might not want to answer."

"Your cousin couldn't be—a little—ah—paranoid, could he?"

"More than a little—but that's from living in this isolation. Two years ago I *had* to get away, or I'd have gone crazy." She sighed, and I saw sadness in her face. "Mostly it had to do with my husband's death."

"He died here?"

"In Medellín—I don't want to talk about it now."

Having gained the security of home turf, Yolanda was becoming evasive. Even so, I'd managed to plant a subversive thought in her mind, and I was going to nourish it whenever opportunity arose. Isolated as I was, I needed the benefit of every psychological advantage I could conjure up. And as for Omar, he was sounding even crazier than the late Luis. Well, I reflected, the jungle could do that to a man even if he was normal at the outset—as Luis Parra never was.

Yolanda's touch brought me back to the present. "Better get on some clothes," she said. "If you go like that, the bugs will eat you alive."

"I was reserving that for you," I remarked, squeezed her hand and left the table.

Jungle camo would have been appropriate for the occasion, but lacking it, I dressed as protectively as I could. The jeep arrived a few minutes later, and the Indian corporal accelerated away from the chateau, heedless of screeching rubber. The rutted jungle road began near the tennis court, and soon it was as though we were burrowing along some

179

long-lost trail. Unseen birds shrilled and cawed, monkeys chittered high above the jungle floor, and I noticed an anaconda nestled in the crotch of a dying tree.

After a while we came to a metal shed and stopped. The driver had me change into a bugproof uniform, with gloves and a hat hung with mosquito netting.

Even in dense shadows the heat was formidable, humidity close to a hundred percent. All of it brought back negative memories of Nam. The Guajira jungle had all the discomforts of the Vietnamese wetlands, but I had none of the weapons I'd carried during long-range recons. So far, my situation was a net minus.

As we continued deeper into the jungle the driver muttered to himself in what sounded like bastard Spanish but was probably a tribal tongue. He, too, had probably been too long in the jungle.

Another few minutes' bouncing and jouncing over the ruts, and the trail dropped down to a shallow stream. As the jeep forded it I noted sparkling flecks in the clear water, and registered them as gold that might be worth panning—if a fellow had patience and a month's spare time. And while panning, you could always look about for emeralds, water-eroded from protective nodules, and other volcanic gems.

But I wasn't in the Parra empire to seek out precious stones. Mine was a different mission, and any rewards would be paid me by Manny Montijo from his Consular office in Guadalajara.

When I got there.

The stolid-face driver gripped the wheel but never slowed. I was on the rear seat, bouncing on thin cushions until my rump and thighs ached. And as the jeep plunged deeper into the jungle I tried to register trail features that would help me if I came this way again.

Set back from the side of the trail was a thatched lean-to above a crude stone altar. Fire-blackened stones were strewn with goat horns and bird claws, and on either side a bleached human skull, impaled on a stake, stared sightlessly.

The area was scattered with fragments of cowrie and coconut shells, twigs, dried leaves and sunflower seeds. A votive altar for the *santería* cult that looked long unused, and I wondered when Yolanda would resume officiating at the dark and sinister rites. Narrowing my eyelids, I could almost see her bronzed body swaying back and forth before leaping flames as she streaked her naked flesh with gouting blood. That would really be something for the natives, I reflected; occult entertainment designed to gain their devotion.

Then we were beyond the shrine, jungle walls again enclosing the narrow trail. It was almost as though we were tunneling through thick foliage.

From the near distance came a burst of automatic weapons fire. I stiffened and glanced at the driver, but his Indian face was impassive. Two more rounds echoed through the vaulting trees, and the air filled with cries of frightened birds. I jerked the driver's .45 from his holster and cocked it. He shrugged, muttered, *"No hay caso,"* and steered into a smoky clearing.

There were six uniformed soldiers holding weapons. A man in white gripped a MAC-10 submachine gun and stared at me. Through head-netting I could see the dark features of Omar Parra.

As the jeep braked I gave the driver his .45 and got out. For a moment I stood staring at a branch-stripped tree in the center of the clearing. Tied to it was the sagging, blood-spattered body of a nearly naked man.

Parra blew smoke from the short muzzle of his gun and came toward me. "Another *chivato* has embraced the tree of forgetfulness. This one was sent by your countrymen to destroy me." He spat on the ground. "Come, see how we preserve the memory of spies and traitors."

He pointed at a large thatched hut in the background.

181

Smoke drifted upward from its conical roof. Parra gestured to me and I began walking toward him as two soldiers started cutting down the bullet-riddled corpse.

The low hut entrance was hung with a length of burlap sacking. Parra flung it aside, and we stooped and went in.

The interior was filled with low-hanging smoke from a fire whose coals I could barely see. Above the fire, suspended from a long pole, were about a dozen loosely woven baskets. Each one held what looked like a small, smoke-blackened replica of a human head. The teeth seemed disproportionately large until I realized that they were the only features not shrunken by the prolonged heat and smoke.

"*Chivatos*," Parra said, voice thick with hatred as he pointed at the grinning array. "The *índios* preserve them for me."

I swallowed. "Why?"

"To show new employees the price of betrayal."

I coughed smoke from my lungs and left the hut to gulp cleaner air. I lifted my mosquito veil long enough to wipe my dripping face, and saw that two soldiers had dragged the executed body onto the trunk of a fallen tree. One held it in place while the other swung his machete to hack off the dead man's head. Behind me, Parra rasped, "A month from now, his mother wouldn't know him. Get in the jeep, *Señor* Reynolds. I am going to show you something even more unusual—the reason spies keep coming here."

TWENTY

Overhead, intermingling branches screened the trail, and I understood why aerial photos failed to show anything but green jungle. The hut full of shrunken heads explained why DEA infiltrators failed to make their expected reports—and why Manny was willing to pay me so much government money to take the agents' place.

I gazed at the back of Parra's neck and felt an impulse to loop it with a strangling wire. Not only to avenge the slaughtered agents, but as reprisal for the countless thousands his drugs had crippled and destroyed.

By now, a variety of insects had collected on my mosquito netting, further obscuring vision. Even so, as the jeep slowed, I could make out a series of low buildings set among thinned-out trees. All were constructed of rough wood, with the exception of a one-story concrete blockhouse. An iron-shod entrance door and air vents suggested ammunition storage. Parra's armory? Hidden generators hummed loudly.

Log-and-sandbag revetments were set deeper into the jungle. Separately, they sheltered drums of acetone and

ether to reduce risk of conflagration. The jeep stopped and
we got out.

Wordlessly, Parra led me toward the largest building, motioned gate guards aside and went in. Following, I
first smelled, then saw, a narcotics laboratory like the one
near Mazatlán, but much larger. Big cooking vats, dryer
setups, digital scales and packaging. From a railed enclosure a uniformed man left his office table and greeted Parra
with an *abrazo*. He wore the insigne of an Army captain
and Parra introduced him as Eloy Quinto. "My chief of
security," he added with a thin smile, and pulled off his hat
and netting.

I didn't, because Quinto's *mestizo* face looked familiar,
and I didn't want him staring too closely at mine while I
tried to remember where we'd met before—if we had.

Then, as his face turned, I remembered him from four
years ago. Though I didn't know his name at the time,
Quinto had been one of Luis's bodyguards the night I'd
snatched Luis from his Freeport hotel and taken him across
the Gulf Stream to Fort Lauderdale and federal arrest. Had
Quinto spotted me that night? Or had Bahamian police
grabbed him earlier, as I'd arranged? And if Quinto was
here, what about other bodyguards who might recall the
kidnapper's face? To Parra I said, "This is quite a setup."

He nodded with satisfaction. "I'm going to enlarge it now
that we're closing down the Mexican lab." Turning to
Quinto, he said, "*Señor* Reynolds will be running a load for
us. Yolanda made the arrangement."

Quinto pulled at a mustache tip. "Was that wise, *compadre*?"

"At first I thought not, then Yolanda explained the circumstances, and I agree with her judgment."

"That's a relief," I said. "I wasn't sure we were going to
work things out." To get out of Quinto's line of sight I
walked further into the lab and looked slowly around as
though stupefied by the magnitude of it all. The bubbling

vats, the clanking machinery, the ventilation blowers and overhead fans, the masked, white-coated chemists and the leaf wrapped bundles of coca paste. With Parra out of business, I told myself, DEA could pay more attention to Mid-East narcotics connections. Iran and Afghanistan.

I continued looking around until I noticed Quinto return to his work area, where he picked up an electric personnel detector and examined it with the help of a check-off sheet. Strewing the lab perimeter with a few hundred EPDs would give instant, silent notice of infiltrators, enabling Quinto to dispatch troops to the precise point within minutes of detection.

I remembered how we'd used the EPDs in Nam. The sensors had saved hundreds, even thousands of lives, one of our few technological successes in a losing war.

And now the drug kings had appropriated it for their own ends. At least I knew what lay in the surrounding jungle.

The scent of chemicals was strong and penetrating. I began to cough, covered my face and hurried out of the lab. Once outside—away from Quinto's eyes—I pulled off the headnet and wiped my streaming face.

Presently, Parra came out and said, "I forgot that others are not accustomed to the odors. Well, you've seen the heart of my operation. Any questions?"

"How much can you refine?"

"Of cocaine, a thousand kilos per month. Of heroin, four hundred. By expanding, I will be able to double the amounts—if I can arrange a steady supply of acetone and ether."

"There's a problem?"

"To appease the Americans, the government has outlawed those chemicals except in such small quantities as pharmacies might consume. So, the price has risen from twenty to eight hundred dollars a drum."

"And you can't sell at a profit?"

"Narcotics will sell at any price, no matter how high. It

is a question of maintaining supply. So I am considering bringing the chemicals on one of my ships from—" He glanced slyly at me. "That's something you don't need to know."

As we began walking to the jeep, Omar said, "Did Yolanda say how else I might employ you after your California delivery?"

"No—only that you could always use good men."

"True. And while you're away I'll be deciding where to fit you in. Don't worry, there will be a place for you."

He poked the driver awake and faced me. "When you get back to Casa Dorada, tell my cousin we will have a guest at dinner tonight. A distinguished one."

"She'll ask his name."

"I don't suppose you follow Colombian politics—but the guest is Jaime Alvarez."

I gave him a blank stare.

"Alvarez," he said, "leads one of the big guerrilla bands against the government. His operations keep the army busy and away from me."

"Sounds helpful."

"Of course I pay him well for that service—and for the coca paste he brings here from Bolivia. It is one of those ideal business arrangements, *Señor* Reynolds, where both parties are supremely satisfied."

I got into the jeep and the corporal started the engine. I adjusted my mosquito net as we turned back toward the relocated French chateau.

At the entrance a servant told me that *Señora* Yolanda wanted to be informed of my return. In my room I got out of sticky clothing and gave it to a maid before soaking in the tub. There were insect bites on my hands and ankles, some on my back that I rubbed with strong soap as well as I could. After a while Yolanda glided in and completed the treatment before pulling down the bed covers and inviting me to a pre-dinner quickie.

Lying together, we made small talk about my jungle trip and the laboratory Omar had shown me. "I'm not a chemist," I said, "but everything looks shipshape and productive."

"Did you see the—place where spies are killed?"

"Omar called it the 'tree of forgetfulness.' What's it mean?"

"In *santería* legend we are born descending the tree of forgetfulness. When we die, we ascend it again."

"How poetic. I saw the shrunken heads, too. Much less poetic." I felt her body shiver against mine.

"It's for our own security."

"Yeah, but Omar doesn't have to enjoy it so much."

"He is an extremely cruel man." Her hand stroked the side of my face. "I believe Omar killed my husband, Mauricio—or had him killed."

"In Medellín?"

"Yes. It was just after Luis was killed in Miami, and Omar said my husband was trying to take over. I don't know if he believed that, or if it was an excuse to get rid of him. My husband came of a much better family than the Parras, and my cousins resented him."

"But you loved him."

"The only man I ever really loved. Then, not long after Mauricio was murdered, Omar came to my room one night and wanted to make love to me. When I told him to get out he tried to rape me, but I managed to get my gun and wound him in the thigh. After that I went to California."

"Think he'll try again?"

"Without his wife . . ." She let the thought trail off, but I understood her meaning.

"Bringing us back," I said, "to the logic of having you run this place without him. Avenging your husband's murder would leave you in full control."

"I'd need help," she said thoughtfully. "Would you help me, Jack?"

"If that's what you really want."

"I've decided—I do." She kissed my lips. "You'll take care of Omar?"

"After the California trip. That'll give you time to make plans, decide who you can trust without Omar around." I stroked the small of her back. "What about Eloy Quinto—does he go, too?"

"I'd feel better if he did. Eloy has always been very loyal to Omar—after Luis."

"Well," I said, "that's two down, and I imagine the list will grow."

From above I heard the Learjet whining down into a landing approach at the nearby field. Yolanda said, "Back from Baranquilla. The sooner you leave, the better for us both. Do you want two or three men for your crew?"

"Two are enough—if they're bluewater sailors."

"You'll have to decide for yourself. They'll be here tomorrow, and if you accept them, the Lear will take you back to Mazatlán."

After she left I dozed for a while, and my thoughts drifted to Melody in Miami and my life on Cozumel. I hadn't been gone a week, but it all seemed very far away. No point in pondering what I'd left behind, because if I got back I'd pick up slack lines, and if I didn't, it wouldn't matter anyway.

Just before sleep washed over me, I recalled Billy Joe's face as the bounty hunter hauled him away, and found myself wondering whether Tara had been able to track them down. What could she do to free her father? The problem was too complex for my tired mind, and I let it ebb away on the tide of sleep.

Jaime Alvarez arrived by helicopter from one of his jungle redoubts. As expected, he wore a thick beard, but I hadn't expected to find him over six feet tall. In place of jungle uniform he wore cream-colored polyester slacks and a lavishly embroidered guayabera, tailored to his broad shoulders. Parra remarked that his guest had been a star hammer-thrower during university days before Alvarez formed his S-21 movement from anti-government classmates and rebellious ideologues like himself. S-21, I was told, symbolized the 21st of September, a date on which, a decade earlier, three bomb-throwing students had been shot by Bogotá police.

Alvarez puffed a long, thin cigar and smiled indulgently while his background was clarified for the *gringo*. But his eyes ravished Yolanda to the point of irritating our host. The guerrilla chief complimented her extravagantly and said she'd never been far from his thoughts during her two-year absence. "But at last you've returned," he intoned, "and I intend to see much of you—lest the bird fly away again."

"That," said Parra sourly, "is not likely to happen. Yolanda will be occupied with our business"—he used the word *asuntos*—"so I advise you to seek elsewhere for a sweetheart."

Alvarez's heavy eyebrows drew together, then he chuckled and exhaled blue smoke toward the ceiling. This one, I mused, could qualify as Number Three on our hit list, and there was probably a considerable reward on his head. Yolanda's gaze met mine, and I wondered if our thoughts were the same.

Presently, a servant announced dinner, and we went in to a slate-floored dining hall. The table was at least thirty feet long, covered with embroidered linen and set with antique silver and goblets. Four massive candelabra provided mellow lighting for a scene so luxurious as to make unimaginable the thought that we were in the heart of the Guajira jungle.

Omar was at the head of the table, Yolanda and Alvarez across from me. The men's table manners would have earned a good many demerits at Annapolis, but I kept my thoughts to myself, though Yolanda's eyebrows raised when the slurping got overloud. For my part I thought it characteristic of the family that killing a man a few hours ago hadn't interfered with Omar's appetite. Even Yolanda was blessed with the ability to rise above the sufferings of others.

Throughout dinner, Jaime and Omar bent each other's ears, talking prices, routes and weapons, and the location of government troops. I heard of a planned offensive by the Colombian army, details of which had come to Alvarez through a well-placed army spy. No wonder the army couldn't prevail, I thought, when S-21 knew every move in advance.

For a Socialist, anti-imperialist fighter, Alvarez took what I saw as unseemly pleasure from our opulent surroundings, and was apparently quite at home amid luxury. That was not the usually projected image of Spartan jungle combatants, but perhaps Alvarez was canny enough to let his cadres do the fighting while he managed finance and philosophy for the endless insurrection. The precedent for that division of revolutionary tasks had been sanctified by V.I. Lenin. Who was Alvarez to ignore it?

Four courses later, dinner ended, and coffee was served in a drawing room laid with thick oriental rugs. Omar got out a map of the Guajira, and with Alvarez began figuring out where future shipments of acetone and ether should unload—after the voyage from Guayana. My disinterest was genuine, because if I was able to destroy the lab, Parra's chemicals would have no place to go. Besides, I was beginning to think of ways to get back there—and get out alive. For that I was going to need weapons, jungle clothing, food and water—in that order. A compass would be a nice addition, but I was accustomed to navigating by sun and stars. And if I got disoriented in the sunless jungle I could always fashion a compass with a knife and a sliver of iron. In the SEALs we called it a field expedient.

Looking bored, Yolanda came over to me and murmured, "I've never liked being involved with guerrillas, and I like it even less now."

"I can understand how it might enrage the government—and you don't need more enemies."

"No."

I lowered my voice. "Are you suggesting he's expendable?"

"Uh-huh. With Omar gone, I think Jaime would try to take over."

"I was thinking the same," I confessed, "and he has the troops to do it. How many do you have guarding the *estancia*?"

"Two years ago we had between three and four hundred, so I assume it's stayed the same."

That was an interesting slice of information, and it had surfaced in an entirely casual way. "Radio contact?" I asked.

She nodded. "There's a big radio room in the basement so Omar can keep in touch with guards, our aircraft, and boats." She smiled. "Also, they listen to army radio signals."

"That's real organization," I said admiringly.

"Otherwise, we couldn't have lasted until now."

A beeper sounded, and I saw Omar fumble at his belt to shut it off. He left the room and Jaime Alvarez strolled over. To Yolanda he said, "You're more beautiful than ever, *mi amor*. Could I persuade you to spend a day or so visiting my camps?"

"Next year, perhaps. As Omar told you, I'm becoming reacquainted with our business. By the way, is Carmen well? Has she borne more revolutionaries to carry on the Alvarez name?"

"My wife is well," he said irritably, "and living in Bucaramanga with the children. Our daughter was born a year ago."

"Congratulations. My affection to them both."

191

Having found only a dry well, Alvarez turned to me. "So, *yanqui* adventurer, are you enjoying Colombia?"

"What I've seen of it."

"Staying long?"

"That's up to Omar."

"You have heard of me in America? The S-21 Movement?"

"I don't follow politics."

"It is the only vocation for a man of talent and intelligence."

"That disqualifies me," I said, and saw Omar, frowning, return.

Alvarez bent over Yolanda's hand and pressed it briefly. "I must rejoin my brave compatriots, but with the hope of seeing you soon again."

"Yes," she said, noncommittally, "that may come to pass."

When Omar took Alvarez out to his helicopter, I said, "This has been a long day, *querida*, think I'll turn in. Will you . . . ?"

"I'll come as soon as it's safe." She squeezed my hand, and I climbed up to my room.

About an hour later I felt her weight on the bed, and woke to hear her whisper, "Jack—something very bad has happened. Omar has it in his head that you're an American narcotics agent named Novak."

TWENTY-ONE

I was glad she couldn't see my face in the dark, because it must have stiffened in shock. I managed a curt laugh that sounded more like a grunt. "Crazy. Surely he doesn't believe it? More importantly, do you?" I sat up and gripped her shoulders.

"I—I don't want to, Jack. It doesn't make sense."

I kissed the side of her face. "Who would give Omar such an idea?"

"The security chief, Quinto."

"Hmmm. Met him today, but didn't realize I'd made a poor impression. I think Quinto's been so long in the jungle he figures every arrival is a *chivato*."

"Could be," she sighed, "but where did he get that name from—Novak?"

"Where, indeed?" I wondered if she could feel the accelerated pounding of my heart.

"*Now* I know," she said suddenly. "Omar's always said a *yanqui* named Novak killed Luis."

"Ah—so they're paranoid on the subject." Lying back, I

193

drew her against me. "Is your cousin planning to shoot me and shrink my head?"

Her body shuddered. "Unless you can convince him your name is Reynolds, he'll torture you until you 'confess.'"

"It's hard to prove a negative, but would I have saved you from the sniper or loaded your boat with cocaine if I was an agent?"

Slowly she nodded. "That's so—unless you had another plan."

Mouth dry, I swallowed. "Such as?"

"Oh, coming here, learning about our *estancia*—I don't know, it's such a bizarre idea."

"Exactly. But Omar isn't the most balanced fellow I've come across lately. What seems ridiculous to us may look logical to him. Especially with Quinto feeding his doubts and suspicions."

She kissed me, then, and murmured, "Omar said you know too much to live."

"Terrific. And I'm not supposed to know what you've told me."

"That would put me in a difficult position—you can see that."

"Yeah—also that unless I do something, I'm dead." I stared up at the ceiling. "How did Quinto come by his idea?"

"Omar didn't say—but Quinto has informants in America—perhaps at DEA headquarters."

"Then he's buying trash information."

"The call Omar took just before Jaime left—that was Quinto denouncing you."

"What should I do?"

"I don't think there's anything you can do—but in the morning I can talk to my cousin, try to persuade him you're not this Novak." Her face turned to me. "Jack, I'm frightened."

"Think I'm not? Will they grab me tonight?"

"Probably not until morning."

I disentangled myself from her body, went to my suitcase and got out the Browning pistol. Lying back beside her, I shoved the pistol under my pillow. "You're my only advocate," I told her, "so be persuasive."

"You know I will." Moving against me, she warmed my chilled body, and after a while I said, "Omar killed your husband because he wanted you. He probably sees me as another rival and needs a motive to remove me."

"You know, it's a possibility."

"Hell, he's crazier than a caged baboon, and you'll be better off without him around."

"Crazy and dangerous. But I need time to eliminate him." Her hands were doing things to me, exciting things that finally blotted thoughts of death and betrayal from my mind so that passion could prevail.

After she left, I locked the door, got dressed and lay on the bed, pistol at hand. If Omar decided to take me tonight, he was going to be unpleasantly surprised.

What woke me was not Omar's voice and the click of weapons but sunlight streaming through my room. So much for night fears, I thought, shaved and tucked the Browning into my belt under the guayabera shirt. Then I went down to breakfast on the patio.

I heard Yolanda and Omar arguing before I saw them seated at a table. As I appeared, Yolanda said, "Omar, I'm going to tell him—he has a right to know."

"I'll tell him." Omar stared hostilely at me as I picked up a plate at the buffet.

"Me?" I said. "Tell what?"

"There's information you are a *chivato* named Novak."

I forked a sweet bun onto my plate. "I've been called a lot of names, but not that one."

"Novak killed my brother."

I smiled tolerantly. "Either you see Novaks everywhere or this is some sort of loyalty test."

"You don't take me seriously? This is very serious."

I added a slice of grilled ham to my plate and set it on the table. "How can I be serious about something so preposterous? What do I have to do to get a cup of coffee?" Sitting down, I looked around helplessly and noticed a restrained smile on Yolanda's lips. She said, "Coffee is coming, Jack. Be patient—I think my cousin has more to say."

"Go ahead," I told him. "Let it all hang out." I broke the pastry and stuffed part of it in my mouth.

"Good sources say you're Novak."

"Since I'm not Novak, your sources can't be good. *Wait a minute*—maybe this Novak is expected to come here. Okay, let him come—you'll be ready for him."

The thought hadn't occurred to Parra. His gaze left me, and Yolanda said, "That's the explanation, cousin. Considering all Jack did to protect me in Mazatlán, he couldn't be that Novak."

"No hard feelings," I said, and tapped my cup with the knife edge. "Can I have coffee now?"

Abruptly, Parra scraped back his chair. "I'll look into this further," he snapped, and began striding away.

"While you're looking into things," I called, "let's see those crewmen I was promised."

He halted. "Why?"

"Mazatlán to California can be a long, dirty trip. Are these men bluewater sailors, or have they never handled more than a raft on Lake Maracaibo? You talk about being serious—well, sailing a big boat is serious."

He grunted. "Maybe you'll never see that big boat again."

"Same to me, *amigo*. Get another captain and I'll be on my way," I said cheerfully. "And when you see this Novak, give him my thanks for showing up."

"From a gun barrel."

"Whatever." I cut a portion of ham and watched Parra disappear inside his chateau. Yolanda expelled pent-up breath. "You did that beautifully, Jack, and the danger's over—for now. But he trusts Eloy Quinto more than he trusts me."

"Mmmm. I had hopes for Quinto, but he's got to go."

A servant filled our coffee cups, and after she plodded away I said, "I'm serious about those crewmen. I ain' gonna set out with no lubbers."

"I don't expect you to." She glanced at her watch. "While you were still sleeping I sent a plane for them."

"Where?"

"Santa Marta, this side of Baranquilla."

"Your men, or—his?"

"You'll have to decide."

I stirred brown crystals into my coffee. "I'll want to decide pretty fast. I have this nightmare of arriving at wherever we're going and one of Omar's men blowing off my head."

"If I thought that could happen, I wouldn't let you go, Jack."

"And if I think it could happen, I won't be going." I took her hand. "Will that end a beautiful friendship?"

She shook her head. "It shouldn't—because we've made plans, haven't we?"

"Right. And I want to be damn sure that when I come back to Casa Dorada you'll be waiting."

"I promise." Furtively, her lips brushed my cheek.

That took away some of the tension generated by Omar's accusation, but his suspicions meant I couldn't stay around much longer and stay alive.

It troubled me that I'd been fingered, because when I took Manny's mission I'd expected to come in clean. Somehow, his office had been penetrated, and if I survived betrayal on top of everything else, Manny would have some catch-up vetting to do.

Yolanda said, "Anything special you'd like to do until the plane comes?"

"I had the grand tour yesterday, without knowing where I was. Any maps around to show where things are located?"

"Omar keeps them in his office."

They were fixed to the wall and covered with acetate overlays. In a far corner stood a heavy, six-foot European safe that probably contained cash, account ledgers and bankbooks. Four sticks of dynamite would have as much effect on its thick steel as a spitball.

Moving close to the maps, I pretended an interest in Baranquilla and Santa Marta but managed an extended look at the *estancia* map—from airstrip to laboratory complex, troop barracks, field radio stations and topographical features: rivers, and especially the *sierra* foothills I planned to cross. It was going to be one hell of a rough journey.

Yolanda said, "Memorizing it?"

"Familiarizing myself with the layout, after the coup. We can't expect a hell of a lot of cooperation from the loyalists."

She nodded understandingly, and we moved on to the grill-door radio room where three operators monitored massive consoles. They, too, had wall maps with boxes and call signs scattered around the Caribbean rim, and as we left, Yolanda said, "If Luis hadn't installed all this, we'd have no way to communicate with suppliers and distributors."

"A man ahead of his time," I remarked, and as we climbed back to the main floor I heard a plane come in.

It was an old DC-3 drifting over the trees, full flaps and sputtering engines as it fishtailed into the wind. Trees screened it, and after a while I heard the engines rev as the plane taxied back.

An army jeep brought us two salty-looking fellows—if salty means tough. I hadn't expected effete yachtsmen, but this pair looked like hard-fisted stevedores, and while they guzzled cold beer from bottles I probed their level of incompetence. Raul had been bos'n on a tramp steamer, Javier, AB on an oiler, and neither had been under canvas. To string things out for Yolanda's benefit, I asked them about sheets and ballast, keels, jibing and tacking, and what it meant to sail close-hauled, but their response was silence and visible irritation. Even had they been qualified, I wasn't going to accept them for an ocean voyage, and when I turned to Yolanda she shook her head. "Sorry, Jack, we'll try again."

"Pay them for their time," I suggested, "and if the plane's fueled they can leave."

After the jeep drove off with the nautical aspirants I said, "Omar confused sail with steam. I can find better crewmen on the Mazatlán waterfront."

"Omar won't want you hiring men he hasn't approved."

"He had his chance—anyway, it's your operation."

"And I have confidence in you. When do you want to leave?"

I took her hand. "Leaving tomorrow, I can get back here in about two weeks—if Omar lets me go. Will you be okay?"

"Yes."

"And my down payment?"

"I'll give it to you at the plane—with charts and contact instructions. I'll work on them tonight."

"All night?"

"No. Before I left here I was more than a *santera*—I was a priestess—*iyalocha*. The faithful want me to become one again, but because I was away so long the *santero* must test me. Re-initiate me."

"At that jungle altar?"

She nodded. "The *bembe*. All the believers will attend. The ceremony will take several hours, and you'll hear the *ilu* drums. But, before dawn I'll come to you."

That solved a major problem—how to leave the chateau without being missed by Yolanda. And the *santería* celebrants would include troops, giving me more space and opportunity to move. So far, things were going better than I'd dared hope.

During lunch I stayed in this upbeat frame of mind, then Yolanda was called down to the airstrip—I didn't ask why— and I finished lunch alone. Afterward, I went into the chateau and was heading for an energy-storing *siesta* when I heard a jeep roar up in front. Thinking it was Yolanda returning, I walked out of the entrance and saw Parra, Quinto and two armed guards getting out of their jeep.

At sight of me Parra jerked out his gold-plated Dragoon and pointed it at my belly. There was a wild look on his face as he yelled, "Novak, you killed my brother, and you're going to die!"

TWENTY-TWO

I didn't resist when they took my Browning, tied my hands behind my back and hustled me into the jeep. Then we drove away, Parra staying at the chateau to gloat at Yolanda over his victory.

Quinto said, "You shouldn't have come here, *chivato*. That was a bad mistake."

"What makes you think I'm Novak?"

"This," he said, and from his pocket brought out a crumpled photograph. Copied from my old DEA file, it showed my face and profile above my ID number. My stomach became a ball of ice but I managed to say, "Nice work, Eloy. Where'd you get it?"

"I collect information," he said in a pleased tone. "When Omar was traded for you I offered big money for your photograph. Well, it was worth every *centavo*."

"Who got the payoff?"

"A woman who works for your friend, Montijo. She reported you were coming here."

"Fantastic," I said, "a penetration in Manny's office. No wonder you guys do so well."

That brought a grunt of satisfaction and I decided to say no more. About then, the jeep bounced past the *santería* shrine where four half-naked men were preparing for the night's celebration, laying flowers around the stones, placing bizarre-looking figurines with conical heads and huge eyes. At one side was a mesh crate of clucking chickens, and near them, tied and grazing, a white goat and a black one. It was going to be a great night for the *santeros*, I thought, but a bad one for chickens, goats and me. Well, I'd had a good life, wasted some bad guys, and done pretty much what I wanted to. But very few people were going to mourn me. Melody, for sure, possibly Delores, and even Tara, if she ever learned of my demise. Yolanda? She might give me a passing thought some night when she was in bed and lonely, then she'd recall how I'd used her, beginning at Mazatlán, and no woman enjoys being deceived.

Of course, Yolanda had used the Preacher for her own ends, but she wasn't likely to see things that way.

Quinto didn't have to tell me we were heading for the execution site, the place of shrunken heads; the question in my mind was when they planned to kill me. In Nam there had been a dozen times I thought I was going to die, and in that Guadalajara police dungeon I'd resigned myself to death. From those occasions I'd experienced the curious peace that comes when no hope remains, the feeling of indifference to what happens.

I hadn't reached that transcendental stage, but if I lived a little longer it would come, destroying my will to survive. And perhaps it was better that way; nothing exhausted the mind more than false hope.

When the jeep occasionally slowed, mosquitoes settled on my face and hands. Quinto and his guards wore protective netting, but without it, my lips and eyelids were beginning to swell from dozens of bites. Then the jeep would accelerate a little and the insects would vanish.

Finally, the jeep entered the clearing and I saw the stark tree trunk, bullet-scarred from who knew how many executions. Not everyone has the opportunity to see where and how he's going to die, but that bit of questionable fortune had been granted me, and as I stared at the tree of forgetfulness a sudden breeze gusted smoke from the shrinking hut.

My head would be hung with the others. A basket case at last, I told myself, and chuckled at the thought.

Quinto turned quickly, stared at me as though I was crazy, and at that moment I could have been. Then his men jerked me out of the jeep and hauled me over to the execution tree. While Quinto's MAC-10 covered me, they retied my wrists around the trunk behind me. Then one of the *indios* spat in my face. I kicked him in the balls, and while he hopped around, crouching and yelping, the other two howled with laughter. Finally, the injured guard hauled out his pistol, but Quinto made him put it away, saying, "He's not for you to kill, *niño*. The *chivato*'s head belongs to *Señor* Omar, by right of blood."

Surlily the *indio* limped away and got gingerly into the jeep, where he lay back, face twitching with pain. He was out of it for a while, and I was glad I'd damaged him.

To prevent repetition, Quinto had the other guard tie my feet together. Then he stood off to the side, lighted a thin cigar and stared at me.

My throat felt choked with sand, but I managed to grate, "What's the delay? Let's get on with it."

For a while he kept on studying my face, then said, "Omar will bring a crowd to witness your death. Until then, you have much to think about." Half-turning, he glanced at the smokehouse.

"Charming. Anyway, I'll join the company of honorable men."

"It is not honorable to be a *chivato*."

"Not in your slimy world."

His face hardened, then relaxed. Walking past me to the jeep, he said, "Still, you are a man of spirit. I shall never forget how you captured Luis single-handed."

"Wasted effort."

"So you killed him in Miami."

"He had a gun on me and my girl. Sure, I wanted him dead." I slid down the trunk until I was sitting on soft ground, legs outstretched, ankles tied.

"Enjoy your memories." Quinto poked the suffering driver, who started the jeep as Quinto got in. After a villainous look at me, the driver clashed gears and the jeep moved away. Toward the manufacturing complex. The remaining guard unshouldered his weapon and sat down against the smokehouse wall. Within moments he was asleep.

Mosquitoes settled on my head and neck. They feasted for a while, then smoke would roll out of the hut and disperse them. When the smoke cleared, they returned. I tried rubbing my wrist ropes against the trunk, but the surface was too smooth to abrade the fibers. So I tried pulling at the strands with my fingers and finally reached the knot. My nails bent and broke as I worked on unloosening it, until finally I gave up, having gained nothing.

The guard snored, and slid further down the wall. Clearly, he had the gift of peace.

This was the time to make my move, I thought, but I had no moves to make. There was nothing complicated about my situation, it was elemental. I was trussed like a hog, and there was nothing I could do to get free. The simplicity of the problem aggravated me, and I realized that I had ceased scanning for solutions. I could neither bribe the guard nor disable him, and once Parra and his slavering group arrived, my execution would begin.

But when was that to be? Before or after the *santería* celebration? Yolanda was to take part in it tonight. Would she also watch her cousin's bullets tear me apart?

As I sat there, sweat rolling down my face, a loinclothed Indian came into the clearing, sticks of wood in his arms. From his face paint and bird-claw necklace, he could be Jívaro. Usually they ranged to the south, but this one could be an import, doing what his tribe did best—miniaturizing human heads. He glanced at me impassively and entered the hut. I could hear the sound of tumbling wood, and after a while fresh smoke lifted from the hut. The Indian came out, and smoke wafted across the clearing. As mosquitoes left my flesh, the Indian glanced at me again, and I shook my wrists. He touched his machete. I nodded back. Enthusiastically. The Indian shook his head and disappeared into the jungle.

Well, I thought, so much for that. Trade goods might have persuaded him—needles, fishhooks or shiny beads. Unfortunately, I hadn't come equipped for barter. Take a memo to DEA: Pogey Bait for Field Agent Use.

The insects returned, and the clearing was silent while they fed. Now and then I'd rub my cheeks against the tree trunk, but it was a losing contest; I was outnumbered two thousand to one.

Time passed. The guard blinked, sat up and cleared his throat. He spat in my direction. Looking dully around, he readjusted his position and relapsed into sleep.

At least he wasn't goading me, I thought, so let's be grateful for small things.

Small things, however, were sucking at my blood supply. The insects must be almost too bloated to fly. If I could get free, my swollen face would disguise me from the curious—but first I had to free my wrists.

Halfheartedly, I tried to rub the cords against the trunk behind me. I didn't expect results, but it kept my mind occupied, circulation flowing.

A snake slithered into the clearing. It was an anaconda, nine feet long, and it looked hungry. If he coiled himself around my neck and squeezed, Parra was going to be cheated of his spectacle. Well, I'd killed plenty of snakes in Nam's jungles, maybe it was their turn to work on me.

The snake stopped moving, formed a half-circle and lifted its head. The tongue flicked out, sensing the situation. I stayed very still. The guard snored and the snake's head turned. More tongue-flicking. The head lowered, and the snake began undulating toward the guard. I watched with interest as the scene unfolded.

A foot from the guard's body the anaconda coiled, thrust up its head and scented with its tongue. The guard's hand lifted to brush away an insect, and in that second the anaconda struck. With a scream the guard shot to his feet, trying to fight off the snake, whose fangs had penetrated his palm. More screaming and yelling as the snake heaved its coils around the man's thighs. The guard's hopping reminded me of a potato-sack race, and I began to guffaw.

The guard's free hand was simultaneously trying to choke the snake and separate its jaws. Nothing worked, and now, with firm leverage, the snake's coils began inching up the guard's body. Once the anaconda's head was within striking distance of the man's throat, the guard was a goner. And I was rooting for the snake.

Suddenly the guard remembered his belt knife, snatched it from the sheath and began stabbing the snake's body. He'd jab and yell, and I realized the knife was also piercing his thigh. Finally the guard began hacking desperately at the anaconda's neck. The long, muscular body reacted violently, thrashing around, tail flailing wildly, seeking another anchor.

This went on for a while as blood spouted from snake and man, and finally a savage knife stroke decapitated the snake, and the man's arm lifted free.

The snake's body writhed in postmortem convulsions,

but its jaws still clamped the hand. The coils slackened and the guard stepped from them as he tried to pry off the deadlocked jaws, but they were as deeply sunk as steel rivets.

He saw blood gouting from stab wounds in his thigh, stared at the snake jaws in his hand and turned. Limping toward me, he held out the snake head. *"Por favor, señor,"* he pleaded.

In answer, I shook my bound wrists. The guard knelt and, with his knife hand, cut me free. Then he came around and sawed my ankle cords. I chafed my wrists and stood up. Okay, I thought, and thrust out my open palm. The guard stared at it, swallowed and handed me his knife. I stabbed it into the tree trunk above his reach, and gripped the snake's jaws. Fighting their rictus was like opening a bear trap, for they were fully closed, all fangs penetrating his flesh. Some snake, I thought, as I put more muscle into the effort.

Gradually the jaws parted, and blood pumped from his hand. The guard grunted as I pried out the curved fangs, and when his hand was free I tossed the severed head among its still-shuddering coils.

"Help me," the guard begged, "I'm bleeding."

I cut strips of cloth from his uniform, twisted a tourniquet above the self-inflicted wounds and just below his groin. While he held the cloth tightly I bandaged his wounded hand. "Good boy," I said, "you put up a great fight. Next time try cutting just the snake."

Sticking the knife in my belt, I walked to where he'd left his automatic rifle.

Whimpering in pain, the guard watched me arm myself. His tourniquet and deeply bitten hand gave him plenty to focus on without trying to stop me from leaving.

I was congratulating myself on unexpected freedom, and blessing the reptile deity, when from beside the smokehouse

Eloy Quinto got the drop on me and ordered me to down the rifle. He cursed me, fired two shots above my head, and presently a jeep roared into the clearing.

I was a prisoner again.

TWENTY-THREE

This time they stood me against the tree trunk and wound cord around me from ankle to neck, mummy-style. When Quinto was satisfied I couldn't move, he drove off with the injured guard, leaving another guard to watch me.

After a while the wood-carrier brought another load to the hut and caught sight of the anaconda. He squatted, plumped the body with his fingers and lugged it into the hut. Probably to toast anaconda steaks over his charcoal fire. I was getting hungry myself, but the Indian didn't offer to share, so I reflected that dying with full or empty stomach was all the same.

Time passed. Darkness dropped like a shroud, and tree toads and lizards began to chirp and croak. I was thirsty enough to drink reptile blood and enjoy it.

The guard went into the hut and came out, presently, a chunk of meat on the point of his knife. He sat near the entrance and munched the white flesh until my mouth watered. The Indian came out with half the snake looped over one shoulder, and disappeared into jungle darkness.

From the distance came a slow pounding of drums.

The guard listened intently, and his expression told me that, as a *santero*, he would rather be at the ceremony than guarding me. But Quinto had threatened to kill him if I escaped, so he shook his head and swallowed the last of his meat.

I was bound so tightly to the trunk that I couldn't disturb the feeding insects. These were nocturnal reinforcements, a new wave thirstier than the first assault group. From Nam there was malaria in my bloodstream, so perhaps my final act would be to propagate the disease through the Guajira.

Blood pounded in my head, almost in rhythm with what I was hearing from the *bembe*. Three *ilu* drums now, pitched differently, and soon I heard an eerie wailing, some background jabbering, and more chanting, as voices joined the chorus. I wasn't sure whether goats or chickens were sacrificed first, or if the priest or priestess alternated animals to extend the ritual tension. What I was sure of was that, after all the animals were killed, the crowd would assemble around me while Parra and his weapons completed the night's bloody entertainment.

Like his snake-bitten partner, the guard stretched out by the hut. He'd filled his stomach, no concern of his that I was going to die.

Because snakes usually travel in pairs, I hoped the dead one's mate would now enter Stage Right and energize the set, as once before. But the hope was only vagrant, and as the *santeros'* voices gained volume, I realized nothing was going to save me this time, and so I let my mind relax and slide into lethargy.

Time ceased.

The guard's snoring broke into my reverie, bringing me back to the present. *Santero* drums were still beating, and over them I heard a goat bray its death agony. My flesh crawled.

A twig snapped at the edge of the clearing. I looked in the direction of the sound, and with night-adjusted vision saw a crouched figure moving around the perimeter, toward the smoking hut. The unexpected arrival engaged my interest, and I watched its stealthy progress toward the sleeping guard. A ray of moonlight glinted briefly from a blade in the figure's hand, and I felt my muscles tense. I decided it was the guard I'd kicked, returning for personal revenge.

The figure reached the guard, and a hand shoved aside his weapon. A swift slash at the unprotected throat, and the body convulsed, as gurgling sounds carried to my ears.

The figure padded toward me, and I saw not the guard but a near-naked Yolanda. Her breasts and torso were bare, crotch covered by a dark loincloth, and for a moment I thought she was coming to kill me herself. Instead, I heard and felt her knife slit my ropes, and as they dropped free, she whispered, "I may die for it, but I owe you this much."

Turning, I almost toppled as blood began coursing into dulled legs and arms. She steadied me, and hissed, "Now, go. I can't do more for you."

"Thank you," I said. "Bless you."

"I don't care where you go, Jack Novak, just go." She drew herself erect, proud and beautiful. "You *are* Novak, aren't you?"

"Yes," I said, "but Novak the Slovak was never going to harm Yolanda."

"And you would have killed Omar and Quinto?"

"That's why I came." I reached for her shoulders, but she pressed the knife point against my chest. I pushed it aside and kissed her. She struggled for a moment, her throat making hostile sounds, then her body sagged, and her mouth opened against mine. "Go," she repeated, "they're coming now. God, I hope you make it—somehow. Don't ever return."

I kissed her again. "I'll always remember," I said, and let her go. Like a wraith she vanished in darkness, and I heard the sound of engines and oncoming voices.

From the dead guard I took mosquito-net hat, weapons

belt and shirt. Grabbing up his automatic rifle, I stumbled across the clearing to the trail that led through encroaching jungle toward the guarded laboratory I had come to destroy.

Because of stiffness and recovering circulation, I had to jog slowly for the first quarter-mile. Then things went better and I increased my pace. Unseen potholes and ruts made going uncertain, but I had to widen the distance from Parra's gang, which eventually would figure out my course.

As I moved through the night I began to marvel at Yolanda's bravery in killing the guard and setting me free. Even more astonishing was her willingness to do it when she knew I was a narc and the killer of Luis. She'd told me her motive, but I suspected there was more than that.

Anyway, she'd come through, and now I had weapons and a chance to get away. I slanted off the trail and stopped long enough to pull on the dead guard's shirt—still sticky around the throat—and fit on the weapons belt. It held two loaded clips for the automatic rifle, a sheathed knife, a canteen and a Colt .45 pistol with extra magazines. The canteen water was far from fresh, but to my dried mouth and throat it was more delicious than the finest champagne. I didn't want my stomach to cramp so I drank less than I wanted, capped the rest and jogged on.

Because the jungle around the complex would be seeded with electronic sensors, I stayed on the trail until I saw a dim glow ahead. To me it seemed as bright as a quarter of a million dollars in silver coins.

To begin the night's activity I needed items from Parra's armory. By day there had been two guards at the ironwork entrance; perhaps the *santería* ceremony had drawn one away.

Staying close to the road edge, I reached the border of the clearing, knelt and looked around. There was a military truck parked beside the acetone and ether drum revetments. A light over the armory door showed a lone guard leaning back on a stool, rifle across his thighs. Two guards sat on either side of the laboratory entrance. In the night's stillness the generators sounded raucously loud.

As I considered an approach, I reasoned that in semidarkness my uniform shirt, weapons belt, rifle and netting hat might get me past the stationary guards. If that didn't work, I'd shoot before they could—but let's try it rather than crawl on elbows, knees and belly, which was the alternative. After all, the guards wouldn't be expecting Señor Omar's prisoner to appear out of the night, dressed like one of them.

So, I slung my AR, muzzle down, as they did, and walked bravely ahead. I'd covered about eighty yards before the armory guard challenged me. Cupping my hands, I yelled, "*Cabrón*, mind your own business. I am on an errand for Señor Eloy."

"Pass, *compadre*," he called, and I continued on.

After traversing a long section of the clearing, I reached the generators' thatched shelter. Both were big amp Phillips rigs driven by Mercedes truck diesels, and noisy. Mounted on steel-and-concrete foundations, each was about ten feet tall. Ladders led up to their fuel intake pipes, and before I mounted the nearest one I filled two pockets with gravelly sand. I unscrewed the big cap and dumped in the saboteur's field expedient, climbed down and repeated the operation on the other engine. Then I walked behind the shelter and waited.

It took about three minutes for the engines to start coughing and sputtering. They died within seconds of each other, and lights around the complex dimmed and faded out. The lab probably functioned for a time on emergency batteries, because its machinery kept on clacking and pounding away.

As soon as I heard yelling and pounding feet I cut out

from the shelter wall and headed for the armory. The guard had moved out from the entrance and stood fingering his trigger in a nonplussed way, waiting for orders or explanations.

I strode directly to him. "Get over there and lend a hand." I gestured at the generator shelter.

"But—I'm not supposed to leave here."

"I'm relieving you." I gave his back a shove, and when he moved off I tried the grilled gate. It was locked, but with Latin practicality the key had been hung on the doorjamb. So I unlocked the gate and went in.

A battery-run battle light gave enough illumination to show an astonishing array of military weaponry, most from the USA.

There were racks of automatic rifles, revolvers and MAC-10 machine pistols. On the concrete floor, tripod machine guns stood belted and ready to fire. Open cases of ammunition and grenades. I selected four frags and two smoke, and dropped them into a handy musette bag, plucked a MAC-10 from the display and jammed in a magazine. I discarded the rifle magazines from my belt and replaced them with two for the MAC-10. From one of the longer cases I extracted a rocket launcher and picked up two rockets; one could stop a tank or destroy a good-sized building. I was getting pretty well loaded down, so I took another frag grenade and backed out of the armory.

Men were running back and forth across the clearing. Jeep headlights made a macabre display as their beams crossed and recrossed like searchlights intersecting over Hanoi.

No one was paying attention to the armory, so I pulled the pin and tossed the grenade inside, aiming at the ammo cases.

Then I headed for the truck.

Ten seconds later the grenade detonated, along with several cases of cartridges, and the roof lifted off in a crazy spurt of flame. It vomited from the doorway like a flamethrower jet, curled back like a dragon's tongue to thrust out again before the walls collapsed.

Heat was setting off ammo primers in a continuum of hellish destruction that lighted the clearing as brightly as midday. It seemed reasonable to run from the scene, so I clutched rockets and launcher and made directly for the truck.

A clump of men stood near the generator shed, but they were staring at the burning, exploding armory, not at me. I passed them as rapidly as I could, and reached the sand-bagged revetments at the jungle's edge. I climbed into the big Ford truck and started the engine. Leaving rockets and launchers on the seat, I jumped down.

Beyond the sandbags I found about a hundred steel drums of ether. There was no cap wrench, so I returned to the truck and unclamped the emergency axe. With it I holed a drum, leaving quickly as noxious fumes filled the air. From there I climbed among the acetone drums, holed one, and when the smelly liquid was flowing I got back into the truck. After turning it around for fast getaway, I flung a grenade at the acetone, another at the ether, and gunned the engine.

As the truck gathered speed the grenades detonated behind me. Drums began exploding deafeningly, and the rear-view mirror showed flames and containers shooting high in the sky.

This was congenial work, I thought, with the payoff a good deal more profitable than the last time I blew a Cong ammo dump.

Twenty yards from the laboratory entrance I braked the truck and crawled under it with my launcher and two rockets. Flames showed one with a phosphorous head, an unexpected bonus. So I loaded the AP rocket first, adjusted the sight for forty yards and steadied the tube on my shoulder. When I pressed the trigger the rocket whooshed off, trailing flame like Hailey's comet.

It sped through the entrance and exploded deep inside the

lab. I sighted the phosphorous rocket and fired again. The detonation was awesome as portions of the laboratory roof disintegrated in sheets of flame. More chemicals ignited as I got behind the wheel and hauled ass for the trail.

A few disoriented *índios* fired rifles at me, then fled as the truck plunged toward the enveloping jungle. I'd decided to try the airfield to see what planes were available, then I remembered Yolanda, and knew I couldn't leave without trying to learn her fate.

As I bounced up to the execution site I saw only the guard's dead body, so I braked and got out. Holding my cocked MAC-10, I went into the hut and plucked a burning stick from the fire below the agents' heads. I couldn't bury them but I could cremate them with cleansing flames. So I set fire to the thatched walls and walked back to the truck, the conflagration crackling as it swept upward behind me.

The *santería* shrine was abandoned too; just white-feathered bodies and the headless carcasses of two goats. Everyone was at the laboratory roast, it seemed, and I was the only one heading the other way.

When I reached the chateau, the grounds were floodlit, Parra's jeep parked in front. That gave me an idea, so I left the truck in shadows by the tennis court and went inside. Even within those thick and ancient walls the distant detonations came loud and clear.

As I walked toward the staircase I saw a maid hurrying down. Pointing my machine pistol, I called, "Where is Señora Yolanda?"

"Upstairs, *señor*," she gasped.

"Alone?"

She hesitated, and I waved the pistol menacingly.

"With Señor Omar."

"Show me," I ordered, and began climbing the stairs.

The master suite was on the second floor, and through the thick oak door I could hear voices, one angry, one desperate.

To the maid I said, "Tell Omar he's wanted downstairs—by Eloy Quinto."

After knocking on the panel, the maid called Omar, who yelled, "Go away, I'm busy now."

"Tell him this won't wait," I whispered.

She repeated my words, but it only made Omar more furious. I shoved the maid aside and tried the door lever. Locked. Stepping back, I fired the MAC-10, splintering a circle around the lock, then kicked the door open.

There wasn't much light in the spacious room, but what there was showed an extraordinary scene.

Yolanda, naked, was tied spread-eagled on the big bed. Omar, wearing only shirt and socks, was on the bed, kneeling between her legs. He stared at me as though seeing the Devil, and Yolanda screamed.

"Get off," I snarled. "Now!"

Slowly he moved off the bed, stood beside it on thin, hairy legs, face contorted with hatred.

"Untie her." I moved closer.

He turned from me and bent over. I saw his hand reach for her nearest wrist, then dart under the pillow. Whirling around, he fired a pistol at me. I dropped to my knees and got off a burst at his chest. Fired again before he dropped backward, head striking his cousin's hip. Yolanda screamed and struggled until I shoved Parra's body aside and cut her free.

She lay there in an uncomprehending daze until I pulled her erect. "Clothes," I told her, "you're coming with me."

She didn't respond, so I had to repeat it. Finally she said dully, "I can't leave. This is my home."

"There's nothing left," I said, "it's all blown away. Quinto will blame you for all this, and I can't stay to protect you. By morning you'd be dead—after being raped by him and his men."

I hauled her to her feet, half-carried her down the hallway

to her room. Like an automaton she pulled on bluejeans and a blouse, took some jewelry from a box and came toward me. "Not with bare feet," I told her.

She stepped into leather *huaraches*, and I kept her behind me as we went down the broad staircase to the door. I didn't need the truck any longer, so I got her into the jeep and headed down the airfield road, keeping within the Day-glo markers. In a distant voice Yolanda said, "He was raping me—Omar, my own cousin."

"Well, he won't rape anymore. And he would have killed you. Whatever else you forget, remember that."

Her mind seemed fogged. "Why would he kill me?"

"Because you brought me here and I destroyed everything he had." Suddenly I remembered the big office safe with its cash and bankbooks. "Not quite everything," I muttered, "but enough for tonight."

Shivering, she huddled against me, clutching the crusted collar of my shirt. After a while she said, "Where are we going?"

"I don't know," I said, "but we're doing well to stay alive. Do you trust me?"

She smiled faintly. "Not with my property, just my life."

"Fair enough." I turned off the road into high grass, bounced the jeep into concealment fifty yards away. Then I turned off engine and lights.

I walked back to the road and saw a distant light in the control tower. The airstrip itself was dark. Even if we could make it to a place, I couldn't risk night takeoff. Besides, it was hours until dawn, and before then I'd have to find a place to land.

There was an old blanket on the floor of the jeep. I got out the rear seat cushion and spread the blanket over it. "Try to rest," I said. "We're safe until morning."

We were two miles from the explosions, but they penetrated the jungle like bass drumbeats. She looked at me and shrugged. "I should hate you for everything you've done,

218

Novak, but there's too much between us now. What are you going to do with me? Take me to America and prison?"

"I'm not a cop," I said curtly, "and first things first. Let's get away from Quinto and his men, then figure something out." I helped her onto the makeshift mattress, noticing that her wrists were raw from Omar's cords. She'd put up a hell of a struggle, but Omar's pistol changed the odds.

Sitting on the jeep, I took inventory: Machine pistol and spare magazines, two smoke grenades, a loaded Colt .45 with two magazines, sheath knife and canteen. There was a rusty machete on the jeep floor by the pedals.

Against that was Quinto and at least three hundred armed guards who, by now, were spreading out and searching for me.

Yolanda lay near my feet, eyes closed, chest rising and falling as she slept.

Then I heard the dogs.

TWENTY-FOUR

Bloodhounds.

I heard their deep, mournful baying in the distance, stiffened when I realized they were heading our way. I got the gas jerrican from the jeep, opened the cap and laid gasoline in a wide circle around us, hoping to obliterate our scent. Men would be following the hounds, but not closely because they moved slower through the thick undergrowth.

For a time I let Yolanda sleep on, but when the baying grew louder I woke her. She heard the dogs and her eyes widened in fear. Then she scented gasoline fumes and understood. "Get into the jeep," I told her. "They sound like big brutes."

"They are—oh, they're hideous." Her hands covered her face.

"If I shoot them," I said, "your whole damn army will close in on us, so I'll have to try something less dramatic."

She stood up, and I took the old machete and slashed the blanket into strips. As she watched, I twisted material around each forearm, and Yolanda wound a protective strip around my throat. I gave her my Colt .45 and said, "If they get me down, use it, but only as a last resort. Ah—the dogs, not me."

She smiled faintly. "You're my lifeline."

I helped her into the jeep and began sharpening the machete blade with my sheath knife. I kept working on the blade until the barking sounded like the hounds of hell. Then I set my back against the jeep hood, knife in my left hand, machete in my right.

Waited.

I heard their heavy bodies crashing through the undergrowth before I saw their eyes. Both beasts came lunging toward me, but stopped at the gasoline perimeter, dipped their noses, yelped and backed away.

For a moment I thought that could end things, but I was very wrong. If their sense of smell was gone, they could see me five yards off, and after plodding back and forth with occasional yowls, they jumped the perimeter and charged.

Like tacklers, they hit me high and low, slamming me back on the hood under their heavy bodies. One had his teeth in the wrapping of my left arm, while the other kept snapping and lunging at my throat. I kicked to make him back off, and before he lunged again I slashed the machete at his head. The blade cut off an ear and laid a long gash across his shoulder, but he wasn't disabled. The other dog was pulling me down, so I did some stabbing and carving under his jaws. They opened, and both my hands were free. Steadying myself, gasping, I watched them ready for another assault, and briefly admired their bred-in courage. One lunged at my head. I ducked, and he went over the hood. As the other came at me, I swung the machete and caught his chest. While he toppled sideways I lopped off his head, and saw the first one menacing Yolanda. Terrified, she sighted the pistol at him, but I yelled, "No!" and jumped into the jeep. I was off balance when the hound flung himself at me, and we hit the ground together. I tried protecting my face while he snapped and snarled and my knife slashed and stabbed. Finally, I pried up the machete and ran it through his belly.

With a drawn-out howl, the hound began biting the blade. Rising on one elbow, I stabbed the knife into the base of his skull in a matador's coup de grace. The animal coughed and died atop me.

I shoved the heavy body aside, withdrew the machete and drank from the canteen. That steadied me enough to drag the bodies away into deep undergrowth, where I left them.

Yolanda unwrapped my arms and neck, then sucked blood from teeth marks in my hands to cleanse the wounds. After spitting, she said, "There are medications at the chateau."

"Maybe," I said, "and I appreciate the thought, but by now Quinto's men will be there."

"If I could get to the safe," she said, "we'd have all the money we could ever possibly need, Jack."

"I thought of that," I admitted, "but I guess Eloy Quinto will get it now. Does he know the combination?"

"He can find it in Omar's billfold, but I wouldn't worry about that."

"Do you want him to get it all?"

"Of course I don't. Eloy doesn't know there's a thermite bomb inside. After the door opens there's a five-second delay."

"That's foresight. Omar's idea?"

"Mine. But I have money elsewhere in the world, Jack—I'll never starve." She pressed my lacerated hands. "I don't suppose you'd let me get that cocaine from my boat?"

When I shook my head, she said, "That's what I thought. All right, I'll forget it. What happens to me is up to you."

"True. And now that I think of it, you had Billy Joe in that dungeon. Were you going to kill him?"

"No," she said, shaking her head, "just keep him there until *Paz Paloma* sailed away. But he escaped—I guess you know that."

"I helped him."

There in the night's stillness, as we clung together, it seemed like a time for confessions. So I told her how I'd met Tara Vaill and why I'd come to Mazatlán. I didn't tell her that Freddy Gomez had been a DEA informant, or how his death had cleared the way for me to get next to her—in time she might figure it out for herself. So I lied a little and said that after she and I had been noticed together I'd been approached by an old friend, and agreed to do what I could to put the Parras out of business."

"Which you've certainly done," she said thinly. "Other *chivatos* tried the rear door—you came in by the front entrance, with me. Congratulations. You've earned whatever they pay you."

It was true, also self-evident, so I said nothing, just held her close, wondering if we'd ever be together again.

Finally she said, "When morning comes, what will we do?"

"Get to the airstrip, try to steal a plane."

"But—I can't fly—you mean *you* can?"

"One of my concealed skills," I admitted. "We'll start out early, on foot. Quinto doesn't know I'm a pilot—he won't be looking for us there."

"But the guards will be alerted."

"I know."

What woke me were birds racketing in branches high above. Greeting the first light of dawn, invisible to me below.

Time to get going.

Despite stiff and painful hands, I cut a foot of insulated wire from the ignition and made a wrist lanyard for the machete. Just beyond where I'd spilled gasoline I found a porous jungle plant, severed the stem and squeezed liquid into my mouth. I cut another, woke Yolanda, and showed her how to drink. Afterward she said, "It doesn't taste very good."

"It's life-sustaining, and if we get out of here, there'll be champagne." As I drew her to her feet, she said, "Your hands look terrible."

"They feel worse."

So we started off, Yolanda with the .45, me with everything else, keeping within sight of the airfield road, but far enough into the jungle that we wouldn't be seen if a patrol went by.

It was less than half a mile to the airstrip, but we didn't reach it until the pre-dawn purple was graying. Another few minutes and sunlight would rim the mountain range.

Both of us were hot, sweaty and mosquito-bitten as we rested against trees and peered at the airstrip. Through the dimness I could make out a couple of ancient Lodestars, a DC-3, a sag-winged DC-4, and—the family Learjet. All parked in the vicinity of the hangar. "Is the Lear fueled?"

"Should be. In case any of us had to fly out of here in a hurry."

"Like now."

She nodded. "Can you really fly the Lear?"

"I can try. Now, where are the guards? I don't see them."

"In the hangar or control tower." Her hand tightened on my arm. "Jack, even if we don't make it, I'm grateful for everything you've done for me. I know you could go alone, and having me along makes things much harder."

"Pish, tush." I kissed her swollen, reddened cheek. "We're in this together." I scanned the airstrip again and pointed at the Lear. "When I'm rolling I'll come as close to you as I can, so get ready to run out and climb aboard. There won't be a second to waste."

"But the guards—if you have to fight, I should be with you."

"If I'm in trouble, use your discretion. But that pistol's no good beyond forty yards. *Hasta luego.*" I shifted the musette bag and opened the flap, cocked the MAC-10 and left the tree.

Then froze.

About ten feet away lay a motion sensor, the type I'd seen on Quinto's desk. It was painted green to blend with the foliage, and all that attracted my attention was a streak of rust across it. Yolanda noticed it too, and I said, "Stay clear of it, and let's hope it hasn't done its dirty work."

Nodding, she blew me a parting kiss.

I moved away from the old EPD and kept a rank of trees between myself and the cleared edge of the airstrip as I headed toward the Lear. I figured to leave concealment near the hangar and follow its side to the end. From there it was only about twenty yards to the turbojet, but I couldn't see if the clamshell door was open. If not, I'd need a key to open it—and I had no key.

Glancing back, I fixed Yolanda's location in my mind, then moved on, looking for more sensors and scanning the field for movement.

Behind the hangar I broke into open space and stayed low beside the building as I inched ahead. The nearest window was broken, letting me look inside.

Crewmen were loading an old Stearman biplane with insecticide tanks, probably to spray marijuana and poppy acreage. The tanks were heavy, and the workers were having trouble with the under-wing shackles. Fine, I thought, stay with it, boys.

In a far corner, a group of armed guards were helping themselves to coffee. Morning breeze wafted the delicious odor to me, making my mouth salivate. Two mechanics were working at the open cowling of a Cessna, and seemed to be without weapons.

The control tower, such as it was, stood on the hangar's far side, out of sight. There could be more guards there, according to Yolanda, but I wasn't going there for a weather check.

Kneeling, I got out a smoke grenade and drew the pin, clenched the grenade in my left hand. Then, gripping the machine pistol, I crouched and moved ahead.

Just then I heard an engine coming down the access road. Too loud for a jeep, it sounded like the truck I'd abandoned at the Casa Dorada, and that was bad joss. Hell, I'd known this wouldn't be easy.

So I sprinted for the Lear and made the offside without looking back. Then I ducked under and found—thank God—the clamshell door open.

Looking back, I decided I hadn't been seen, so I settled in the left-hand seat and prepared to Blow and Go. The grenade was in my left hand, so I hit the battery and inverter switches with my right, noticing that the fuel gauge registered half-full—all four tanks. As the left engine whined a rising crescendo, I punched the other starter button and heard the right engine catch. Release brakes, flaps at twenty degrees—my overburdened mind trying to mesh what I remembered from Mazatlán takeoff with F-16 start-up. The rear-view mirror showed guards running toward me, firing wildly, as a truck bounced onto the tarmac and braked. From it spilled Eloy Quinto and the two pilots. Quinto joined the running soldiers, and as I throttled ahead, I tossed the smoke grenade from the open door.

Scanning the instrument display, I turned on the pilot heat switches and the Emergency Attitude Indicator, then steered toward where I'd left Yolanda.

The mirror showed my pursuers breaking through the heavy smoke, but I was well ahead of them. Suddenly I sniffed jet fuel, and saw drainage from the left wing tank. Shit! Where else had their bullets hit?

When I could see Yolanda behind the undergrowth, I accelerated to the edge of the strip and braked the left wheel. The plane pivoted, so that the open door faced her and I was staring at the oncoming soldiers. Behind them came the truck. I left my seat and climbed back to the doorway. As she ran toward me I fired the machine pistol at the soldiers, and two fell down. Quinto was racing and shooting crazily, then he had to change magazines. As he stood there, he made a splendid target. I fired a final burst in his direction and saw him jackknife, fall backward. By then, Yolanda had one foot on the steps, and I reached down to help her aboard. Her left arm jerked as a bullet impacted, and blood spurted below her shoulder. She would have fallen back onto the tarmac, but I scrambled down and grabbed her right hand. Jerking her into the cabin, I tossed my last smoke grenade toward the soldiers, then climbed into my seat.

As I throttled toward the runway's far end I closed the door sections and spotted the wind sock. It showed light breeze, not enough to worry about, and I tried to figure what liftoff speed should be. Half-fuel meant about three thousand pounds of aviation-grade kerosene in the unpunctured tanks, shortening takeoff distance. The basic gauges and instrumentation looked good, but doubtless I'd ignored a number of checkoff formalities. If I could get this baby airborne, I'd have time to see what was lacking.

Reaching the runway's end, I spun the plane around and ran up the engines while the truck began racing across the airstrip. I waited until it was directionally committed, then released the brakes and shoved both throttles ahead. G-force pushed me into the seat before I realized I wasn't buckled in. As the plane lunged ahead, I steered at the slowing truck, seeing soldiers flattening themselves as the plane screamed past. At the last second I altered direction and the fleeing truck bounced off the runway.

Eighty mph, ninety, a hundred and ten. The plane lightened under winglift. I'd need another thousand feet of airstrip—did I have it? A hundred twenty-five and jungle wall seemed just ahead. Here goes everything.

I pulled back the yoke and hit the wheel retractor as the nose pulled up. The landing gear whined and ground into the belly as I rose over verdant jungle, gaining altitude fast.

At two thousand feet I raised flaps, set the trim and turned east toward Venezuela. Then I locked on autopilot, figuring I could follow the coastline to Caracas.

After that, I went back to Yolanda.

She'd tied a rough tourniquet around her armpit and gave me a weak smile. "Bravo," she said huskily, "we made it."

I helped her into sitting position on the lounge seat and buckled her in place. Then I examined her wound.

The bullet had pierced her triceps, leaving an ugly exit wound. "Can you move your arm?"

"Yes—why?"

"Then the bone's not shattered. Anything resembling a first-aid kit on board?"

She gestured at the forward bulkhead, and when I opened the compartment I found a picked-over kit, but it still contained bandages and antibiotic powder. And a half-liter of Red Label scotch.

I fed her a double shot, drank as much myself, and covered her body with a blanket. Then I bandaged her wounds with gauze compresses and tape. When I eased the tourniquet, blood seeped through. She needed surgical attention now.

Her teeth began to chatter, so to keep her from sliding into shock I fed her more liquor, then went forward to check instruments. We were leaving the blunt head of the Guajira peninsula, with the Gulf of Venezuela beyond.

That gave me my first visual location, so I turned another five degrees east and got out Laurel and Hardy's plotting board. Max range with six thousand pounds of fuel was two thousand nautical miles. I'd lifted off with less than half of that, reducing range to, say, eight hundred miles. At thirty thousand feet, optimum cruising speed was 440 knots. We were doing less, because I didn't want to push an unfamiliar plane.

A smudged air chart showed Caracas about two hundred and fifty miles east of Maracaibo, and that was a close enough estimate. North of me lay the Dutch islands of

Aruba, Willemstad and Bonaire. They were attractively near, but I didn't want to risk over-water flying. Following the Venezuelan coast gave me the option of a beach landing if things went wrong—like running out of fuel. At four hundred knots we could cover the distance to Caracas in— what? I used the plotting board and came up with thirty-six minutes. Close enough, and we'd been airborne about ten. Roughly twenty-five minutes to go. I looked down and saw coastline slide by.

The radio manual gave me the call-in frequency of Maiquetía's airport tower. I set the receiver, put on headphones and listened in. Everything calm and matter-of-fact at the Caracas airport.

Ten minutes out, I broke in with my call sign and asked permission to land. They gave me a runway number and asked my point of origin. Baranquilla, I told the controller, in case he'd had me on radar for a while.

I wanted a low-profile arrival. Yolanda was dozing, drowsy from scotch, stress and blood loss. Her bandages were sopped with blood, so I tightened the tourniquet and replaced them. She bore up without whimpering, and when I'd finished I said, "Just a little longer, *querida*. To hide the bandages, wear this blanket as a poncho. Speak only English, and as little as possible. Let me do the talking."

She nodded. "You're good at that. Who am I?"

"My wife—Mrs. John Reynolds of Houston. I've got a few dollars and some Mexican pesos."

"And I have some jewelry we can sell."

"First stop is the nearest clinic. The *médico* will know better, but tell him we were wandering around and a jaguar nipped you. As far as Immigration is concerned, we're rich Texans island-hopping on our honeymoon. We'll stay near the airport while we sort things out."

She nodded again. I kissed her and took over the controls.

From the sea, it was an easy approach to Runway Four, but with a stall speed of 110 mph the Lear came in hot, reminding me I'd made smoother landings on a pitching carrier.

After parking the plane among other private aircraft I cut a hole in Yolanda's blanket and fitted it over her head, then helped her down the steps to the tarmac. Together we went over to the Transient Arrivals building, where I told my tale and displayed Reynolds ID. The officer gave us overnight permission, saying he'd extend it if we found Caracas to our liking. And he directed us to the airport clinic when I told him my Señora had a stomach bug.

A shuttle bus took us there, and while Yolanda was being treated I changed what money I had into *bolivares* and bought a flask of Pampero rum. She came out of the treatment room, pale and unsteady, and rested in a chair. The physician looked at me. "Jaguar?"

"Well, not really. My wife was fooling with a pistol and it went off. She's too embarrassed to admit it."

"Guns are terribly dangerous," he admonished, and I asked him to treat my hands.

He cleansed and bandaged the bites and lacerations, gave me a receipt for payment, and showed us out.

The nearest hotel gave us a large, air-conditioned room with twin beds. I helped Yolanda undress and got her under the covers, then ordered food and drink from room service. While waiting, I placed a collect call to Miami, and to my surprise heard Melody answer.

After telling her my location I asked her to cable a thousand dollars so I could get home. She was too accustomed to my vagaries to bug me with questions, her only query being whether a thousand was enough. I said it was and asked her to phone Manny Montijo and tell him, personally, where I was.

"I'll do it," she said reluctantly, "and that tells me what you've been doing. Up front, Jack, I'm displeased with the way you abandoned Tara and her father."

"Well, after I found him, there wasn't much I could do. *Force majeure*," I explained. "You've heard from Tara?"

"They're in Mazatlán, getting their boat ready to sail back to California."

"Fascinating. Well, I'd kind of like to see them before they leave."

"I've been hoping you would. But don't do anything more for Manny, okay?"

"Agreed."

"Meanwhile, I'm pining for you. Terribly."

"And I for you, pumpkin."

She breathed a kiss into my ear, and the line went dead.

Well, well, I thought, so daughter and Pa are reunited. Despite the Mean Mutha—or maybe because of him. I didn't want that coke-stuffed keel leaving Mexican waters, so there was further work to do.

While I was talking, Yolanda had dozed off, but after I'd made inroads on my plate of *carne mechada* I woke her and insisted she eat some of the local specialty, which consisted of meat hash, rice, fried plantains, black beans and yucca. It tasted better than it looked, and was highly nourishing. We shared a large bottle of cold white wine, after which I took a much-needed shower and helped Yolanda with her bath.

"I'll be leaving tomorrow," I said, "and you're free to do whatever you want. If you'd like, I'll sell some of your jewelry in Caracas, get you some travel money."

She nodded. "I'd like to sell the plane, too, but I suppose that will take time."

"And papers. Leave it for now."

I toweled her body dry and got her into bed again. Before leaving, I had a bellboy bring me a razor, and after I'd shaved around the bite-lumps, I left Yolanda sleeping and caught a bus for the capital.

From the coast, the *autopista* wound up and around

mountains and hills into cooler air, and finally Caracas was ahead, its towers and skyscrapers rising from a long, narrow valley.

I left the bus on Avenida Francisco de Miranda, and after some haggling sold Yolanda's emerald ring for eight thousand dollars in *bolivares*. In New York it would have brought five times that amount, but we weren't in Manhattan, and Yolanda needed walking-around money.

From there I taxied to the Embassy and asked the receptionist if Eddie Moscrip was still on the rolls. He wasn't, but his replacement was named Marc Gorrin, and after a while a secretary escorted me to the DEA office.

Gorrin was on his way out to lunch and kept glancing at his wristwatch until he heard the Parra name. Then he got interested and implored me to tell him more. I said, "What I need from you is a *laissez-passer* out of the country and a Mexican tourist card that'll get me to Guadalajara. Also, a message to Montijo."

He shoved a pad across his desk, and I wrote: "Mission accomplished. Start counting," signing it Novak.

Gorrin read it and his eyes widened. "You're Jack Novak?"

"In the flesh. How long for the papers?"

"Tonight? This evening?"

"Morning's okay." I told him where I was staying and suggested he get a courier there before breakfast.

Gorrin agreed, we shook hands, and I left the Embassy.

My taxi driver recommended a clothing store near the Plaza Bolivar where I used some of Yolanda's cash to buy clothing for us both, including a long-sleeved blouse to conceal her bandages. I changed in the store, discarding my tattered apparel and badly scuffed shoes, and bought two valises. Then I took a taxi back to Maiquetía.

At the airport I reserved a seat to Mexico City on Viasa's mid-morning flight and returned to the hotel room.

Yolanda was still sleeping, so I placed her clothing-filled

valise beside her bed and laid her ring money on the night table where she would see it when she woke.

For me it was long past siesta time, and accumulated fatigue was dragging me down. I got into my bed and turned out the lights.

The telephone's ringing woke me, and I was half-expecting to hear Melody's voice when I answered. Instead it was Gorrin's man, and I realized it was morning.

Yolanda's bed was empty, her valise was gone, so was the money. In its place a note was propped against the lamp.

Dear Jack—We've said everything there is to say, and I hate partings. Thank you for everything. Maybe we'll meet again.

Y.

So, she was gone—sooner than later—and maybe it was better for both of us, because I'd been wondering how to end it without just walking away. The last of the Parra clan, but I couldn't help wishing her well. And—who knows—our paths might cross again.

The courier delivered the papers I needed, so I checked out of the hotel. The airport cable office produced my thousand dollars, and I paid Viasa for my ticket.

An hour later I was flying back to Mexico.

TWENTY-FIVE

While the big plane bore northwest across the Caribbean, it occurred to me briefly—very, very briefly—that Tara had persuaded her daddy to return *Paz Paloma* to its owners, present himself to the San Diego DA and cop a plea. Then Dad would take up honest work and, with the support of his adoring daughter, steer a straight course for the rest of their lives.

The thought was attractive, but it defied accumulated evidence. In theory, rehabilitation was possible, but for career criminals it was statistically negligible. So the pair had to be entertaining other plans.

What they were would have held no interest for me had it not involved the cocaine-laden ketch. Did they know about the keel compartment and the illegal fortune it contained? The prospect of twenty million dollars could corrupt almost anyone, and Billy Joe had a sad history of moral lassitude.

Because I'd loaded the keel, I had a moral responsibility to prevent more than a thousand pounds of coke from reaching the States. And that was why I was heading for Mazatlán—not for high tea with the Vaills.

An after-breakfast shot of Anejo inevitably made me think of Yolanda. I was going to miss her, but I wasn't going to worry about her. She was a self-contained, resourceful and capable female, and she'd had the foresight to stash assets abroad. Cosmetic surgery would repair her arm wound so that, in time, the scar would be only a conversational opening at some lush resort. It might even make her think of me.

Unwittingly she'd helped me earn a quarter of a million dollars from DEA, we'd saved each other's lives, and only twenty-four hours ago I'd airlifted her from destruction and death at the Parra hacienda. So I couldn't let her go to prison.

Besides, I mused, who was going to prosecute her, and on what charge?

I sipped my drink and wondered where she was.

One hell of a woman.

I worked through the confusion of Mexico City's airport and boarded a small feeder plane to Guadalajara and Mazatlán. At Guadalajara's airport I left the plane and went into the terminal. I phoned Manny, and told him I was heading for Mazatlán.

"Mind telling me why?"

"Loose ends. You'll get the full tale later."

"How much later?"

"Couple of days. Vault hinges well-oiled? No trouble opening?"

"Depends what you accomplished."

"Heavy work," I told him, "so send over a photo-recon plane. Let the pictures do the talking."

"Because you're so modest."

"And because photos will show that lab complex in plain

sight. It was never concealed, Manny. It wasn't underground as you led me to believe."

When he said nothing, I said, "*Compadre*, you lied to me."

"The job had to be done, Jack. You were the one to do it. No apologies."

So, he'd known there was never going to be any government assault on Parra's place, and he hadn't wanted to tell me how many agents had been lost infiltrating the target area. Instead, he'd let me dazzle myself with a quarter of a million dollars and wished me well. I'll remember that.

"That's bad enough," I told him. "What's worse is Parra knew I was coming."

"You kidding?"

"You've got a mole in your office, Manny, and you damn well better get rid of her."

He thought it over before saying, "Her?"

"You heard me. Check it out before some other poor bastard has his head whacked off. And shrunk."

"All right—I'll get on it."

Over the jagged Sierra the little plane bounced around, and two of the passengers got sick in their barf bags. So I was glad when we touched down at the airport I'd last left in Yolanda's Lear. That had been only a few days before, but so much had happened that the interval seemed like a month.

I hired a Fiat and took the coast road toward the cove where *Paz Paloma* had been anchored. The time was mid-afternoon, and I was missing my siesta.

Lying along the escarpment, I peered down at the anchorage. Tara was stretched out on the foredeck, body sleek with sun oil. The dinghy bobbed amidships. A tranquil scene.

As I studied it I reflected that my quarter-million was as good as in the bank. Why couldn't I leave well enough alone?

Then, as often happened, the face of my drug-destroyed

wife drifted into my mind, lips parted, pleading for a fix, and I felt my jaw set.

Tara turned slightly, adjusting her glistening body to the rays. Did she know about the keel? I wondered. Daddy knew the original plan, because he claimed to have protested it. Where was Billy Joe?

I heard a slight sound behind me and started to turn my head. Not anticipating danger, I moved too slowly, and from the blue sky a comet whooshed down and slammed my skull.

The galaxy exploded.

It seemed that I was lying on stone bottom while a giant 'cuda crushed my head between his jaws. The fish became a snake whose coils replaced the 'cuda's jaws, and as its coils constricted, the pain become enormous. My mind saw my skull squeezed like pulp through eye sockets and nostrils, so the flesh could be smoked over a charcoal fire.

What was I doing underwater? My lips were wet, but my fingers clawed dry clothing. I managed to open my eyes and the anaconda vanished, replaced by the face of Tara Vaill.

Squatting beside me, she dabbed a wet rag at my mouth and wiped my fragile forehead. "Jack—thank goodness. I was afraid you weren't ever going to come to."

Without moving my head, I could glimpse a nearby gunwale. I was stretched out on deck. "Liquor," I croaked.

"Won't aspirin do?"

"*Liquor.*" I tried to sit up, nearly fainted and rolled on my side, as a man's voice said, "I'll get the bottle."

The Preacher. Billy Joe Vaill. "Sonofabitch," I muttered, "you coldcocked me."

"That was me, boy." A second male voice, so deep and guttural that it had to be the Mean Mutha. "Coulda killed you, but the folks are glad I didn't."

He stood above me, towering like the Green Giant. From

the studded belt up he was bare and bronzed. Pectorals like bulges of steel. Twirling a mustache point, he frowned down at me. "You coulda been anyone."

I gasped as Tara lifted my head enough that her father could get the bottle to my mouth. I gulped thirstily even though the rye tasted like rotten grain. She said, "What were you doing up there?"

"Making sure a visit was in order." I sipped more liquor. "Melody said you were here. I assumed you wanted to tell me how everything worked out." I lay back and stared up at the three of them. "All frictions resolved? Enemies no more?"

The men looked at each other. Mean Mutha shrugged. Billy Joe said, "We worked out a deal, brother."

"That's good news, Preacher. Congratulations." I pried myself up on one elbow. The horizon slanted as a wave of giddiness swept over me, but thanks to the booze, skull pain was dulling.

"So," I said, "the three of you are hoisting sail and returning this here boat to its rightful owners."

"Something like that," Billy Joe said. "By the way, brother, where's Sister Grace?"

"Haven't a clue."

"Let her slip away—or she paid you?"

I smiled. "You know how charming she can be."

His face tightened. "Sure she's not in Mazatlán?"

"I'm not sure of anything. My guess is she's thousands of miles from here."

Billy Joe swore, and I reached for the bottle. Two more pulls and I was able to crawl onto a transom. "Forget her, Preacher," I said, "you're way outclassed. Right, Tara?"

"I'm glad she's out of our lives."

"And you can thank me for that."

Mean Mutha's hand curved possessively around her hip. Tara didn't move away so I figured she didn't mind. A few things were now becoming clear. Her protector said, "Boy, I don't grab how you fit into all this."

"Simple," I said. "Tara got me to come here and look for Dad. I found Graciela and she led me to him. With my help, the Preacher got away. You snatched him, and I faded off the tube." Blinking, I shaded sensitive eyes. "I like a girl who has her own plane. Graciela flew me down to Caracas for a little fling, and that's where I've been." I looked around. "Not sure I should have come back."

Mean Mutha grunted nastily. "Took you for a nosey spy." His arms lifted, and the triceps stood out like hawsers.

"Well, now that we've established who I am and why I came, I'll get on back to Miami." I looked at Tara. "Melody will be glad to know you and Dad are together at last. To her that was important."

She said nothing. Unsteadily I got up, bracing myself on the gunwale. "When you get to Dago you might drop her a thank-you note. For her kindness, and my services."

"San Diego," she said reflexively. "Jack, would you want to sail with us?"

Before I could reply, her father barked, "Not a good idea. We're short on food and space."

She glanced at him and shrugged.

Mean Mutha said, "Grace tell you she's a Parra?"

"A what?"

Billy Joe said, "A wealthy Colombian family."

"We didn't talk family," I lied. "She didn't ask about mine, I didn't ask about hers. Anyway, we were having too much fun to get serious." I added that to see the effect on her husband. His mouth tightened, but that was all. Despite everything, he still had a thing for her. He also had Yolanda's cocaine, and that was now his paramount interest. Take the coke and let the lassie go. I said, "Tara, maybe you'd row me back to the beach?"

She looked at the big guy.

"Go ahead, honey," he boomed. "Or I'll toss him ashore."

The males didn't like the idea. They didn't shake hands, either, or apologize for my concussion. Among the three of us I could feel suppressed hostility. Still, seeing me go would pacify Tara's shipmates, so I got down into the dinghy. Tara followed me and began rowing me ashore.

When we were clear of the boat, she said, "I'm sorry about what Axel did to you."

"Thanks. When are you leaving?"

"Tomorrow morning, with the tide."

"Ummm. En route Dago, bear in mind that Axel's a dangerous man. He could crack Dad's neck with one hand, twist off his head with the other."

Stolidly she said, "He's nice to me. I don't think he means any harm."

"Let's hope. Who cut the deal with him? You or Dad?"

She swallowed. "He likes me—and my father promised him a lot of money."

"From what?"

She shook her head.

"Since Dad's principles dissolved, you'd better be very damned sure what you're involved in," I told her. "The boat's been nothing but trouble, and I see more ahead."

"You mean—if Axel gets violent?"

"Even beyond that—and you know what I mean."

As the bow ground on sand she shipped oars and I got out. "Anyway," she said, "it was disgusting of you to have an affair with Graciela."

"Because I didn't tell you—or because you think it was disloyal?"

"Both," she snapped, and I shoved the little boat off the sand, grinned at her. "Why should Dad be the only chump who gets to sleep with Graciela? When he had her he wasn't man enough to keep her."

240

With a little cry she snatched up the oars and the blades dug water. For a moment I watched her pulling away, then trudged toward the cliffside stairs.

Slowly, painfully, I made my way to the top of the scarp and looked down. The three of them were sitting in the cockpit. Tara looked up but didn't wave. I figured they were discussing my visit, and what its deeper meaning could be.

Aside from a very tender skull, my recon had gained me information I needed to make up my mind. I drove to the *posada*, took a room, swallowed aspirin and rum, and passed out until evening.

When I woke I felt well enough to shuck a bowl of steamed shrimp at the waterfront café, and while there, I noticed that the Ramirez boat, *El Chango*, was in its slip and lighted.

At the dive shop I bought flippers, mask, flashlight and leg knife; considered a bangstick and decided to do without. Then I went back to my room and waited until it was time to go.

TWENTY-SIX

I entered cove water about fifty yards up-current from the ketch. The big boat was dark, the dinghy snubbed to the ladder. There wasn't enough moonlight to show if anyone was on deck.

If things went according to plan, I wouldn't disturb anyone's sleep.

Just before submerging, I noticed distant running lights off the mouth of the cove, then I was in warm water and letting the current help me swim quietly toward the boat.

When I reached the stern, I clung to the rudder and rested awhile. No sounds aboard, but I could hear the engine of a fishing boat somewhere offshore. Underwater, I flicked on my rubberized flashlight and played it the length of the hull. The keel plate was still in place.

I kicked down to the bottom and played the beam around. The two burned-out lanterns were where we'd dropped them, Yolanda and I, and the scuba tank lay under a light sifting of sand. I clung to it as I fitted the regulator into my mouth and began to breathe. The gauge showed 1100 psi, which should be enough for the job. I strapped on the tank, and while I was searching for the Phillips screwdriver, my beam showed the bone-clean head of the big barracuda, part of its spine attached. Scavengers and the moray had done their work.

To find the screwdriver I had to scuffle through a layer of sand, but presently its shaft gleamed and, gripping it, I slid upward along the keel.

This time I let the retaining screws drop away, and when the plate was free I released it and watched it fall to the bottom. My ears picked up underwater vibrations, but I ignored them while I tried to pull a cocaine pod from the open hole. Vibrations increased, and I decided to find out what was causing them.

Poking my head up, I saw a good-sized sportfisher gliding into the cove. Probably the one I'd noticed offshore, except that it showed no running lights—just a glow behind the wheelhouse windscreen.

It seemed a strange time of night for game fishing, but perhaps the skipper was coming in to net extra bait. The boat turned toward the ketch, and moonlight showed me the name lettered on its bow.

El Chango. The Ramirez brothers' boat.

My pulse began racing. *El Chango* had stopped Billy Joe at sea, now it was back again.

Why?

Not to tow *Paz Paloma/Delfin* out to the sea lanes and help it on its way.

I turned off my flashlight.

Because the brothers worked for Yolanda, their arrival made sense. She'd told them to guard her cocaine, get it to the States.

Without knowing there were squatters aboard.

As *El Chango* came alongside, its engine reversed and its hull bumped against the ketch. On the far side, I swam aft and surfaced under the sailboat's stern. Holding to the rudder, I could see a man carry snub lines over to the sailboat. By tying alongside the ketch, Ramirez avoided having to anchor *El Chango*.

Inside the sailboat, lights went on. Aboard *El Chango* I heard startled voices.

From the companionway, Axel Jorgensen climbed into the cockpit, sawed-off in hand. He looked around, caught sight of the boarder and yelled, *"Freeze!"*

The man dropped his lines, straightened, and thrust up his arms. Mean Mutha turned toward *El Chango*. "On deck," he ordered, "anyone who don't want to get cut in two."

From the water there wasn't much I could do but watch. Besides, this was their party, not mine.

Pedro Ramirez strolled from the wheelhouse, arms raised. Between his legs I glimpsed the face of his brother, and Miguel was holding a gun. Flame shot from the barrel, and Mean Mutha grunted and staggered back. Miguel shot again, but not before the big man had fired one barrel at the boarder, the other at Pedro. Both men went down, and Miguel kept firing.

Jorgensen's chest was spouting blood. His shotgun was empty but he went after Miguel anyway. He made it to the gunwale before he died. His body toppled like a stubby tree and the sawed-off clattered away. Miguel ran out of the wheelhouse and aimed at Axel's head. The firing pin clicked on an empty casing.

Two frightened faces appeared in the yacht's companion-way: Tara and Billy Joe. Their mouths were open, but nothing came out. Miguel pulled an automatic from his belt and covered them.

He clambered aboard the ketch, and I swam quickly to the stern of his fishing boat. I kicked off my fins, dropped the scuba tank and pulled myself onto the stern platform. Knife in hand, I looked beyond the wheelhouse and saw Miguel patting down the Preacher.

Under deck planking the boat's engine idled in neutral.

Keeping low, I made it to the wheelhouse and crept inside.

The first thing I noticed was a Very pistol clamped to the bulkhead. Quietly I opened it, saw the rocket shell in the chamber and closed the breech.

Set against the overhead, above the wheel, was an AR-16. I pulled it down and peered through the windshield glass.

Very deliberately, Miguel Ramirez pulled down Tara's panties. As she stood naked before him, Billy Joe lunged at him. But he'd started too far away, and Ramirez slammed his pistol against the Preacher's head. Billy Joe dropped, Ramirez yelled, "*Cabrón!*" and Tara screamed.

In that moment I jerked the clutch into reverse and hit the throttle. Shouting "*Get down!*" at Tara, I stuck my right hand through the doorway and fired the signal rocket at the sky. The sound startled Ramirez, who began firing wildly at the wheelhouse. Flat on deck, Tara was crawling away.

The rocket burst above, flooding the scene with brilliant light. Kneeling, I sighted the AR at Ramirez and fired a three-shot burst, then another. Tara was screaming hysterically. Ramirez fell on his back. I thought he was dead, but I didn't want any surprises.

So I throttled back and shifted to forward. As the boat closed with the yacht, I stood on deck and gave the body two more shots. It jumped at each impact, and that was all. Billy Joe rose from the deck and gazed around.

The bow of the boat hit hard amidships, glanced off. I stopped the engine and went forward to pull trailing lines from the water. Tossing them at the foredeck, I told Tara to secure them where she could.

Unsteadily, Billy Joe helped, and I jumped onto their deck, holding the automatic rifle. Both stared at me like jack-lighted deer. Then Tara ran to me, half-stumbling on Miguel's body. Gasping and shivering, she clung to me as the Preacher watched with a hostile face.

"Henceforth," I said, "you'll do what I tell you—both of you. Forget the coke, Preacher, you'll be lucky to put this night behind you."

"Get dressed," he snapped at his daughter, "you're bare as a skinned rat."

She'd forgotten her nudity, but at his words her face hardened. "You let him strip me," she screeched. "Where was the tough jailbird when I needed him?"

"Ah, Jesus," he groaned. "Bitch, you're like your mother," and came at us, hand raised to strike.

I shoved it aside with the rifle barrel. "Get hold of yourself," I told him. "Tara, get clothes on. Anything you want to save, take to the other boat. You, too, Preacher."

She went first, walking slowly to the companionway, her body lighted by the rocket's dying glow. Billy Joe stared at me, muscles working in his jaw.

I said, "Due to unforeseen circumstances, there's a change in plans. Forget the tide, we're putting to sea now."

He thought it over. "You'll make the run with us?"

"Partway," I said. "The coke goes down with your boat."

He howled unintelligibly, and when he stopped I said, "You're not worth much, Preacher, but maybe you can rig for a tow. Bowline from *Paz Paloma* to *El Chango*'s stern." I prodded the rifle. "Now."

Barefoot, wearing only jeans, he started obeying. Tara came on deck carrying the bag she'd brought from Dago to Miami, then Mazatlán. "What's going on?" she asked.

"Dad's not happy I'm going to sink this mother." I tapped the deck with my rifle butt. "Any objections?"

"You're crazy—walk away from all that money?"

"Crazy or not, you'll do what I say. Otherwise, try swimming home."

She bit her lip. "This was our only chance," she murmured.

"No—because I'd have had you boarded off Baja. There was never anything in this for you, for anybody. Now get on the boat."

Sullenly she climbed aboard. I slung the rifle over my

shoulder and began dragging corpses, one after the other, four in all, from where they'd fallen, to the companionway.

Billy Joe appeared, saying, "It's all tied tight."

"Good. Now dump those fellows down the companionway."

My head and hands ached from everything I'd been doing. While adrenalin was pumping I'd forgotten the pain, but now my *manos* really hurt.

I slipped the anchor cable from the capstan, and it clattered off the deck, snaked into the water. "All aboard," I said, and swung aboard *El Chango*.

I towed the ketch out of the cove and headed out to sea, hoping the lines would stand the strain. Once beyond the first line of waves, things smoothed out, and the boat hummed along, *Paz Paloma* twenty feet astern.

The chart drawer held a bottle of rum. I swigged some to dull pain in my head, and figured how the story would be told.

If *Paz Paloma* were ever found in the blue depths, there would be four bodies in the saloon and a thousand pounds of coke in the open keel. The yacht had already been reported under attack by pirates, then missing. In the saloon were three of those same pirates. And Mean Mutha looked enough like one to pass.

Tara had been corrupted, too, whether through loyalty to her father or from greed—it didn't matter. I no longer saw anything wholesome about her, and that wouldn't be easy to explain to Melody.

My passengers were down in the cabin. I heard moaning and wondered if Billy Joe was hurting his daughter.

Moonlight showed them together on a bunk. There was a blanket over them, and their bodies were moving. It was the ultimate in family togetherness, and something clogged my throat. Then I thought, hell, maybe she's not really his daughter. And when I went back to the wheel, I understood why Tara had no boyfriend, why she hadn't hit on me. Dad was her world. He was all she needed. No wonder she hated Sister Grace.

While they were consoling each other I didn't disturb the lovers, not even when I shut off the engine and let the yacht bump the stern.

Taking my rifle along, I boarded the yacht, went below and got into the auxiliary engine compartment. My light showed two seacocks, and I opened both.

Then I returned to the sportfisher and cut the towing lines.

Paz Paloma was settling by the stern when father and daughter finally came on deck. Arms around each other, they watched the boat go down, with it their cocaine and their dreams of a bright future.

I said, "We're about eighteen miles offshore, on a thousand feet of water."

The Preacher groaned.

Tara said, "What happens to us?" Her face was taut, strained.

"I'll leave at the cove. Where you go and what you do is your problem."

"Narc," she spat. "Dirty bastard."

"Maybe," I said wearily, "but I'm used to ugly names." I gazed at both of them. "Are you?"

She flushed, they looked at each other and walked toward the stern, away from me.

The fuel tanks were more than half-full. If they headed south, that much should take them to Manzanillo. Or they could cross the Gulf to Baja California, put in at La Paz, and make their way back to Dago. Or hang around La Paz and work a scam—the old badger game would be about right. The twist would be outraged father instead of outraged husband. Never mind, Billy Joe would figure out something— he always had.

The lights of Mazatlán guided me back to the cove. I let

the boat coast until the bow ground on sand. Then I jumped into the water. Separating the magazine from the rifle, I heaved them back aboard the boat, rifle on the foredeck, magazine to the stern. Before Billy Joe could assemble them, I headed up the beach, out of range.

For a while nothing happened. Then I heard the engine grumble as the boat strained off the sand. When it was free, Billy Joe backed around and headed toward sea.

God knows what would become of them, I thought, but I wasn't going to worry.

I climbed the old, uncertain stairway for the last time, walked to my car and got dressed.

In the morning I phoned Melody to tell her I was on my way. Next, I called Manny and asked him to have my fee at the airport when the plane came through.

At the waterfront café I shelled cold shrimp and drank Tecates. The waiter—a youngster I hadn't seen before—remarked that most *gringos* didn't eat shrimp for breakfast.

I said I wasn't the average *gringo*. He nodded reflectively and strolled away.

Looking out over the water, I saw the empty slip where the Ramirez boat had been. Where it was now, I couldn't begin to guess.

But I thought of Yolanda with her dark hair and bronzed body, and tried to remember all we'd been through together—before memory began to fade. I remembered her soft breasts and warm lips, the way she'd caressed me the night we first made love, and I knew that I could never forget her. The good things were all I wanted to recall.

Then it was time to hit the airport for my plane.

THE END